JUSTICE REBORN

JUSTICE REBORN

Cowboy Justice Association
Book Eight

Olivia Jaymes
www.OliviaJaymes.com

JUSTICE REBORN

ISBN: 1944490086
ISBN 13: 9781944490089

CHAPTER ONE

Evan Davis slapped his sheriff's badge down on the mayor's expansive desk and then planted his palms on the smooth oak surface. A wave of pure happiness washed over him and he couldn't suppress a smile.

"I quit."

Mayor Morris Gladstone hadn't looked all that happy when Evan entered the room and he looked even less so now. "What do you mean? What are you talking about? You can't quit. You have a contract."

Evan's smile grew wider. "Your office never forwarded the revised copy to me so I never signed one. Although I think I would have grounds to break it since you haven't been keeping up your side of the bargain. You had to know this day was coming, Morris. How many head lawmen have you gone through in the last five years? Did it ever cross your mind that it wasn't them but you?"

It wasn't fair to blame Morris for everything but he'd played his part. Evan might have tried to stick it out in hopes things would get better but every day was more miserable than the one before it. He wasn't cut out to be a small town cop. The fact was he didn't know what he was supposed to be when he grew up. He was too tall for an astronaut, too citified for a cowboy, he couldn't sing a lick which left out rock star, and he'd been shot in the leg so rich and famous athlete was off the table as well.

"Shit," the harangued mayor muttered under his breath. "Sherry! Come in here and bring Sheriff Evan's contract."

Straightening, Evan just shrugged. He wouldn't be changing his mind. It had taken a long time to get here but now that he was? There was no turning back. "She's not going to find it. I didn't sign one. No one cared until this minute. The town was just glad to have someone take this thankless, God-forsaken job and I was dumb enough to do it. No more. Deputy Steve can be the acting sheriff until you find someone. Hell, if you were smart you'd offer it to him at double the salary. He's got more patience than anyone I know. If I'd been doing this job for five years I would have shot you by now."

Red creeped up Morris's neck and a sheen of sweat had broken out on the older man's pasty white forehead. Morris needed to get some sun. "It's not that bad. Sherry!"

"Stop yelling. She's not going to find it. It doesn't exist. Did you ever think your stubborn resistance to reality might be part of the problem around here?"

Morris slapped the table and then winced. "We don't have a problem. Except maybe you. You're the problem."

If only that were the case, then things could be fixed.

"Then you'll be glad to be rid of me," Evan retorted, wandering over to the windows on one side of the large room. Morris's office looked over the rolling green lawns outside the courthouse and city hall. It looked pretty and serene with large maple trees and park benches but Evan wasn't fooled. The town was eating at itself, unwilling to invest in services or infrastructure.

He'd been fighting local crime with one hand tied behind his back and he was sick and tired of it. This year's budget was worse than the last and he was already operating way under optimum. He needed at least three more full-time deputies and a canine unit. As it was he was looking to have to lay off at least one full-time man.

Morris took a deep breath and stood although Evan still towered over him. "Let's just calm down and step back a minute. I know things look grim but we have to make cuts in response to a smaller tax base. I don't have any choice."

Politicians. It was amazing how smoothly they could lie.

"Bullshit. There always seems to be money for raises for the mayor and the city manager. I can't be a part of this anymore and honestly, Morris, you ought to be ashamed. Your daddy must be rolling over in his grave seeing how you've used your position to enrich yourself and your cronies. I hear you're putting in a swimming pool at your house."

Scraping his fingers through his hair, Evan exhaled in frustration. He'd grown more discontented with each passing day and now he was simply making everyone around him miserable.

"These contracts are going to bring in jobs, Evan, and with jobs come people. People who pay taxes. In a few years maybe we can do something about the budget issues."

Evan was sick and tired of hearing about these so-called job creators. They never hired anyone at a decent salary or gave benefits. But they all seemed to get rich off the working men and women in this town.

"A few years? What should I do in the meantime? Wire the bumpers onto the cars and make bullets out of ice? How am I supposed to keep the peace when I don't have the tools? I went into law enforcement because I wanted to make a difference. Why did you become mayor?"

Morris coughed a few times and puffed out his chest. "For the same reason. I wanted to make a difference."

"Congratulations, you have. This town is completely different than the one I grew up in. Now it's like every other place on earth. Corrupt and falling apart."

Perhaps it always had been. Evan had grown up in a sheltered household, living a Norman Rockwell childhood. It was that idealism that had driven him into the military and then to law enforcement. His years as a US Marshal had been good and if he hadn't been injured in the line of duty he'd still be there, climbing the chain of command even though he'd become increasingly bored with the duties he'd been assigned. The job had lost its challenge and the bureaucratic red tape had become a daily impediment to getting anything done, but dammit, it had been a career. He'd put in years toward it and now it was all gone.

He'd been shot and had taken the sheriff's job out of desperation, wanting someone or something to give him a direction in his now rudderless existence.

It had been a mistake.

He'd never taken to the job. Didn't enjoy it. He liked variety and there wasn't much in a small town sheriff's day to day world. Everyone complained, nothing he did was good enough, and there was never enough money for the resources he needed. Frankly, he hadn't had a decent night's sleep since he took the job. Invariably he was dragged out of bed by a middle of the night call because he didn't have enough deputies to do the job correctly.

He was tired, disgusted, and over it all. He wanted a comfortable bed and to sleep for a week.

Sherry tentatively stepped into the office at that moment, looking like she didn't want to be there. "Um, Morris? I don't see any contract on file."

The mayor fell back into the chair, a heavy sigh on his lips. "Thank you, Sherry. Can you get me some coffee, please?"

The young woman nodded and hastily exited the office, obviously glad to be away from the tension. Evan shook his head and inwardly groaned. He hadn't wanted this to go so badly. He hadn't wanted a shouting match or the two of them pointing fingers, blaming the other. He simply wasn't cut out for this job and that made him sad. He'd wanted to enjoy it but it was making him miserable. He had to cut his losses and start all over again.

"I don't want to argue with you, Morris. I'm quitting and you can't talk me out of it. If I keep doing this, I won't be good for this town. Let's not pretend you didn't see this coming, okay? You've known for a long time I wasn't happy."

Morris looked up, resignation showing in his eyes. "What will you do? Are you going back to the Marshal Service?"

Evan had thought about that and it was a possibility. A very minute possibility. But right now nothing was for certain.

"I don't know," he answered honestly. "I just know that I can't do this anymore. I've already talked to Hazel about renting out my house. I'm going to go somewhere I can be alone and think about what I want to do with my life."

The older man's eyes widened. "You're leaving? Your family has lived in this town for three generations, Evan. Where will you go?"

Evan smiled but didn't answer. Morris wouldn't understand and it wasn't anyone's business anyway. Even in a town as small as this one, a person could sometimes manage to keep a few secrets.

"Away," he replied simply, feeling the oppressive weight of the job lift from his shoulders. He hadn't felt this good in a long time. "I'm leaving in the morning."

Morris tossed his pen on the desk and chuckled, knowing he might have won a few of the battles but ultimately he'd lost the war. "I wish you well, son. You know that, right? There's always a place for you here if you want it. I hate to say it because I know you despised every day on the job but you were the best sheriff we've had in my lifetime. Maybe my daddy's too. Have a seat for a few minutes and I'll get your last paycheck."

Morris started to rise but Evan shook his head. "Keep it since I didn't give you any notice. I do feel badly about that but once a man decides something…Hell, I just need to be on my own for awhile."

"A man has to do what a man has to do. Keep in touch."

Evan wasn't sure he'd ever be back, to be honest, but he nodded his head in agreement. Anything else would have appeared churlish and he didn't want this to be a bitter ending.

Slapping his hat back on his head, he turned on his heel and strode out of the building before pausing on the steps of city hall. He took a deep, long breath and looked up at the shining sun.

It was a good day to be alive and unencumbered.

He wouldn't waste another day looking back. Full speed ahead.

CHAPTER TWO

Josie Carlton stepped off of the bus and stretched her cramped, tired limbs as the fresh air caressed her face. Exhausted to the bone, she'd slept during the ride albeit with one eye open, still unsettled by the events of the night before. Terrified and unsure as to what to do, she'd jumped on the next bus leaving the station, not caring where it was going, only wanting to get away as quickly as possible.

Now she was standing on the sidewalk of a little town in central Florida, about an hour from Orlando. She'd never been to the Sunshine State before and had pictured palm trees and beaches. There were a few palm trees but there wasn't an ocean in sight. From what she had seen from the bus windows, there were trees and horses.

And heat. Sidewalk melting heat. That old saying about frying an egg on the sidewalk must have been coined right here in this little town.

She lifted her long hair off of her neck where a pool of sweat had gathered in the stifling humidity. It was the beginning of May and summer was just beginning in most of the country, but here it was obviously in full swing.

Hitching her backpack higher on her shoulder, she struck out toward what appeared to be the center of town. She wanted desperately to sleep but even more she wanted food. She hadn't eaten in hours and at this point pretty much anything sounded good, which was fortunate as the first eatery she came upon looked like a diner straight from the 1950s complete with pink vinyl booths and juke box in the corner. She slid into a seat and looked around for Fonzie, but if he was there he was hiding in the kitchen or the bathroom.

A young waitress who couldn't have been more than twenty sidled up as Josie studied the menu. "I'm Tammy, and I'll be taking care of you today. What can I get you?"

Stomach gurgling with hunger, Josie pointed to the laminated menu. "How are the shakes here?"

"To die for," the girl giggled. "If you like burgers and fries, you just stepped into heaven."

Josie slapped the menu closed decisively. "I'll have a cheeseburger, fries, and a chocolate shake. Oh, and a glass of water, if you don't mind as well." The waitress nodded and scribbled down the order. "Can you please tell me where the ladies room is? I need to freshen up."

Tammy pointed to a hallway near the jukebox. "Right back there. Did you just get off the bus?"

That subject was the last thing she wanted to discuss. "Uh yes, I'll be right back. You won't give away my table, will you?"

Tammy laughed and shook her head. "It's safe. The lunch rush is over so you can sit there for a few hours if you want to."

Slipping back to the restroom while the waitress put in her order, Josie surveyed the damage in the mirror. Dark smudges under her eyes from lack of sleep and too much worry and stress. Hair sticking every which way. Clothes that looked like she'd slept in them. Because she had.

"Aren't you a beauteous sight," she muttered as she pulled a brush through her wavy auburn hair and tied it back into a ponytail before splashing cold water on her blotchy skin. Right now, the only thing she was fit to do was scare small children.

By the time she returned to her table her chocolate milkshake was waiting for her. She made short work of it along with the cheeseburger and fries, cleaning her plate except for some lettuce and tomato she'd pulled off the bun. Now pleasantly full, she needed to find a place to sleep. Once she'd rested and her brain worked again she could start figuring out what she was going to do. Nothing she'd experienced in her life had prepared her for this. If she thought about it too much, she'd sit down and cry for the rest of the day.

Tammy slid the bill on the table and gathered the dirty dishes. "Looks like you enjoyed it. Can I get you anything else? We have homemade pies."

Josie patted her stomach. "I'm stuffed but thank you. I don't suppose you know of a cheap but clean motel around here? I don't need anything fancy."

And I can't afford it either.

"Sure I do. Go down two blocks that way and then turn right. Cypress Corner Motorlodge will be down about a block. Hank owns it and he's a good man. Runs a clean place and has decent prices." Tammy leaned forward, her eyes sparkling with mirth. "And it's the only hotel in this one horse town. Tell him I sent you."

Josie nodded and thanked the young woman who bustled back to the kitchen. Unzipping her backpack, Josie carefully counted out the bills for her meal plus tip and placed it on the table. She'd pulled money from her checking account before leaving home but this wouldn't last forever and she didn't dare use her ATM card again or any of her credit cards either. The stress of her situation hit her straight in the abdomen again and a lump rose in her throat, threatening to bring her burger and fries back up.

Swallowing hard, she breathed in and out until her stomach settled. Frankly, she didn't have the luxury of throwing up lunch as she couldn't really afford to waste food and money like that.

She zipped her backpack closed and headed toward the door, pausing at a large bulletin board on the wall which had everything from puppies up for adoption to cars for sale. One advert caught her eye and she untacked it from the cork backing to take a closer look.

Temporary housekeeper wanted ASAP.

Lord knew she needed the money so she could keep moving or get to her final destination...whatever that was going to be. Her cash would run out faster than she wanted it to and this might be the answer.

Suddenly Tammy was leaning over Josie's shoulder. "Evan put that up today at breakfast time. He owns an old house outside of town that's been empty for years. Looking for someone to help him clean it up and make it habitable."

Josie's fingers tightened on the index card. She wasn't sure she could trust someone she didn't know from Adam and her concern must have shown on her face. "He seems like the respectable sort. In this business you can always tell the creepers and he's not one of them. You should give him a call. I think he's anxious to find someone."

Anxious enough to hire her with a fake name and references? Could she persuade him to pay her cash? When this was all over, she'd be sure to pay the IRS the tax she owed but right now banking wasn't the best idea.

Josie looked around the diner for a payphone but like most places they'd done away with them. "I don't have a phone."

She'd chucked her cell before getting on the bus in case someone used it to trace her.

"Then come back around six-thirty. He's here every night for dinner. Says his kitchen is only fit for coffee and donuts. I'll introduce you."

Turning, Josie gave the young woman her most grateful smile. Small towns really were friendly. She hadn't felt this calm in over twelve hours. It felt nice not shaking in her shoes like a Chihuahua.

"Thank you. You've been more than helpful. I really appreciate it."

Tammy patted her on the shoulder. "My pleasure. We don't get many new people around here. It's kind of exciting."

The one thing Josie hoped for with all her heart? That she didn't bring any action to this little town. If for no one's sake but her own.

People might ask the question why she hadn't gone to any of her friends for help but she'd learned early on in life that she truly didn't have anyone but herself. Trust wasn't something she offered easily. She'd learned to stand on her own two feet and take care of herself.

She hadn't had much of a choice then and she didn't now. Josie didn't want to put people she cared about in danger. She wouldn't pull anyone else into the mess she'd found herself in.

CHAPTER THREE

"How are you doin' tonight, Evan? You look tired."

Tammy slid an iced tea in front of him as per their usual routine. The kitchen in the house Evan was living in was a disaster so he'd taken to getting most of his meals at the diner. Sometimes for variety he ate at the pizza place or maybe the barbecue joint that was only open on the weekends.

"I am tired." Evan stretched his shoulders with a groan. "I was working on the garage today and I must be getting old because it kicked my ass royally. After I eat, I'm heading straight home to sleep."

Except that he wasn't sleeping much no matter how exhausted he was. His brain wouldn't shut down and he spent the hours between sundown and dawn thinking about his past and possible futures until his head ached and he could barely hold his eyes open.

Then the alarm would go off.

Tammy smiled and almost bounced with excitement. He hadn't seen her this animated in the weeks he'd been in town. Did she have a new boyfriend?

"I have someone who can help you with that. New girl in town, just off the bus, and looking for some temporary employment. She's perfect for the job."

His brows shot up in surprise as he'd just placed the ad on the bulletin board at breakfast time that very day. In a town this small he'd met about everyone around and he hadn't much hope of getting any applicants.

"What's her name?"

Tammy bit her lip and giggled. "I don't know. I didn't ask and she paid with cash."

Evan sighed. His years in law enforcement had made him wary. "Then what makes you think she's perfect? Obviously you just met her today."

"She was real sweet and she didn't seem like she was going to rob us or anything." The waitress shrugged her shoulders as if Evan had asked a stupid question. "Do you have anyone else in mind?"

He didn't and he hated to clean. He should have gone on a cruise or something instead of taking on this project.

"No one," he admitted with a heavy sigh. "I just want to make sure that anyone I hire - even for temporary work - isn't going to abscond with the family silver."

Tammy's eyes widened. "I didn't realize. You have a lot of family valuables?"

Well, shit.

"Not exactly." There was no family silver and even the dishes had chips. There wasn't even a television, only a clock radio from about 1975. "I just want somebody honest."

"You sure wouldn't have to worry about her hurting you or anything. She was just a bitty slip of a thing compared to you but it looked like she needed the work." Her pen poised over her order pad. "What will you have tonight?"

Evan held out the menu. "The roasted chicken with mashed potatoes. Thanks, Tammy."

"You got it." She tucked the menu under her arm. "I told that girl if she was interested in the job she should come meet you here at dinnertime so keep a look out."

Tammy started to move away but Evan had one more question. "How will I know it's her?"

"For one, you've never met her before and two, she has pretty red hair. You'll know her."

She had a point. Unfamiliar faces were a big deal around here.

He had just ordered his dessert when a young woman tentatively entered the diner, her gaze sweeping around the room as she twisted her hands together nervously. Her hair was more auburn than red but she had the traditionally fair complexion that went with it, along with bright green eyes that seemed to take everything in at once. Average height and curvy, especially back behind and on top, she wasn't what he'd had in mind for the job of cleaning his house. She didn't look all that strong but if she was willing to work hard he'd give her a chance.

Beggars couldn't be choosers. Or whatever his grandma used to say to him.

Tammy stuck her head out of the kitchen and pointed to Evan and the girl nodded, approaching him as if he was going to scream or wield a knife. The closer she came, the prettier and younger she looked. Hell, how old was she? She barely looked twenty-one.

"Hello," she said, her eyes firmly fixed on the tile floor. "I'm…I'm Lisa Halliday."

"Hi, Lisa. Tammy told me I might meet you tonight. Why don't you join me for some pie?"

She looked up, her lips pressed together in what appeared to be real fear and his heart softened in response. The girl was plum scared and she had no need to be. He might not give her the job but he could talk to her for a few minutes. He wasn't that much of a hermit.

Yet.

"Um…"

Evan patted the table and gave her an encouraging smile. "Come join me. I hate to eat alone. I'm Evan Davis, by the way. It's nice to meet you."

She smiled then, showing off pearly white teeth as she slid into the booth. Still fidgeting, he signaled to Tammy who quickly came over, order pad in hand. "What can I do you for?"

"The coconut cream pie here is really delicious," Evan said, hoping she'd loosen up a little bit. He was beginning to wonder if he'd grown horns in the last five minutes.

Lisa nodded. "That sounds good. I'll have that. Thank you."

Tammy shot back into the kitchen, leaving the two of them alone at the table although the diner itself was quite busy. The sound of clattering dishes and lively conversation was loud enough to give them the privacy they needed.

"Thank you for speaking with me. I'm sure you're a busy man."

Evan couldn't bottle up the laughter that bubbled out at her statement. "Lisa, I am far from busy. In fact, I have lots of free time. So why don't you tell me a little about yourself. How did you come to be in Cypress Corner?"

Her fingers wound around the paper napkin. "Actually, I lost my job not long ago and I decided that this was the time to travel. You know, see the country. This might be the only chance I get. I've been taking the bus and I figured I could get odd jobs along the way."

Two pieces of coconut cream pie were placed in front of them along with a glass of water for Lisa and a refill of coffee for him. He picked up his fork and waited for her to do the same. She lifted a mouthful to her lips and her tongue snaked out and licked at the velvety custard.

"That is good."

"The only one better is the peach cobbler but they only have that on Wednesdays." He shoveled a forkful into his mouth. He had a major sweet tooth and this hit the spot. "You were saying?"

"Actually, I was done. I'm just traveling the country and seeing the out of the way spots. Places that aren't touristy."

Evan almost choked on his pie. "You've come to the right place. The only tourists we get here are people lost on their way to Disney World."

"I've never been."

"It's fun. You should go while you're down in this area. So how come you're not driving? I would think that would be much easier than riding the bus."

Lisa wrinkled her nose and sighed. "It would be, but my vehicle has seen better days and I didn't want to be stranded on some dusty side road in the middle of nowhere. If I work hard I might be able to buy a cheap used car but the bus isn't so bad. It's air conditioned and there's plenty of interesting people too."

"You're very polite, Lisa," Evan chuckled although he still thought it was strange that she'd set out to see the USA on a bus instead of a car, but then he was a guy that liked to be behind the wheel. She might hate driving for all he knew. Maybe she wasn't good at it, either. "Why don't I tell you about this job? Once you hear about it you might not even be interested."

"I'm interested," she replied quickly, almost too quickly. When she was laid off she must not have had much money in savings. Evan was already feeling sorry for her, which was a bad thing because his emotions had no part in making this decision. He needed the best person for the job, not the person who needed the job the most.

"We'll see."

He watched her expression closely, looking for a tell of some sort. Just from their short conversation he could tell she was well-educated and well-spoken. Not the sort of person who threw over their entire life to bum around the country seeing the sights. She seemed like someone who should be dressed in business attire and carrying a briefcase.

"This house has been in my family for a few generations. My grandparents on my mother's side lived in it for forty years before she passed on and it was just my grandfather. His health as well as his mental state went downhill and he became something of a hoarder. It's not as bad as what you might see on television but it is bad. Add in the fact that the house hasn't been maintained and it's pretty much a nightmare. I won't make anything but coffee in the kitchen as I'm sure there are molds and fungus that haven't been identified by medical science yet."

He might as well tell her the bare truth and maybe scare her off. There was nothing glamorous about this job. In fact, he'd been sure that no one would take it and he'd be stuck doing it. By himself it might take months. But that was okay. He had the time. So far he hadn't made any progress in figuring out what he was going to do with the rest of his life.

Sucking in a breath, Lisa contemplated his words. "I'm no stranger to hard work, if that's what you're worried about. I spent a summer detassling corn and believe me that is some hot, sweaty, backbreaking work right there and for very little money. I'm not afraid of getting my hands dirty."

That prompted Evan to glance down at Lisa's hands, which were small but capable with short nails. There was no way she'd be able to keep a manicure with the kind of labor he was needing.

"You'll get them dirty all right. Along with the rest of you. There's cleaning and painting and stacks of crap that have to be sorted through. But I will pay a fair wage and if you stick it out until the end I'll pay you a five hundred dollar bonus."

Her expression brightened considerably which solidified his thought that she was down on her luck. He ought to do a thorough background check plus references on her but hell…would he have done that with anyone local? If Barney or Darrell down at the horse farm had offered to help him out part-time he would have been grateful as hell and took them up on their offer and he didn't know them much better than this woman.

There wasn't anything of value for her to steal and he'd be with her pretty much the whole time. His only real fear was that she'd do a good job but would hate the work and quit. That's why he'd dangled the carrot of a bonus if she finished.

"Are you thinking by the hour or a flat rate for the job?"

He took the last bite of pie and pushed the plate away, his stomach pleasantly full. "I wouldn't know how to price it flat so I think hourly is the most fair."

He cautiously named a rate that he hoped wouldn't send her running from the building.

She tilted her head and nodded. "I can do that."

She must be desperate to take this crappy job for little pay.

"How about we have a one week trial?" he offered. "If it goes well we continue. If not, then we go our separate ways with no hard feelings?"

"Sounds like a plan. Do you want me to start tomorrow?"

He liked that she was eager but then it was probably because she really needed the money. His heart twisted in his chest a little bit at the idea. He was surprised by how much he genuinely wanted to help her out. That's why he'd gone into law enforcement - to help people - although it had rarely worked out that way. If this worked, she'd be helping him out just as much. This was no giveaway job. She'd earn every penny he paid her.

"I would. I know you don't have a car so how about we meet here for breakfast at seven? Then I'll drive you to the house and we can get started." He appraised her from head to toe. "I'd wear the oldest clothes you have because you're going to get filthy."

Lisa frowned and looked down at her attire. "I don't have much with me but I didn't bring anything fancy either." She held out her hand. "Should we shake on it?"

He reached out and enclosed her small hand in his much larger one. It felt small and delicate, and for a moment he wasn't sure hiring her was the best idea. But she was the only option he had and frankly she seemed to need the help.

"Deal. I'll see you tomorrow."

"Tomorrow," she echoed, a real smile blooming on her face. Lisa was a lovely woman and he'd do well to not notice that in the future. They'd help each other and then she'd move on while he figured out what in the hell he was going to do with his life. But it did feel good.

He actually had plans and a reason not to oversleep.

◈ ◈ ◈

Back at her hotel room later that evening, Josie slumped against the headboard of the bed lost in her own thoughts. The television played in the background but she'd kept it low enough that she could hear if a car passed by the window or footsteps echoed on the stairs outside. She hadn't slept well since the night her entire life changed and she honestly wasn't sure if she ever would again.

She was filled with a black, clawing fear.

Every minute of every day she worried that they'd find her. She'd been so naive when she'd ran from home in her own vehicle, her cell phone tucked in her backpack. When the sinister-looking men had showed up at that motel at the edge of D.C., she'd known immediately she had been incredibly foolish. Of course they could trace her car or phone. Heck, she'd even used her own credit card to pay for the room. She might as well have posted a neon sign with a giant arrow pointing to her location.

With her adrenaline pumping and true fear strangling her throat, she'd called the poor night manager of the motel and screamed about armed men in the parking lot, which had sent him running out of his office with a shotgun. That had created just enough of a distraction that she'd been able to slip out of her room and dart onto a passing city bus that she'd ridden into the center of town. From there, she'd hiked the mile and a half to the seedy bus station where she'd purchased a ticket - cash this time after cleaning out her account at an ATM at the drugstore - for the next departing bus.

Florida.

She could have ridden the bus all the way to Orlando but she feared the cost of hotel rooms and food would be way out of her budget in a tourist town. So far she'd made the right choice. The room here was clean and cheap and so was the food. Evan had even insisted on buying her pie at the diner this evening, although she'd argued with him until she'd realized it was a futile action. He seemed like a nice man.

Josie had decent instincts about people and Evan seemed like one of the good guys. He had an easy way about him, his expression open and honest. It wasn't in her nature to trust much, but she could extend enough to take the job.

Sliding off of the bed, she stripped off her clothes and placed her panties and socks in the bathroom sink to soak using some of the free shampoo provided by the hotel. Clothes she'd washed this morning, hung on the shower rod already so she would have something to wear in the morning. She hadn't had time to grab much when she'd ran and she certainly hadn't packed for a trip to a semi-tropical location. Two pairs of jeans, two pairs of shorts, four t-shirts, four pairs of panties, bras, and socks, plus one hoodie wasn't going to be enough and she'd need to think about buying a few things when Evan paid her. She might also need to think about a prepaid phone in case she needed to contact someone.

Right now all she could hope for was a little peace while she made some money before moving on once again.

She was just nodding off when she heard the growl of an engine and then the slamming of car doors. A quick glance at the illuminated face of the bedside clock told her it was three in the morning. Her heart stuttered in her chest before accelerating, her palms damp with perspiration.

Hushed voices outside her window and door had her crawling out from under the covers and across the carpeted floor to the front windows overlooking the parking lot so she was stationed right below. Staying low to the floor, she strained to make out even part of what they were saying but they were being too quiet. Slowly rising to her knees, she lifted one corner of the drapes and peeked outside, her heart hammering like a timpani in her ears.

A man and a woman stood on the pavement in front of Josie's door, luggage thrown over the man's shoulder and in both of his hands. A small child was held in the woman's arms and even in the dim light Josie could tell the toddler was deeply asleep, a thumb stuck in its cupid bow mouth. The couple pointed one direction and then another before heading off to the right about three doors down and disappearing inside.

She slowly let out the breath that she'd been holding. They were simply a harmless couple with an exhausted kid. No threat. No danger. She'd overreacted, but then what happened when they finally found her and she under-reacted? It was better to stay vigilant, always keeping an eye on her surroundings as if her life depended on it. She couldn't allow herself to get sloppy because that's how people ended up dead.

Like Amy. Those wide, unblinking eyes staring up at Josie still haunted her, asleep or awake.

With unsteady hands Josie let go of the drapes and fell back down to the carpet, ignoring the rough texture against her bare legs. She began to tremble in a delayed reaction and she could only sit there on the floor, propped against the wall as sobs began to shake her entire body. Hot tears ran down her cheeks and she rocked back and forth, trying to somehow self-soothe but knowing inside that this situation she found herself in was only going to get worse.

It might never get better.

Everything was about as bad as it could be and her options were few and far between. Cops were chasing her, bad people were chasing her, and now she was scared of her own shadow.

She didn't know how much more of this she could take.

CHAPTER FOUR

Nothing had prepared Josie for what she found at Evan's home the next morning.

Dirt and grime an inch thick. Stacks of newspapers, magazines, and general crap everywhere she looked to the point that he'd dug a path through the house so he could get from point A to point B. There wasn't a surface that wasn't piled high except for a patch of table in the kitchen where he had a drip coffee maker.

"I hope you don't take cream in your coffee because I don't have any milk." Grimacing, Evan handed her a bottle of chilled water. "The fridge is unusable in its current state so I have a cooler filled with water, juice, and soda. It's going to be hot today so you'll need to stay hydrated."

She did a three-sixty, taking in as much as she could. It might be easier to just bulldoze the whole place and start again. "You weren't kidding. I've never seen anything like this."

His shoulders slumped and he sighed heavily. "I wouldn't blame you if you've changed your mind. The fact is I ought to be kissing your feet for even thinking about taking this on with me."

Josie had a distinct feeling it was that desperation that had snagged this job for her; no references and very few questions asked so she couldn't complain. At the moment, a regular job wasn't available to her.

Besides, she was getting to like Evan.

He appeared to be a nice man who had a near impossible job ahead of him and could use the help. He'd also been funny and charming as they'd talked over breakfast. He had interesting stories of visiting here in the summers between school years.

"Can I ask you a question? Are you fixing up this house to live in or to sell?"

Careful not to knock over a stack of magazines, Evan leaned across the door frame. "Good question. The fact is I don't know. You say that you were laid off so you're planning to travel the country. Well, I quit my job not long ago and I still don't know what I'm going to do with my life now. My family has owned this house for a long time and something needed to be done with it. But my parents aren't in the best of health to do that so it seemed like a good project while I figure things out. I used to work down here near Tampa a few years ago and I've always liked the area, although I'm originally from Montana."

She frowned, having a difficult time picturing him in boots and a cowboy hat. He was currently dressed in khaki cargo shorts, a yellow t-shirt, and beat-up tennis shoes. He was a handsome man by any criteria with his close-cropped dark hair, slight beard, and light blue eyes. His shirt strained at his wide shoulders and his abdomen looked trim. Heck, even his legs were tanned and muscular. If he hadn't been hiding himself away in this backwater burg he would probably have a few females following him around.

He might have them anyway for all she knew. There were certainly plenty of hiding places in this house, or spots to hide a body too. Which considering her recent history immediately creeped her out.

"You don't think there are any bodies here, do you?"

His brows shot up and he threw back his head and laughed, clearly amused by her semi-serious question.

"I'm not sure how we got onto this subject but I can state categorically that there are not any dead people under one of these stacks. We'd smell them by now."

Her gaze swept the room, landing on a particularly suspicious mound of newspapers on the couch. "Okay, but if I find a body or even a hand or a leg I'm going to need a raise."

"If you manage to find anything like that I'll double your hourly rate. It would only be fair since I'd bet I would be scarring you for life."

She was smiling at him and then her current predicament slapped her in the face, wiping any trace of happiness from her expression. She'd been enjoying his company so much she'd almost forgotten how incredibly screwed she was and that it wouldn't be her first dead body. That cherry had been well and truly popped a few nights before. Despite what she'd told him, this wasn't a fun, adventurous lark around the country. This was life and death.

She'd do well to keep her head down, make some money, and then get the hell out of town.

◈ ◈ ◈

Pushing a sweaty and dusty lock of hair out of her eyes, Josie dug into another stack of papers in the kitchen. After much discussion, they'd decided she should start here since the quicker they could get the room cleaned out, the quicker they could actually cook a meal in it.

So far she'd looked through mostly stacks of old periodicals, dusty and torn. She'd carefully set aside the *Life* magazines she'd found, wondering if perhaps they might be worth a few dollars to a collector. Surprisingly, they weren't in terrible shape despite how they'd been stored, although they weren't pristine enough to fetch top dollar. The photos in the magazines had been seductive and she'd found herself flipping through the pages of pictures from the Vietnam War and hippies at Haight-Ashbury. If she had time, she could easily get lost in the history of an era before she was born and only seen in movies.

Sipping at her water bottle, she almost choked mid-gulp when she tossed an old newspaper from 1973 aside, revealing her find. Her fingers ran down the cover reverently as she reminded herself to breathe. Carefully, she lifted it off the stack and paged through the magazine. Tears, not from the dust but from a swell of emotion, pricked the back of her eyes and she swiped at the moisture dragging more dirt across her cheek.

"Evan," she called, although the sound came out more like a croak. "Evan, I think you need to see this."

He strode through the doorway, wiping his hands with a towel. "Is everything okay? Did you see a spider?"

She couldn't hold in a laugh at the thought of her cowering in a corner from the mere sight of an arachnid.

"I'm not afraid of spiders unless it's a real big one. No, I wanted you to see this. It's quite a find."

Even tossed the towel aside and grinned. "You haven't seen any of our Florida spiders. They get big, all right. And hairy. Actually, being careful about them is a good idea. There might be some brown recluse spiders in here and they are poisonous."

He looked completely serious.

Now that was something she didn't want to hear. Maybe spiders were creepy after all. The one thing she didn't want to see was a palmetto bug, although she was pretty sure she was going to in all this mess.

"You're full of good news. I should have asked for hazard pay." She held up the magazine. "Take a look at this."

He took it from her hand and perused the cover, his brows shooting up almost to his hair line. "Holy shit. This is the *Life* magazine from JFK's assassination."

Evan sat down on the floor next to Josie. "Isn't it amazing? I got so emotional when I saw the picture of his little boy saluting. It was so sad."

"I remember my mom and dad telling me stories of where they were that day. They talked about Camelot and how magical it was. I don't think we have anything to compare to that now."

Josie would gladly take a time machine back to anywhere before Saturday night. "I'm sure you'll want to keep that. It might even be worth some money."

Evan shrugged but smiled. "Maybe, but it's not in the best of condition. I think I'd like to keep it though. If you come across anything else you think is interesting just set it in a separate stack and I'll look through it later."

So far, Evan Davis was proving to be an easy going boss. She was also overjoyed to see that he didn't own a television, which boded well for her. It would make it more difficult for him to find out who she was.

"How's the bedroom coming? Found any spiders or snakes?"

Evan scowled as if she'd insulted his mother. "I do not like snakes. At all. So let's not joke about that."

Josie held up her hands in a sign of surrender. Evan actually looked kind of cute at the moment, like a little boy who had been told he couldn't play outside. "I don't like them either. I was simply inquiring as to how the work was going. Do you want me to continue in here or help you?"

Evan sighed and looked around the chaos that surrounded them. "I was hoping for a divide and conquer strategy but I think you might be onto something. It might be more efficient for both of us to work on one room before moving to another. The question is should it be the bedroom or the kitchen?"

Every room was daunting except for the bathroom, which Evan had cleared upon his arrival. "The bedroom, I think. You can eat out but you have to sleep here."

Giving her an approving look, Evan nodded in agreement. "Good point. Let's hit the bedroom and then we'll head to the pizza place for dinner. How does that sound?"

It sounded like a good deal and she'd be a fool to turn it down. Unlike the kitchen, the bedroom had an adequate cross-breeze through the windows and would be much more pleasant to work in. It hadn't figured into her opinion of which room they should work on but it was a nice bonus. She'd only worked in the kitchen for a few hours but she'd almost melted with the sticky heat and stale air.

"I say it sounds like a plan. Let me grab another bottle of water and we'll tackle it."

This job wasn't so bad. She was sweaty and dirty but Evan was pleasant to be around and not a slave driver. The wage was fair and she was tucked out of the way in a home miles off the beaten path. Surely no one would look for her out here. Maybe…just maybe…she could relax. Just a little bit. Because if she didn't, she might break into a thousand brittle pieces and blow away with a puff of wind.

CHAPTER FIVE

One short week later Evan was feeling like he'd won the lottery. Hell, better than that. Hiring Lisa had turned out to be the best damn decision he'd ever made. She worked tirelessly until she was sweaty and dirty from head to toe without a single complaint. No whining or bitching. When they were done he was going to build a statue in her honor right out in the front yard. There was no way he would have managed to finish the bedroom this week without her.

He dipped his paintbrush in the paint can and brushed a spot on the wall before stepping back to survey his work. "I'm not sure about this color. It's so...blue."

Lisa put down her own paint roller and came to stand beside him. "That's because *it is* blue. And need I remind you, we spent a couple of hours at the hardware store picking out that particular shade. You wanted it to be blue, but not too blue. It had to be masculine but not harsh. Giddy with just a hint of playfulness."

He sure as hell hadn't said that last part but he'd learned she was a sarcastic little shit and he had to admit he liked that about her. She could make him laugh until his sides hurt.

But he had stretched her patience badly when looking at paint colors. The looks she'd given him that day had been priceless. He was pretty sure she wanted to haul off and smack him a few times. He wouldn't have blamed her if she had. He'd annoyed himself, if the truth were known.

"I think you're confusing the paint with wine. Seriously, I don't remember it looking this bright in the store."

"It will dry darker," she pointed out. "But if you're truly spooked I guess we could go back to the store and get three gallons of the beige you were eyeing. If you don't mind it being boring as hell."

"The beige was nice."

He didn't know why he was arguing with her. He didn't know shit about color or design and had grabbed the most neutral paint he could find before she'd called a halt to the whole thing and made him start again. She'd dragged him to the home furnishings store where he picked out a comforter, sheets, pillows, and drapes. Then and only then would she let him choose a paint color.

And when he said he'd picked it out he meant that she had. She'd made a show of trying to simply steer him in the right direction, but from the raised eyebrows and exasperated expressions he could tell he had lousy taste. That didn't surprise him as he tried to keep things simple in his own life.

White walls. Beige carpeting. Blue and brown furniture.

So he'd shut his mouth and really taken a look at what she was suggesting, and damned if it wasn't miles better than anything he would have selected. She'd managed to integrate his brown and blue tastes but in a way he never would have expected. He was kind of looking forward to sleeping in this room when it was done.

"I thought you decided you weren't going to be afraid of color," Lisa reminded him with a smirk. "You told me you wanted to live a little and experiment. Have we changed our mind?"

Maybe. No, wait. It was out of his comfort zone but wasn't that why he was doing this? He'd lived his entire life doing the safe thing, the expected thing. The only time he took any chances was when he was at work, and for the most part it had paid off. He'd been climbing the ranks at the Marshal Service when he was shot.

"No, we haven't." Evan blew out of breath, conceding defeat without much of a fight. He wanted this, he was just wary. The last thing he needed was a psychedelic bedroom that would make him get less sleep than he already was. "It's just…"

"Blue. Yes, I know." Lisa laughed and went back to her paint roller and pan. "I'll tell you what. If you don't like how the room looks when we're done with the whole thing, I'll paint it all again myself. For free. That's how confident I am that you're going to love it. Is that a deal? It's a win-win and you can't lose."

She has a great smile.

Evan mentally slapped himself as his mind wandered into dangerous territory. He'd spent the better part of a week usually not more than three feet from Lisa and as each day passed his admiration for her grew. Not only was she a hard worker, she was usually happy too, singing to the radio and even dancing around despite the oppressive heat and humidity. She'd made working on this hovel a great deal of fun.

She wasn't hard on the eyes either. Today she was dressed in cutoff jean shorts that showed off a pair of tanned legs and a worn and faded t-shirt, her long auburn hair pulled back into a braid that went halfway down her back. Her nose was sprinkled with newly-acquired freckles from the Florida sun that only served to make her look even younger than the first day they'd met. He really needed to ask her how old she was but there were few ways to phrase that question without offending a woman.

"It's a deal," he conceded, having no intention of not paying her for the work if she had to repaint. Her efforts so far had been nothing short of heroic. "I do like the color. I'm just unsure about how I'm going to like looking at it on my walls day after day."

Lisa swept her arm toward the bed in the middle of the room. "If we do this right you shouldn't notice the wall color. It's just a backdrop, a canvas really, for the rest of the decor."

"You sound like an interior decorator. Is that what you did before?"

Instantly her bright smile disappeared and her gaze darted around the room. "Nope. I just like color."

She was lying but Evan didn't push her for the truth. Clearly, it was something she didn't want to discuss and she hadn't pushed him for personal information either. In fact, she'd been exceedingly respectful about all the subjects that put him in a bad mood. The least he could do was give her the same courtesy.

"You're more creative than I am so I'm grateful for the help," he said instead. "We better get started or we'll never finish this today. I'm hoping we can get two coats on these walls plus the trim."

"You're an ambitious man but I think we can do it." Lisa's smile was back and he breathed a sigh of relief. He didn't want her to be unhappy. He desperately needed her on this job.

He'd come to depend on her company more than he should. She was friendly, relaxing, and she didn't bug him about what he was going to do with the rest of his life. He hadn't expected it or even wanted it, but Lisa had become important to him in a short space of time. She'd quickly become his friend but eventually she would leave, moving on to the next place in her quest to see the country.

Why did that bother him so damn much?

◈ ◈ ◈

Her muscles protesting every movement, Josie hefted one side of the new mattress up into the air so she and Evan could set it down directly on top of the box spring. They'd finished painting the walls and then assembled the new bedframe, a simple Shaker style stained a medium walnut. Evan had also purchased a large matching dresser and two side tables, and Josie had chosen a few throw rugs to add warmth to the newly refinished hardwood floors. All in all, the room was really coming together.

"I could have done this. You need to be careful or you're going to hurt yourself," Evan warned, shifting the mattress an inch to the left.

Josie reached for the freshly laundered fitted sheet, purchased brand new during their trip into Ocala earlier in the week. "You're sweet to be worried but I'm fine. It wasn't that heavy."

His eyebrow arched and an evil smile spread across his handsome face. "You think I'm worried about you? I'm just concerned about who would help me out around here if something happened to you. I'd have to do all this work myself."

Grabbing one of the matching throw pillows, she lobbed it in the air so it bounced off his head. "I'm going to pretend you didn't say that."

Evan snorted and began to tuck his side of the sheets under the mattress. "You can pretend but I'm seriously worried. I'm thinking I might have to invest in getting you a weekly massage or something. Maybe even wrap you in bubble wrap when you're off duty. You've made yourself indispensable."

She couldn't help the warmth she felt at being so appreciated but it was tempered with the knowledge that she couldn't stay long. At any given time, she might have to grab her meager belongings and get out of town. Each night in her lonely hotel room, she watched the news and scoured the papers for any mention of herself, but so far she'd been lucky. She hoped that luck would hold out at least until she'd earned enough money to move on.

"I think I'll turn down the bubble wrap but say yes to the massage. I will admit my muscles and joints are not happy about this new level of activity. On the bright side, my clothes are beginning to get loose. I think I've lost a few pounds, probably from sweating."

Heat rushed to her cheeks as his appreciative gaze swept her head to toe. She'd never been skinny and she wasn't fat either, but rarely had she been on the receiving end of such male enjoyment.

She could easily get used to it.

Evan had been the perfect gentleman but he also had been warm, friendly, and appreciative. He was the nicest man she'd met in a very long time and it sucked that she had to keep her distance from him. In another time and place they might have become close friends. Maybe even more.

"You don't really have any weight to lose so I'll make sure you eat a big piece of pie or cake tonight for dessert."

She tossed the comforter on the bed and began to spread it over the sheets. "I'm not missing any meals, believe me. I've never been much for dieting or working out. I'll probably die young choking on a piece of chocolate while I trip over a pillow and blanket."

Or by those killers that are after me. Stop! Don't think about that.

"I've seen worse ways to go."

Both Evan and Josie were on all fours on the bed, pulling and tugging at the comforter to smooth out any wrinkles. She tucked the bottom corner down so it laid flat before reaching over the side to grab the bed pillows on the floor. When she looked up, Evan was right there just inches from her face, looking as surprised as she felt.

Their gazes locked and for a moment she was lost in his eyes, just the color of well-washed blue denim. Reminding herself to breathe, she exhaled slowly and sat back on her heels to put some distance between them. She couldn't allow her attraction to Evan to override her common sense. Any relationship she might start wasn't going anywhere. There was a good chance she'd end up dead or in prison and she wouldn't drag someone as nice as he was into the mess that had become her life.

"So," she said, the words sounding way too loud in the silence. "Pillows."

She held up the king-sized pillows as if they were trophies. Sometimes, especially when she was nervous, she couldn't help but act like a total dork.

If he thought she was a big goof he was too polite to say so. He reached for the pillows and tucked them at the headboard. "Thank you. I think the bed looks good. You were right, this all goes together."

Her palms were sweaty and a flush of warmth crawled up her chest, making her shift uncomfortably on the mattress.

Shit, she was on a bed with a gorgeous guy. That hadn't happened in a while.

Move. For the love of God, move.

Jumping up and almost tripping over her own feet, she tried to act casual as if she was simply perusing the room. "It looks good. Really good. Yep, it looks good."

I am such an idiot.

She wasn't talking about him, or at least she didn't want him to think she was talking about him. But he did look good. Very good. It took every ounce of strength she had not to reach out and brush that growth of whiskers on his square jaw or let her fingers trail down the muscles of his arm.

Stop drooling, Josie. It's not polite to pant.

Evan was smiling at her, still kneeling on the bed looking rumpled and sexy. It wasn't fair that men looked good sweaty and dirty and then add in the bed...Dammit, why didn't he get off?

No! No getting off! Remove any images of employer getting off from brain. Dammit, I need a lobotomy and big glass of wine.

"I'd say everything looks good," Evan agreed, finally climbing off the bed much to her relief. "Thanks to you, of course. What do you say I buy you dinner? We'll celebrate finishing a room."

Under any other circumstances, she'd have argued but getting out of this bedroom was priority number one. She heard herself quickly agreeing as she backed out into the hallway.

She was pretty sure Evan was laughing at her when she collided with the door frame, banging her head and almost seeing stars. She laughed it off and bolted down the stairs and into the kitchen where the cooler resided.

She needed a cool drink and ice. Lots and lots of ice.

CHAPTER SIX

After he'd dropped Lisa at her motel later that evening, Evan twisted the top off of a beer and stretched out on his new bed. There was still the faint aroma of new paint in the air but it had lessened quite a bit since the afternoon, thanks to the open windows and a few strategically placed fans. He had a window air conditioner in the bedroom but tonight he'd sleep with the windows open to get rid of the last of the fumes.

He stared at the blank wall and kicked off his shoes, his eyelids already heavy. He was dog-tired after all the work they'd done today and Lisa hadn't complained at all. He was working her like a rented mule and he could tell that her muscles ached with practically every movement, but not one negative word passed her lips.

And pretty lips they were, too.

His employee was quite attractive and he would have had to be blind not to notice. They'd had a moment on this bed earlier today and it had clearly freaked her out. She'd scrambled off the bed as if it was on fire, almost bolting for the door she was in such a hurry to put some distance between them. He, on the other hand, had enjoyed their nearness very much. She looked cute, she smelled good, and she made him laugh. It was a trifecta of attractiveness and he wasn't immune, but it didn't look like she was feeling positive about anything happening between them.

Evan was a typical man when it came to relationships, or at least he'd always thought he was. He liked women. He liked sex. So when the two of them combined he was a pretty happy guy. He wouldn't mind if something more intimate than friendship began between him and Lisa but he wasn't looking for a commitment. He didn't even know where he'd be or what he'd be doing six months from now, so it wasn't a good idea to start something up and Lisa was in the same boat.

It had crossed his mind a few times this week that their friendship was ripe to take the next step but he hadn't pushed the subject, not even when they'd ended up inches from one another on this mattress. He didn't want her to think she had to…put out… to keep her job. Not in the least. His desire to spend more time with her was separate from the work. If she said no, he'd respect it.

But he'd be disappointed. He liked her more than any woman in recent memory, but then part of the reason he liked her was because she was so intelligent. He didn't have a job and nothing on the horizon. He was aimless and the only reason he got up in the morning was to clean out this piece of crap house for his family. That wasn't exactly a recipe for making a woman fall for him. If she had a lick of common sense, she'd stay three feet away at all times.

His chirping phone on the bedside table pulled him from his thoughts. Reaching for it, he checked the screen, hoping it wasn't his former partner Marisa. She'd been bombarding him with calls and texts lately trying to convince him to return to the Marshal Service, despite the fact that he'd be on desk duty.

Seth Reilly. Old Army buddy and sheriff of Harper, Montana.

"Hey Seth. Haven't heard from you in awhile. How's Presley and the kids?"

When Evan had been a marshal he'd hidden Presley in witness protection with Seth. Now they were happily married with two kids and their lives were complete chaos.

"They're good. Bennett is doing T-ball this summer and it's a hoot to watch. Presley even talked me into volunteering to help coach the team. Imagine twenty little kids with the attention span of a gnat. One needs to go potty, one wants to know if he can have a snack, and another just wants his mommy. I'm outnumbered and overwhelmed."

Seth wasn't fooling anybody.

"You love it," Evan pronounced. "Don't even try and deny it. So to what do I owe the honor of a call? Is anything wrong?"

"No, as I said, everything is good. All good." Seth sighed heavily and Evan now had an inkling of what this was all about. "Marisa called me."

It was Evan's turn to sigh. "I had a feeling about that. Let me guess…she wants you to convince me to go back to the Marshal Service. She wants you to tell me being tied to a desk is better than cleaning up an old house and bumming around Florida. Did I miss anything?"

Seth whistled in response. "Only the part about how you weren't very bright to quit your job without a plan. Can I assume that this is not the first you've heard from her? Has she roped in other unsuspecting friends to do her dirty work?"

This must be one of her newer ideas. She was getting desperate.

"You're the first, actually, but I doubt you'll be the last. I'm sure by now she's called any and all of my friends and family."

"She's worried about you," Seth said after a small silence.

It was sweet but Evan was fine. Confused and unsure, but fine. He simply needed time to figure things out.

"Are you worried about me?"

There was one thing Evan knew for sure and it was that Seth Reilly was as honest as the day was long. He'd tell the truth no matter what.

"A little." Seth groaned and Evan hated himself for putting one of his best friends on the spot. Men didn't like to talk about their damn feelings and now Seth had to do just that. "Dammit, it's just that you've always seemed to know what you were doing and where you were going. Now you're just drifting and it has us a little spooked. It's not like you."

Evan wasn't sure he could explain this but he'd try. "That's the whole point, my friend. All my life I've done what was expected of me, what was planned. I went into the Army Rangers and then into law enforcement. I worked hard, dedicated myself and climbed the ladder. Mom and Dad beamed with pride. Then I got shot that day and everything changed. Suddenly I wasn't on the fast track to anywhere but a desk job managing ambitious assholes that were just like me. I couldn't face it, so I retired and took the sheriff's job."

"You hated it," Seth stated flatly before Evan could continue. "Don't deny it because we could all see it. I don't remember the last time I saw you really happy."

Words hadn't been invented yet that could describe the misery Evan had been in while doing that job. It had been a clusterfuck from beginning to end and the day he'd quit had been the happiest in memory. But he did feel sorry for whatever bastard they'd roped into doing it after he left.

"I did hate it," Evan conceded, not wanting to admit to his friend how bad things had become. "That town had many problems and I'm glad to see the back of it, frankly. But I didn't want to just jump back into something blindly. For the first time in my damn life, I'm actually taking time for me and figuring out what I want to do. Not what my parents want me to do or what my superiors want me to do, or even what my friends and co-workers think I should do. This is about me. The fact is, even when I was happy as a marshal I wasn't really happy."

"Are you happy now?"

Evan didn't answer the question immediately, wanting to take his time and think about the truth of the answer.

"I'm happier than I've been in over a year and I think I could be even happier in the future. For the first time in a long time I have the hope of being truly happy. I don't think you know how huge that is, Seth. Shit, you're always happy now."

His friend chuckled before lowering his voice, apparently not wanting anyone to overhear. "I'm not happy every minute of the day. Presley made spaghetti again tonight for dinner. That's the fourth time in two weeks. It tasted funny. Do you think she's trying to poison me?"

Presley would do many things but poisoning Seth wasn't one of them. "No, I don't. I think she's probably overwhelmed by having two kids underfoot all day and then her third grown kid comes home asking what she's made for dinner. Order a pizza, bro, and give her the night off."

A string of choked coughs came through the phone that might have been laughter as well. "You've got a point. She is busy and I probably need to be more sensitive to how hard she works. She even helps out at the station once in awhile when I'm between office help."

Seth went through secretaries like a hot knife through butter. Some didn't even last the entire day, disappearing at lunchtime, never to be heard from again.

"See? She's probably exhausted and is tired of figuring out what's for dinner. I remember my mom telling my dad the same thing. She didn't mind cooking but deciding what to fix was always a quandary."

"I appreciate the advice, although you've never been married so I'm not sure if I should be listening. Let's get back to you. How are things at the house? Have you made any progress?"

"I have, actually. We finished the bedroom today. It turned out amazing."

"We? Did you finally hire someone to do that dirty, thankless job?"

An image of Lisa flashed through Evan's mind and he found himself smiling for no particular reason.

"I did. She's a hard worker and doing a great job. I wish I could clone her a dozen times over."

"She? You're making some poor girl shovel out that mess? You're a real hard ass, Davis. Does she get lunch and coffee breaks? A day off? I saw on the news that it's ninety degrees down there with some kind of inhuman humidity that would turn most people into a sponge. That can't be healthy."

Wincing, Evan realized that Seth had a point. He'd worked Lisa six days in a row and she deserved a day off, time to rest. She probably hadn't complained because she obviously needed the money, but that didn't mean he could work her into an early grave.

"I'm giving her the day off tomorrow and I do give her breaks and lunches. I'm lucky to have her, honestly. She's smart and funny and she really knows how to pick out paint."

Shit, now he was babbling like a fucking idiot. He'd said too much and Seth would pounce on this like a mouse on Swiss cheese.

"Is she now?" Seth drawled, amusement in his tone. "She sounds like a regular paragon of virtue. Tell me, Davis, what does she look like? I bet she's good-looking too."

"I'm not going to answer that."

"He's pleading the fifth, folks." The sounds of laughter filled Evan's ear. "That is an answer, asshole. She must be something else. I think we have our answer as to why you're hanging out down there. It's a woman."

Evan sat up in the bed, suddenly irritated with his old friend. He didn't need this bullshit in his already confused existence. "It's not a woman. I'm taking some time. I told you."

"I bet she–"

"Leave it," Evan growled, putting an end to the subject. "Lisa is off-limits as a topic. Pick something else."

He'd never had a problem talking about women with Seth before, so he wasn't sure what this rush of protectiveness was all about. He'd only known Lisa for a week but he wasn't ready to share her with anyone. He wanted her all to himself, if only for a little while longer.

"I don't have anything else. Just keep in touch and don't be a damn stranger, okay? When you get that house cleaned out why don't you plan a visit up here? I'll get all the guys together and we'll have a cookout or something. Hell, I think I can even get Jason, Jared, and Logan here."

He did miss his friends, even though he didn't miss the job. "Sounds like a plan. Listen, I didn't mean to–"

"Shut the hell up," Seth interrupted with a laugh. "You don't owe me any apologies. I was sticking my nose where it doesn't belong. End of story."

"I appreciate the call though. If Marisa contacts you again tell her to deal directly with me. I'm more than a little pissed off that she went behind my back. She knows how I feel about this."

"If I hear from her I'll tell her, but between you and me I'm hoping I'm off her call sheet, if you know what I mean. I've got to get going. Presley's trying to bathe the kids and Bennett has taken to streaking around the house naked and soapy. I better give her a hand."

"Tell her hello and I'll talk to you soon."

They ended the call and Evan tossed the phone onto the comforter next to him. He reached for it again to call Lisa and let her know she had the day off but then remembered she didn't have a phone. Frowning, he decided to pick her up for breakfast like it was any other morning and let her know over bacon and eggs. She had to eat regardless, and so did he.

Which then led to a few thoughts of how he'd spend the day as well. He needed some rest but he was beginning to feel a little claustrophobic in the house. They'd spent most of the week here and he was itching to get outside and enjoy some sunshine.

Which gave him an idea.

Lisa wanted to see the country. He could help with that goal and they could both have a nice time doing it.

Hopefully she'd be up for a little fun and adventure.

Or she'd turn him down flat.

He knew which one he wanted, but what did Lisa want? He simply wanted to get to know her better.

He might even talk about himself if she asked, and if that didn't scare her off, nothing would.

CHAPTER SEVEN

Josie popped the last bite of hash brown into her mouth and hummed with appreciation. With all the hard labor she'd been putting in the last week, her appetite was booming and everything seemed to taste so darn good. Funny how she'd been too busy running the rat race back home to stop and truly enjoy her food but now she had no career and no ladder to climb. She was distraction free.

Except for those people that wanted her dead and the other ones that wanted her in prison.

Strangely, since coming here to Cypress Corner she felt safer with each passing day. Those menacing men hadn't shown up and neither had the police, so she was beginning to settle into her new life in the tiny town. People were friendly and Evan was nice and easy to work for, which added up to very little stress on top of what she already had. The job might be dirty and sweaty but it kept her mind off of her problems. Evan was truly thankful for everything she did and praised her often, which she hadn't been the norm at her last crappy gig. The only reward there for a job well done was more work. Other people's work.

There was something about Evan that made her world seem like she was wrapped in a safe cocoon. Perhaps it was how calm he was no matter what was going on. Or maybe it was how strong and capable he appeared to be in all situations. Whatever it was, Josie was certain he could handle whatever monkey poo life threw at him.

That same man was signaling for more coffee while he shoveled down a mound of scrambled eggs. That first night they'd met she'd been shocked by how much food he could put away and she still wasn't used to it. He'd ordered pancakes, eggs, bacon, biscuits and gravy, toast, and fruit.

The plates were now empty. If she'd eaten that much food she'd have to rolled out of the front door on her side like a big balloon. Not to mention the nausea and indigestion that would surely follow.

"So what's on the agenda today?" Josie asked, adding cream and sugar to her warmed-up coffee. "The kitchen again?"

"We're not going to work today," Evan finally replied after a moment. "You've worked hard the last six days and deserve a day off to rest."

That was sweet and everything but she needed the cash. As soon as she had enough money she'd be off to the next town, wherever that might be.

"It's okay. I like to work. I don't mind."

Evan pulled a white envelope from his front jean pocket and slid it across the table. "That's your first week's pay which, by the way, you earned every single cent. I can't tell you how glad I am that you stopped in this town. I couldn't have asked for a better worker than you, Lisa."

Rolling her eyes, she shoved the envelope in her backpack, not bothering to count it. Men like Evan Davis didn't shortchange people.

"You sound a little nervous there, boss. Like you're afraid I'll take this money and catch the next bus out of town. I haven't heard that kind of praise since I was nine and learning to play the piano. Trust me, it wasn't deserved either, but my mother was desperate for me to learn an instrument."

His blue eyes twinkled and his deep laugh caused a few heads to turn. "I'm terrified. There is no way I could do this without you."

She tapped her chin playfully, enjoying teasing him. "You could...but it wouldn't be as much fun. And your bedroom would be ugly."

"Butt ugly," he agreed with a grin. "That's why I keep things simple. Blue and beige. The perfect combination."

She shuddered and took another sip of her coffee. Honestly, if she didn't work today she didn't really know what she'd do. She didn't know many people in town, at least not enough to spend any time with them. Add in that there wasn't much to do on a Sunday and it left her with a long, boring day ahead. The only bright spot was that she might get a nap. Sleep had been in short supply lately.

Pushing her plate away she patted her stomach, feeling pleasantly full. "So what do you have planned today then? What do people do around here for fun?"

Evan snorted and shook his head. "I have no idea what people around here do. The closest movie theatre or mall is a thirty-five minute drive and most of the businesses here in town are closed on Sunday. If I was a betting man, I'd say most of them stay home and watch television."

"You don't own a television."

"Which means I have to find something else to do," he agreed. "How about you do it with me?"

A frisson of electricity ran down her spine at the suggestion in his words, but of course he didn't mean the dirty thoughts that were running through her mind.

"Do...it? I'm scared to ask what that means."

He leaned across the table and waggled his eyebrows. She liked this sexy, teasing side. "Do you trust me?"

Yes. Surprisingly…yes.

"No."

The corners of his lips turn up a little more. "Smart girl. I'm up to no good today."

If he only knew what Josie had been doing before she came to town.

"I'm getting the feeling you have an activity already in mind. Sharing is caring."

"How do you feel about horses?"

"I think they're big, and they probably smell but I can't be sure."

Evan threw down some cash on the check and she tried to add some of her own but he simply gave her a disgusted look and slid it back to her. He obviously felt sorry for her as he never let her pay for anything.

"Have you ever ridden one?"

"Does a merry-go-round count?"

It was his turn to roll his eyes. "I would say no. That is not sufficient training for riding an actual living, breathing animal with a mind of its own. This could be a problem."

Josie had more than one of those and horseback riding wasn't even in the top five.

◈ ◈ ◈

Josie groaned as she dismounted from the dapple-gray horse. "I can't feel my ass."

Evan laughed as he tied the reins to a small branch and then rewarded each horse with a piece of apple from his palm. "It might be a good thing, although it looks like you're not completely numb."

Gingerly she took a few steps, her legs bowed and her back bent awkwardly. Pain shot straight from her lower back down to her ankles and she winced, rubbing her hips and hoping for some relief. All she'd done was sit on the horse. No canter. No gallop. Just sat. It was pathetic and downright sad. This was why she didn't exercise or "work out" or whatever it was called. Sofa surfing was her favorite sport while watching a Netflix marathon.

"Sadly, no. Shit, I am out of shape. How did I let you talk me into this anyway? You're devious and cruel."

Evan spread a large blanket on the ground under a large oak tree and began to pull out the lunch the diner had packed for them. "I've been called much worse. How about I help you sit down and we'll have some lunch. Then maybe an ibuprofen."

"I'll take nothing less than morphine," Josie giggled, not wanting to let her discomfort ruin what had been a lovely day. Since she'd told Evan that her goal was to see America he'd obliged and taken her around some out-of-the-way spots around Cypress Corner. "And I will need your help. My knees don't seem to want to bend any farther than this."

Hovering over the blanket in sort of a half-squat position, she allowed Evan to wrap his arm around her waist, his hand anchored on her ribs. She couldn't help the laughter that bubbled up when she thought of how ridiculous she must look at the moment. It was so funny she couldn't even be bothered to be embarrassed. If she had a phone she would have wanted photos for a good laugh later.

"Just go limp. I've got you."

She placed her hands on his biceps to steady herself but couldn't bring herself to obey. She'd break his back.

"Um, just brace me as I try to sit down."

"No, just listen–"

Of course she didn't listen. She tried to sort of roll back onto her bottom but somehow her legs - which were painfully stiff - tangled with each other and she fell against Evan's muscled body.

He didn't budge. He didn't even breathe heavy or wince.

His hold tightened and he simply grinned down at her as if he helped half-sitting, muscle-hurtin' women every day of his life. Maybe he did for all she knew. He was darn good at it. His arms were like steel bands and his powerful thighs strained against the denim of his jeans, adding to her already flustered state.

"Will you listen to me now? Just go limp. Trust me, I won't drop you."

"I don't want to hurt you. I'm…heavy."

"In the Army I carried packs heavier than you up mountains. Limp. Do it."

His tone brooked no argument and her legs were beginning to give out anyway so she did as he ordered, letting her entire form relax which it turned out lessened the shooting pains down her calves. She let out a sigh of relief as his strong arms lowered her gently to the blanket.

"Thank you, but I think we have an even bigger problem," she said as he settled next to her. "How the hell am I going to get back up? I can feel my muscles tightening already. I may be stuck here for days. Is it supposed to rain?"

Evan handed her a paper plate and plastic fork. "I think I can lift you up without too much effort, although I think I should be insulted that you thought I wasn't strong enough to help you sit down. My leg isn't that bad."

Frowning, Josie eyed his legs for some tell-tale sign of what he was referring to but they both looked perfectly normal. She probably should just let the remark pass but that wasn't who she really was. Too curious to shut up, she plunged forward, hoping she wouldn't upset the man she'd grown quite fond of this week.

"I'm not sure what you're talking about. I don't see anything wrong with your legs."

Evan scowled for a moment but didn't seem upset with her. He slapped his left thigh, which only served to draw her attention there, but it didn't look any different than the other. In fact, it looked nicely muscled, thank you very much.

"Actually, that's the kindest thing you could have said to me. It means that my limp isn't that noticeable, which is good news. I've been working hard on that." He rubbed the denim over the flesh, his expression suddenly far away. "I got shot and they had to put a steel rod and some screws in there. I can tell when it's going to rain."

Sucking in a shocked breath, Josie had to run over the words in her head several times before she could formulate a coherent reply. "Shot? That's not something you hear every day. What the hell happened? Were you in the wrong place at the wrong time?"

Evan chuckled as he set out the chicken, rolls, and thick slabs of chocolate cake for dessert. "I was transporting a prisoner from Canada to a supermax prison in Colorado. The leader of a drug cartel attacked our convoy to break the guy out. I was shot in the process. Luckily, I was wearing a vest so my leg was the only thing that sustained any damage. That and a concussion when I fell off the roof of the armored vehicle."

Transporting a prisoner? Evan was…a cop?

I have the worst luck in the world. How did I not know this?

Josie coughed and cleared her throat a few times. "You're some kind of police officer?"

Evan bit into a drumstick with relish, oblivious to her discomfiture. "I worked for the Marshal Service. Transporting prisoners, witness protection, fugitive retrieval. That sort of thing. I'm retired now."

Her chest squeezed so tightly she forgot about the pain in her lower body. Shit, she couldn't believe this. Out of all the people in the world to meet, like, and work for, she found a police officer.

Someone who hunted fugitives. Holy hell and damn.

He reached across and laid a hand on her knee. "Are you okay? You look pale."

She *was* pale. She'd also broken out into a cold sweat. The fear she'd been feeling earlier in the week was back in glorious Technicolor.

I can't go to jail. I just can't.

"I'm just shocked, that's all," she finally managed to stutter out. "I had no idea. It's just so terrible that you were shot. But you're retired? You look a little young for that."

"They wanted me to ride a desk." He leaned closer, his brows drawn together. "Are you sure you're okay? You haven't touched your lunch."

It was a valid concern as normally she ate like a pig. Reaching out a shaky hand, she plucked the roll from her paper plate and took a tentative bite, trying to smile for Evan as if he hadn't pulled the rug out from under her world.

"It's good," she said between bites. "It's just the heat, I think. It's so hot that it's hard to eat."

He was still frowning but seemed to accept her explanation. "Maybe you should drink some more water. I don't want you getting dehydrated."

She nodded and took a large gulp from the water bottle, her mind still whirling with the new information. He was still Evan her friend but he was also Evan, the former cop, and she wasn't sure what she was supposed to do now. She'd never been on the run before so she was unprepared. She took a few more gulps and tried to calm her racing pulse.

"So you must have a lot of cop friends, I bet. Do you miss it? Being a police officer, I mean."

He took his time answering her question, completely unaware she was holding her breath for the answer.

"I thought I would," he finally said, his gaze far away. Maybe to that day he was shot. "But not really. I liked helping people but I didn't get to do nearly enough of that in the job. Then when I left the Marshal Service, I became the sheriff of my hometown in Montana. Jesus, that was the worst. I hated every damn day of it. So one day I walked in and quit. Slapped my badge down on the mayor's desk, left town, and never looked back. I still don't. I'm trying to figure out what my next phase in life is going to be."

The lump in her throat loosened slightly. It sounded like he was well out of the life. "Your friends must miss you, though."

He shrugged and reached for another piece of chicken. "Some do but so many of them were really just acquaintances. Sometimes a job is all people have in common and when that's gone...My true friends don't care what I do for a living. I'm glad I'm out, honestly. My life is a hell of a lot more peaceful and quiet. I can actually hear myself think now, which might be good or bad depending on the outcome."

"So no regrets?"

"None," he answered promptly. "I'm not sorry I did it but that chapter is closed. I'm moving on to something else. What that is I don't know, but I'm ready to make a change in my life."

Evan didn't care. Josie slowly exhaled all the tension she'd been holding in when he'd told her his past profession. He'd left it behind and wasn't monitoring police scanners hoping to get back on the job. She could relax a little.

But not much.

CHAPTER EIGHT

Evan picked up a pizza at the end of their day before driving them back to his house. He'd take her back to the motel after dinner but he was glad he had another chance to talk with her. Having spent the last eight hours in her company he'd found it wasn't nearly enough. He wanted to spend more time with her, asking her questions about every little thing, wanting to know what she hoped and dreamed about.

He was smitten and that was saying something. He didn't remember the last time a woman had interested him as much as she did. Funny, smart, and gorgeous, she'd kept him laughing and smiling the entire day. It was the best date he'd been on in years. And it wasn't even a real date.

He'd had relationships in the past, including a short friends with benefits thing with his former partner Marisa. They hadn't had much in the way of tender feelings for one another if he was truthful. Mostly he had been convenient for her and she had been the same for him. They worked long hours and having any sort of romantic life was difficult, if not downright impossible. It helped that they both knew how the job worked.

Things had ended long before he'd been shot and without much fanfare. As if it had never happened, they went back to being partners and friends with barely a ripple on the surface of their relationship. But perhaps Marisa had been more involved than he had thought if she couldn't give up on the idea of him returning to the Marshal Service. She was spending way too much of her time worrying about his stupid ass and that wasn't good. He didn't want to hurt her but he simply didn't have any feelings for her…like that. She was a good friend and that was it.

"Are you going to be able to walk?" Evan asked when he pulled in front of his house. "Do you need some help getting out of the car?"

She'd already promised him that she would soak in a hot bath when she returned to her motel room. He reminded himself to pull a tube of muscle cream out of the medicine cabinet as well or she might not even be able to get out of bed tomorrow. If he thought she'd take it, he'd give her another day off but he knew she was desperate for the money. He'd just make sure that whatever he gave her to do tomorrow was relatively easy, like sorting through stacks of newspaper and magazines. She could do that sitting down.

Lisa's lips pressed together and her green eyes sparkled in challenge. "Of course I can walk. I'm just sore. A bath and a few ibuprofen and I'll be good as new."

She was fibbing and putting on a brave show but he could tell she was highly uncomfortable. He wanted to sweep her off her feet and carry her into the house but he'd probably get a knee in the balls for his trouble. She was an independent cuss with a tart tongue and she didn't like him fussing over her like when he reminded her to drink her water or take a break. Independent as hell.

He didn't bother to argue with her, instead grabbing the pizza box from the back seat along with the six-pack of cold soda. It wasn't easy to keep his mouth shut as he watched her take every excruciating step to the front door, especially when she tried to hide her wince at the porch steps, but he somehow managed to keep from remarking on her difficulty. He was skating on thin ice as it was by continuing to push the subject.

Closed up all day, the house was stifling but he opened a few windows and the slight cross breeze was quickly cooling down the living room. Every piece of furniture had stacks of crap on it and he realized they didn't have anywhere to sit and eat.

He hadn't thought this through at all.

"It's such a nice night. Why don't we eat on the front porch?" Lisa suggested, her gaze sweeping the room. Even if the couch had been cleared it clearly wasn't clean enough to eat on.

But the front porch had an old metal table with two rickety chairs he was pretty sure would still hold their weight. It wasn't fancy and it wasn't hygienic but it would have to do.

"That's a good idea."

It had been Lisa's idea to come back here. She had been persuasive, clearly still uneasy around the residents of Cypress Corner. Whenever anyone would stop by their table to chat Lisa would drop her gaze and study her shoes, only interacting if Evan forced her to. He respected that she liked to keep to herself though so he tried to let her have her way. He handed the pizza to Lisa while he retrieved supplies from the kitchen, juggling the sodas, paper plates, and napkins before placing them on the table.

The sun was beginning to sink into the horizon and already he could hear the symphony of crickets in the yard serenading their meal. Evan had always loved this part of the day. After some good hard work, there was nothing better than putting his feet up and relaxing while he listened to the sounds of nature. Whatever his next career in life turned out to be, he had to make sure he made time for this.

"Soda?" Evan held up a can and Lisa nodded, settling into the chair opposite. She opened the pizza box and the smell of tomatoes and garlic wafted around them, making his stomach growl. Lunch seemed far away. "So we talked about me today but we didn't talk much about you. Tell me more about yourself."

Lisa's eyes widened slightly almost in panic, but if he'd alarmed her she quickly hid it. She was a private person and he didn't want to pry but he was curious. He'd opened up to her today in an effort to show her she was safe with him. He wouldn't discuss her life with anyone.

"There's not much to tell." She popped a piece of sausage into her mouth. "I had a pretty normal upbringing in Connecticut. My mom was a single parent and I was an only child so we were pretty close."

"Were?"

The corners of her mouth drooped and she sighed heavily. "She passed away a few years ago. Breast cancer. It all seemed to happen so fast. She'd ignored the warning signs too long, I guess."

"I'm sorry." He truly was. It was obvious from the bright tears in Lisa's eyes that she'd loved her mother a great deal. "Do you have any other family?"

"A few cousins but we're not close. Not long after she passed away I was downsized from my job, probably because I took so much time off to care for her. It didn't matter because I hated that job anyway and I was beginning to hate the city. So I packed up my belongings and moved out of my New York City apartment that I shared with three other girls. Headed down to the D.C. area where my best friend from college lived. She helped me get a job and an apartment. I started over really, and it was the best thing I could have done for myself."

"Then you were laid off again," Evan prompted, wanting her to continue. Not only was he learning about her life but he was also able to listen to her speak. Her voice was soft and strong all at the same time and although he wasn't sure how that was possible, he was sure that he enjoyed it.

She finished the piece of crust she had been chewing before answering. "The economy is cruel."

Evan wasn't a genius but he wasn't a stupid man, either. Lisa was carefully picking and choosing what she shared with him. The bare bones. No flowery details, no anecdotal stories. Just the facts and as few as possible. If he wanted to learn more he was going to have to ask.

"You never said what you did for a living."

Lisa fiddled with her soda can as if deciding whether to answer. "I didn't tell you the whole truth before when you asked because it's hard to talk about it. I haven't exactly set the world on fire with my genius, you see. I do have a degree in design. I worked as a low-level assistant for one of the big fashion houses in New York City. Let me repeat the low-level part. I was one rung above making coffee but that's how you move up in those places. You have to pay your dues. In D.C., I was able to get a job as an assistant to a successful interior designer. I learned a lot and it was a great opportunity but she sold off her business to one of those big corporations. They came through and promptly fired everyone, which she had expressly said wouldn't happen. But of course it did."

Not wanting to spook her but wanting to offer some sort of comfort, Evan placed his own hand over hers, lacing the fingers together. "Life's been tough on you. I admire your grit though. Now you're taking time for yourself while you still can. Seems like a good plan."

She looked up at him and shook her head, a smile playing on her full lips. "Tough? I don't think I really know what that is. Hell, if people don't like chintz sofas they don't shoot at me. They bitch, whine, and complain but I don't need a trip to the hospital afterward. Besides, my mother always told me that I needed to learn to take care of myself. No one was going to offer to do it and that I could only depend on myself."

That was a lonely philosophy.

"I may have made things sound worse than they actually were. I didn't have people shooting at me every single day. Only sometimes. Most of a cop's life is paperwork." He leaned forward so their lips were close together and he could smell the light floral fragrance from her hair. "Although I will admit that I hate chintz. I'm more of a leather sofa type."

For a moment their gazes locked and he instinctually moved nearer, the attraction between them powerful, crackling hot. But at the last minute she jerked back into her chair, her chest rising and falling rapidly as if she'd finished a race.

"I–I have to go to the bathroom."

The legs of her chair made a scraping sound as she shoved it backward and then bolted for the relative safety of the house. He heard her footsteps on the stairs and couldn't suppress a smile of satisfaction. Little Miss Lisa might act all cool and unaffected but it was purely an act. The simmering heat was mutual. He wasn't out there all alone feeling like a fool.

Evan hadn't felt like this about a female in a damn long time and he wasn't going to let this chance pass by. Wasn't this what his new life was about? He was going to go for it.

He'd end up a winner or a fool.

CHAPTER NINE

Josie pressed her cool, wet fingertips to her heated cheeks as she stared at her own reflection in the bathroom mirror. Evan was a good and wonderful man but he was getting too close. Every instinct inside of her was screaming to open up to him but she simply couldn't. He'd been a cop and would turn her in, she was sure of it. No, the best thing to do was continue as if that entire conversation never happened. She'd told him enough of the truth to keep him happy—at least she hoped so. The less he knew the better.

But dammit, she liked him. A whole heck of a lot.

If this wasn't a life or death situation and she didn't need to eventually leave she would have loved to sit back, relax, and see what might happen between the two of them. She already knew some of the good - he was hardworking, smart, and funny. She even knew some of the bad as well - he was impatient as hell, he didn't eat his vegetables, and his politics clashed with her own. But all in all, he was the kind of guy she'd normally be thrilled to meet.

If this wasn't the absolute worst time of her life.

She dried her face with a towel and took several deep breaths to calm her racing heart. When their eyes had met she'd felt a bolt of electricity straight down to her toes. Evan Davis was a gorgeous man and she was only human. She'd have to be dead or in a coma not to notice, but when he turned that attention on her deliberately? Holy moly, she was in big trouble.

The only cleaned up bathroom was in Evan's bedroom and she had to walk back through it to get downstairs. Sorry she hadn't turned on a light, she made her way slowly around the furniture but must have miscalculated where his desk was as her hip connected painfully with something solid. A spate of profanity followed along with a shower of items from the desk falling onto her and then to the floor. With flailing arms, she managed to find the switch on the lamp and turn it on before anything else was destroyed.

"Are you okay?"

Of course she wasn't okay. She'd been trying to hold onto her dignity but that ship had now sailed.

"I think so," she said anyway, rubbing her sore hipbone as he flipped on a few more lights. "I think I made a mess."

Papers, a stapler, and a few folders were strewn across the floor where she'd knocked them off their perch on the desk. Evan wasn't the tidiest of men, although nowhere near his hoarding ancestor.

"I shouldn't have left them on the corner like that. Are you sure you're okay?"

"I'm fine. Really."

They both knelt to retrieve the fallen items but the papers caught Josie's eye, slowing her down. He stacked everything back on the desk as she sat on the floor, absorbed in the words on the page. Finally she looked up at Evan, shocked at what she'd read. "Did you write this?"

Evan shifted from one foot to the other, a red tinge on his cheekbones. "Maybe. It depends on what you think of it."

"I think it's great. Really, really good, actually. Is any of it true?"

She'd only read the one page but it had sucked her right in with the danger and suspense. It was far better than the tattered book she had stuffed in her backpack.

He reached out his hand and she took it, letting him pull her to her feet. "It's all true. That's the case that got me shot the last time and put an end to my career. I did change some names and things to protect identities but for the most part it's all true."

Her mild-mannered employer was kind of a badass and that only made him even sexier. Dammit. Why couldn't he have written about stealing some kid's lunch money or kicking little old ladies when they crossed the street?

"I'd love to read more of it."

"Really? I haven't let anyone look at it yet. I've just sort of been messing around with it when I can't sleep."

He slipped the sheet of paper from her fingers and set it on the top of the stack now placed next to his laptop. He appeared nervous but hopeful and not a little shocked that she wanted to read what he'd written, but it wasn't a surprise to Josie. She was a sucker for a great story.

"I'm a book nerd and this is good, Evan. Are you thinking about writing a book?"

He shook his head and snorted as if her suggestion was ludicrous then stopped and sighed. "No. Well…maybe. It's one of those things, you know. Those things that I've always wanted to do but never get to because life gets in the way. Now I don't really have much of an excuse. It's actually kind of fun reliving all the crazy things I've done."

Josie gave him a hopeful look. "So…can I read it then? I already want to know what happens next."

His fingers hovered over the stack but then he smiled and chuckled, gathering the papers together and sliding them into a folder. "Only if you really give them a true read and tell me the unvarnished truth. Don't be sweet and nice like I know you would be. I want a real critique of the story. In other words, give me hell. Do you think you can do that?"

"In design school we often had to critique each other's work. I once made someone cry."

He held out the folder and she plucked it from his hand before he could change his mind. "You made some poor girl cry? That doesn't sound like you."

"I was doing that *poor girl* a favor. She was new to that instructor and didn't realize what a total dickwad he could be to the students. I gave her that critique in private the day before class so she could clean up some of her work. He hated sloppiness and he was going to come down on her like a ton of bricks. Instead of taking it as helpful, she accused me of being jealous and spiteful. She told me I was ugly and stupid and didn't have a lick of talent. She said I'd be slinging fries for a living while she made the fashion magazines. So I don't think you need to feel sorry for her. She can handle herself just fine."

Just another instructive moment in Josie's life. Not everyone was going to appreciate a helping hand. More evidence that taking care of oneself was the right path.

"Whatever happened to her?"

"The instructor tore her a new asshole in front of the entire class just as I suspected he would. She burst into tears and complained to the dean, which of course didn't change anything. The instructor might have been an asshole but he was brilliant and knew what the hell he was doing. Once she realized that public critiques happened on a regular basis she changed her major to marketing. I'm told they're much more civilized and polite."

"This is a whole new side of you I didn't even know existed. Kind of cruel and really happy about it."

It didn't look like it bothered him much though. If anything, he was regarding her with a grudging respect which almost made her laugh.

"I'm not a Disney princess, boss. I'm a human being and I'm not perfect. Boy, am I not perfect. I'll even let you in on a little secret." She leaned forward and he did the same. "When the signs tell you to merge over to one lane there's always that one person who doesn't and then tries to cut in at the last minute. I'll admit this to you…I never let them in. I think they're selfish and they piss me off so I ride the bumper of the car in front of me so they can't get in. That probably makes me a real bitch."

A wide smile appeared on Evan's handsome face and then he threw back his head and laughed. "Honey, I do exactly the same thing. They should have merged over earlier instead of the last minute. I applaud your tenacity in showing them the error of their ways."

"I thought I was the only one. Everyone else seems to let them in," she admitted, her awareness of their proximity suddenly rising. There were mere single digit inches between them and she could feel the heat from his skin as well as the scent of clean sweat teasing her nostrils. "I guess we should go downstairs, huh?"

Danger. Danger. Get out of the bedroom now.

It was too intimate. Too…everything. She liked being with him way too much. She had to fight the urge to reach out the short distance and place her palm on his chest just to see if it felt as good as she thought it would. Or better.

From his smiling expression she could tell that he clearly saw her inner turmoil and was enjoying it. He was the first man who had turned her into a muddled, addlebrained idiot but he didn't have to be so damn smug about it.

"That's not an attractive quality." Josie's sharp words tumbled out before she could stop them.

His brows pulled down but he didn't stop smiling. "What's not? I'm not sure I follow you."

"You know what I'm talking about."

Now she felt stupid. Blurting things out was a nasty habit she needed to curb but it was too late.

"I honestly don't but that's okay. I'm guessing there are many things about me that aren't attractive but I'm not sure I want a comprehensive list, so I'll just shut the hell up. How does that sound?"

Like a reprieve from heaven.

"I should go."

She regretted her words instantly when a hurt looked crossed Evan's face. It was gone as quickly as it had come but she hadn't imagined it.

"I'll take you home then."

Evan stepped back so she could pass and she walked by him, careful not to let their bodies brush. If he touched her she might possibly give in to the raging hormones dancing inside of her making her say and do things that would make her cringe later.

Nothing good could come from starting a relationship with Evan. There wasn't any future for two of them. Heck, she wasn't even sure she had a future at all. She was simply trying to stay alive.

◈ ◈ ◈

Evan felt like a first-class ass. He'd been too forward, too pushy and now Lisa had retreated inside herself so deeply it would be a wonder if she ever looked him in the eye again. His attraction to this tiny auburn-haired woman was strong but that didn't mean his feelings were reciprocated. He thought he'd seen a kindred spark in her eyes but every time they moved closer…she'd run.

She was now sitting next to him as he drove her back to the hotel, the folder containing his story clutched to her chest like a life preserver. She'd said little since they'd left his place and the silence had grown uncomfortable. Painfully awkward.

"Maybe we should start later tomorrow."

Her head swiveled toward him but he couldn't quite make out her expression in the dark, the only light from the dash. "Why? What's different about tomorrow?"

He should have known she'd object. She had a work ethic to be envied. "Nothing. But today was different. You're going to be sore plus we had a late evening. I was just thinking that we could meet for breakfast a little later, that's all."

She turned back so she was facing the windshield, her posture stiff. "I'll be fine. I'll take a couple of ibuprofen before bed."

More stubborn than a mule.

"I wouldn't mind sleeping in," he said instead, pretending she hadn't spoken. She'd argue with him until they were both blue in the face. They both liked to be right. "How about we meet an hour later?"

Silence then a sigh. "Fine. You're the boss."

Are we sure? Because I don't always feel like it.

"That I am. So it's decided. We'll meet an hour later tomorrow."

He pulled into a parking space in front of her motel room, the headlights shining on the plain white building. Hank had painted the old cedar siding a few years ago but it already needed touching up.

Lisa sat for a moment, not moving. "Thank you for a lovely day. I had a nice time."

Evan slowly let out a breath, an attempt to alleviate some of the tension that had built up in the back of his neck during their silent drive. "I did too and you're welcome. If you need anything call me."

He'd made the same offer every single night for the past week and she had yet to take him up on it. After the fiasco in the bedroom the chances of her ever doing that were basement-bottom low.

"Thank you. Goodnight."

She climbed out of his SUV and hurried to her door, unlocking it and disappearing behind it. He waited until she peeked out of the curtain and gave him a little wave before he backed up and headed to his place. He'd upset her and he hadn't meant to.

But he was determined to make it up to her tomorrow. A good breakfast and some conversation could smooth all of this over and make it better. He'd back off for a little while and give her some space. He wanted to show her he was interested but not a pervert.

He wanted her to know he was worth taking a chance on.

CHAPTER TEN

Josie was coughing, each breath a searing pain in her chest. Her body almost folded in half as she strained to expel whatever foreign object or substance that had taken up residence in the back of her throat. Beginning to panic as sleep dissolved, her gritty eyes burned as she slowly lifted her lids only to find something much worse than a tickle in her throat. The room was filled with smoke and her skin felt prickly due to the heat.

Fire.

The bad guys had found her and were trying to either smoke her out or simply kill her and anyone else that happened to have the bad luck to be anywhere in her vicinity. Remembering Amy's face in those last few moments, Josie knew she couldn't allow her resolve to waver. She had to stay strong and this was a lousy way to die. No way was she going to become some sort of crispy critter in a plastic body bag when the sun came up. She had way too much to live for and high on that list was bringing Amy's killers to justice and clearing her own name.

Remembering what she'd been taught in grade school, Josie slid out of bed and straight to the floor where the air was slightly clearer. Her heart tripped in her chest before accelerating and she shifted into survival mode, letting her instincts rule over her emotions. Fear-induced adrenaline zipped through her veins but she shut out the panicked voices in her head, concentrating solely on escaping the fiery tomb of her motel room.

A sliver of light came through the curtains and the outline of her backpack was clearly visible through the haze. So far there were no flames in her room, which was a blessing. Sending up a prayer of gratitude she crawled on her belly, the acrid smoke stinging her nose and throat while the rough carpet fibers scraped her skin. The room was unbearably hot and by the time she reached her backpack she was slick with dirt and sweat.

Blinking back the tears that had begun to gather in her eyes, she grabbed her backpack and lone pair of shoes sitting next to it before moving the foot and a half to the door. Tentatively, she reached for the doorknob but thankfully the metal was a normal temperature which indicated that there wasn't any fire on the other side. Through the haze of panic and fear, she vaguely registered the sound of sirens and the flash of lights outside but it didn't assuage any of the terror that was clawing its way out of her chest. People who wanted her dead were on the other side of that door. She'd been fooling herself to think she was safe here in this tiny town.

But she couldn't stay on this side of the wall either.

Pulling open the door, she shoved herself outside of the room and into the parking lot, choking and coughing on the fresh oxygen that assailed her pained lungs. Still on her hands and knees, she felt a set of strong arms try to pull her up and frenzied panic took over. She wouldn't allow those men to take her. She kicked and scratched despite the disparity in their sizes and the fact that she was still wearing a set of shortie pajamas. Their arms and legs were covered so she was doing little damage even as their voices began to penetrate her brain.

"Ma'am. Ma'am. I'm trying to help you. Please, I'm trying to help you."

Josie finally looked up at her captor through the glaze of tears and saw the face of one very concerned firefighter who probably thought she'd lost her mind. With a sob of relief, her body went limp and she let him pick her up and carry her to a stretcher where he set her down gently. Two EMTs converged on her simultaneously, asking her non-stop questions that she numbly answered but her gaze was riveted to the burning building. Orange and yellow flames jumped in the air only three rooms from where she'd been sleeping. A few more minutes and it would have probably been all over.

Her face covered in an oxygen mask, the EMT cleaned the scratches in her palms and knees from where she crawled onto the pavement. She didn't have any other injuries so they wrapped her in a blanket and let her sit in the ambulance as they tended to the other guests in the motel.

She pulled the mask from her face and grabbed the jacket of a firefighter as he passed by.

"Hank?"

Her voice came out as a croak but the man appeared to understand. He patted her on the shoulder and nodded with a smile. "He's okay. He rushed into one of the rooms to help someone get out so he has a few minor burns and smoke inhalation but he's going to be fine. The other ambulance took him to the county hospital."

Sighing with relief, Josie leaned her head back against the wall and closed her eyes, exhausted and scared. So far she hadn't seen anything nefarious but she couldn't be too careful. Getting out of town was paramount but she couldn't leave like this. She needed a shower and a change of clothes. And a plan. A plan would be excellent. Last time she'd run she hadn't had time to think anything through but this time she needed to be strategic. She had to think ahead.

The next bus out of town wouldn't even be here until almost lunchtime. She'd memorized the schedules for just an event like this but she didn't have a place to hide until then. That was the problem. There was no other motel in Cypress Corner and that would be the first place they'd look for her anyway. Perhaps she could hide out in the diner bathroom or maybe in the alleyway behind the grocery store.

"Ma'am?"

A voice shattered her stream of consciousness and her eyes flew open, taking a moment to focus on the man in front of her. Dirty and sweaty, he was wearing the typical fireman uniform of yellow jacket and hat. Why he wasn't assisting the other men who were currently pointing high-pressured hoses at the now crumbling building she didn't know, but perhaps they had everything under control.

"Ma'am?" he repeated. "Is there anyone we can call for you?"

She shook her head a trifle forlornly. She was alone and that fact was brought home to her like a freight train against a brick wall at this moment. "No. Is everyone okay? Did everyone get out?"

"Yes, ma'am. Everyone is accounted for." His gaze went back to the building still in flames before returning to her. "There's a motel in the next town about thirty minutes away and there are lots of hotels in Ocala. No one is going to be staying here for awhile. Even in the rooms that weren't burned there's smoke and water damage."

The news just kept getting better. The universe wasn't going to cut her any breaks.

"I don't have a car."

The man's expression was sympathetic but still surprised. She would have bet that not too many people traveled through this town without a vehicle. There was a good reason for her predicament but she wasn't about to tell him.

He turned to the left and the right, looking around the parking lot filled with fire engines and people milling about. This was probably the most exciting thing that had happened in town in years.

"Maybe you could get a ride with someone?" he suggested. "Another traveler?"

Trust a stranger? Amy had told her to trust no one and Josie had already blown that rule out of the water by trusting Evan. She didn't know if anyone here had seen her face on television or read about her in the paper.

Wait...Evan. Damn. She had to trust him one more time. No matter what her mother or Amy said.

"There is someone you can call," she finally replied, pulling the oxygen mask off completely. "Can you call Evan Davis?"

◈ ◈ ◈

Christ on a crutch, this woman was going to be the death of Evan. His fingers tightened on the steering wheel and he gave her a quick glance out of the corner of his eye. Lisa was curled into a ball in the passenger seat almost as if she was trying to see just how small she could get. She'd stared out of the window without saying a word the entire drive back to his place and he loathed the idea of making her relive what had to be a traumatic event but he needed to know she was okay. Or at least that she was going to be okay.

"We're here."

He pushed open the vehicle door and ran around to her side to help her out. When he'd shown up at the motel, she'd been quite a sight sitting there in the ambulance still wearing her pajamas and an oxygen mask. He'd almost passed out with fear until she'd opened her mouth and spoke, thanking him for coming to get her.

The poor girl didn't have anywhere else to go and now he was afraid she was going to get on the first bus out of town. Somehow he had to keep that from happening. Not only was she the best employee he'd ever had, he *liked* her. She was funny and kind and hardworking and intelligent. She was the kind of woman he'd been wanting to meet and now she was in his life. That's where he wanted to keep her.

Keeping an arm around her shoulders as they walked up the front porch steps, his mind was already running through the changes he needed to make in the house to accommodate his new roommate. They entered and she immediately sat down on the arm of the couch, taking another gulp from the bottle of water a fireman had given her. Her expression was almost vacant and lost and he had to restrain himself from pulling her into his arms and telling her everything was going to be fine.

Because he'd be a liar.

Lisa hadn't said much and he had no idea how much she'd lost in the fire. She barely had any belongings to begin with and she said some were destroyed...Somehow he'd make her accept new clothes even if she balked at his offer, but knowing how stubborn she was it wouldn't be easy. He wanted to help her if only she'd let him. He'd actually been shocked when he got the call to come pick her up, which only illustrated just how screwed she was in the situation. She had no place to go and no way to get there even if she did.

"Why don't I go make you some tea? That might feel good on your throat." The few words she'd spoken had sounded hoarse and she'd coughed a few times during the drive home. "You can head upstairs and use the shower. I'll put out a t-shirt and pair of shorts you can wear if you like. I'm not sure what you were able to save."

She had on shoes but he'd bet his last dollar they were her only pair, just like the pink pajama set she was currently wearing.

He'd only known her a week but he was certain he'd seen every piece of clothing in her wardrobe. This girl was seriously down on her luck.

Lisa blinked at him a few times and then nodded. "Don't go to any trouble. I really just want to get clean and get some rest." Her eyes filled with tears and her lips trembled, almost breaking his heart. She looked like her world had imploded. "I hate to leave you without any notice but I'm planning on being on the bus out of town tomorrow."

Her statement was like a dagger to his chest and he had to take a few painful breaths before he could reply, keeping his tone even as though her words didn't send panic flying straight through him. "I bet after some sleep things might look a lot better. Maybe you should put off making any decisions until later when you're well rested."

She shook her head and rose to her feet, holding onto the sofa for support. "I have to go."

"And you look so happy about it," Evan couldn't help but mock. "Listen, you've gone through some shit tonight and are in no position to be making life-altering decisions. Get a shower and some rest. Tomorrow we'll have breakfast and talk. If you feel the same, I'll drive you anywhere you want to go. But I think once you're rested you'll see that this is no reason to leave."

Sniffling, she rubbed at her damn cheeks looking almost like a guilty child. His heart softened and this time he did reach out and pull her into his arms, stroking her back and the tangled strands of her hair while she cried softly into his cotton shirt. "You don't understand. I have to go."

"You're right, I don't understand. You're a free agent from what you've told me. You don't have to be anywhere and have no ties. You can stay."

"No, I have to go."

Her voice was shaking and he was sure she was about to burst into tears again, something he wanted to avoid. He was trying to make her feel better, not worse. "Go on upstairs and get in the shower. I bet you'll feel a hundred percent better if you do."

He led her to the staircase and gave her a gentle push, watching her as she ascended to the second floor, clutching her battered backpack like a lifeline. He'd follow in a few minutes and grab some clothes for her to wear, but in the meantime he'd put on some hot water for tea. Then he'd tuck her into bed.

Tomorrow? He'd find out just why she couldn't stay. Something just wasn't right. He knew she had secrets and he'd respected them but this fire had thrown everything into chaos. Lisa was frightened; anyone with two eyes could see it.

Just what was she frightened of?

He wanted answers and he'd get them. In the morning.

CHAPTER ELEVEN

Josie lay in bed and listened for any movement from Evan. After her bath and tea, he'd insisted that she take his bedroom while he slept on an air mattress in the living room. No amount of argument would budge him so eventually she'd given in, mostly out of sheer exhaustion. Her mind and body were shutting down and she wasn't thinking clearly. If she had been, she'd be hiding in a closet or already on the road out of town. The men who wanted her dead had found her and her fragile sense of security had been ripped to shreds.

A fire was a stupid way to kill someone.

She didn't know much about assassinating another human being but there had to be more efficient methods than setting a fire and crossing your fingers. Not to mention the collateral damage, which just showed these people were heartless bastards who didn't care who they hurt along the way. Stone cold killers and she was their target.

But she was pretty sure they wouldn't try twice in the same night. They might not even yet know if she'd been a casualty unless they were hanging around the scene - which once again - would have been stupid. Strangers stuck out like a sore thumb in this little town. She should know.

Yet she couldn't be sorry that she was alone in Evan's bedroom. There was something in this room she hadn't had access to since she'd left D.C.

A laptop.

She hadn't had time to grab hers when she'd run and Cypress Corner didn't even have a library where she could go to borrow one. If Evan was asleep…

Sliding out of bed, she tiptoed across the room and carefully opened the door so she could sneak a peek over the banister. Evan was lying on the air mattress, one arm thrown over his eyes and the other tucked under a blanket. Dead to the world and softly snoring. It was her lucky day. Something she hadn't had much of in the last week.

Sneaking back into the bedroom she softly closed the door, praying her host and employer was a heavy sleeper. She needed privacy for this little escapade, at least for a few minutes. She didn't know what she was going to find but it had to be something worth killing for.

Settling herself at Evan's desk, she opened his laptop and breathed a sigh of relief that it wasn't password protected. The thumb drive she'd retrieved from a hidden compartment in her backpack felt unnaturally heavy in her palm but it wasn't because of its size, which was actually quite small. It was because of what might be on it. Amy had pressed this into Josie's hand as she lay on the pavement dying, begging her not to trust anyone and to keep it safe. It was time to find out what "it" was.

She slipped the drive into the USB slot and waited for the laptop to recognize the external device before double clicking the lone file that appeared. A video.

Casting a glance over her shoulder as her heart pounded in her ears, she held her breath as the screen flickered and a couple in bed came into view. Scantily clad, they were obviously about to do some very intimate things. The man currently had his back to the camera but the girl wasn't anyone Josie recognized.

Josie didn't have to wait or wonder long as to why Amy had this video in her possession or why someone else wanted it. The man turned toward the camera and revealed his identity, shattering what little peace of mind she had left.

It was former Senator Steve Lydell - a retired attorney and rumored candidate to be appointed to Secretary of Defense - in living color and doing all sorts of kinky shit with someone who wasn't his wife and the mother of his four children.

Sucking in a breath, Josie rubbed her temples where a headache had begun to bloom. She'd known politics was dog eat dog but she hadn't realized that power was something to murder over. Then again, she'd never craved power and prestige. And be willing to do whatever it took to get there.

"Oh Amy," Josie whispered, an ache in her heart as she thought of her best friend. She'd barely allowed herself to mourn this last week but everything was beginning to catch up with her. Amy was gone and she wasn't coming back, and that reality was beginning to settle into Josie's brain. Her friend was gone and the hole in her heart wouldn't be healed for a long time, if ever. "What did you get yourself into? Why do you have this and how did they find out about it? You told me not to trust anyone but I don't know what to do or where to go."

Her voice broke as a sob rose up in her choked throat. Her body shook with a mixture of terror and sadness as she slid to the floor, her back against the desk. Rocking herself back and forth, she silently allowed herself the catharsis of tears until she didn't have any left, her tear ducts drained and sore. All cried out, her eyes swollen and red, she ejected the thumb drive and placed it safely into the small compartment in her backpack. For a moment she'd contemplated hiding it somewhere in the house, but if she needed to make a quick getaway she didn't want to be scrambling to retrieve it. The backpack wasn't perfect, but for now it was the best she could do.

She wasn't some spy or double agent. Amy said not to trust anyone but she couldn't stay on the run the rest of her life. Perhaps sending the evidence to a news outlet might help but there was no guarantee she still wouldn't be accused of Amy's murder. News organizations were owned by large multinational conglomerates and they had political agendas of their own.

Just because the video might become public didn't mean Josie herself was off the hook. It only meant Lydell's political future was in peril. He probably wouldn't take too kindly to that and she was sure it was his men coming after her. It was the only thing that made sense.

Except that nothing really made sense at all.

She'd avoided thinking about her situation or making any decisions but the sand had run out of the hourglass. It was time to put on her big girl panties and figure out what the hell she was going to do.

And whom she was going to trust. Because she had to trust someone. She couldn't do this alone.

CHAPTER TWELVE

Josie opened her lids a mere slit before closing them tightly again. Sun was streaming through the curtains, telling her that without a doubt that it was past the early morning she'd hoped for and well on its way to midday. Groaning with effort, she opened her eyes again and glanced at the clock on the bedside table. Eleven-oh-six.

"Shit. Shit, shit, shit," she chanted, realizing she'd screwed up. Again.

Flying out of bed, she stumbled over her backpack that she'd placed close to the bed so it would be within arm's length. Her knees hit the hardwood as her legs gave way, not completely awake yet, and she let fly a string of curses that would have made a sailor blush. She'd planned to be on the eleven-fifteen bus out of Cypress Corner and that meant she had nine minutes to dress, pack her few belongings, and convince Evan to drive her to the bus station. It would be a miracle but she wanted to believe it could be done.

Despite sore and protesting muscles, she was scrambling through her backpack for a pair of semi-clean jeans when the door flew open, banging against the wall. Evan stood there, his chest rising and falling rapidly as if he'd charged up the stairs two at a time.

"Are you okay?" he asked urgently, his gaze sweeping her from head to toe and then back up again. She must look quite a sight with her bedhead and creases on her face from the sheets but she was too frantic to care.

"I'm fine. Just in a hurry. I have a bus to catch in nine minutes."

Yanking pants and a t-shirt out of her backpack along with a clean pair of panties and socks, she gave him a look that she hoped said something like *thank you for the concern but go away while I dress.*

He didn't get the message.

"I heard something crash."

She sighed and got to her feet, time ticking away. "That was me getting out of bed. I think I mentioned that I was kind of accident prone, plus I'm still kind of sore. Now if you don't mind..."

He just stood there. Scowling.

"I need to get dressed," she prompted, sighing in exasperation and not bothering to hide it any longer. "Right away. They won't let me on the bus in just your t-shirt no matter how much they love AC/DC. So if you could..."

She made a shooing motion with her hands and that seemed to get his attention.

"You'll never make it so you might as well relax."

She shook her head and glanced back at the clock. "I have nine–wait, make that seven minutes. I can do it but I need to get dressed."

Instead of leaving he stepped into the room, a smile tugging at his lips. "You have two minutes and it's a ten minute drive into town anyway. You won't make it, honey. Just relax and we'll go into town for some lunch."

He wasn't making the whole leaving thing easy for her.

"I have seven–"

"Two," Evan interrupted. "That clock runs five minutes slow. At least. Even when I reset it the darn thing loses time. Trust me, at most you have two minutes. If I had a rocket ship I couldn't get you there on time."

"Fuck," Josie muttered, her entire body sagging with disappointment. She fell back onto the mattress with a groan and buried her face in her hands. She was stuck here another day and there were men out there who were willing to burn down a motel to make sure she was dead. "Dammit, I needed to be on that bus."

Evan leaned against the desk, his arms crossed over his chest. "There will be another bus tomorrow—what does it matter?"

"It matters. I need to leave."

A part of her desperately wanted to trust Evan with the burden she was carrying but another part, the part that was trying to keep her alive, stayed silent. He was a good man and he sure as hell didn't deserve to be dragged into this…mess. It might make her feel better not to be in danger all alone but it wouldn't help Evan in the least. She'd keep her mouth shut and move along. Maybe when this was all over, she could write him a letter and tell him the truth. She was so grateful for everything he'd done so far. He didn't have any idea how much he'd helped her already.

She was shoving her pajamas into her backpack when he shocked her.

"What if I don't want you to leave? What if I want you to stay?"

Evan wasn't smiling anymore and his expression was intensely…intense. She watched as he swallowed hard, his Adam's apple bobbing in his throat and his jaw growing tight at the silence that followed his question. The last thing she wanted was to have this conversation.

Sitting down on the bed, she abandoned packing. This had to be dealt with first. "We don't always get what we want. I sure don't, anyway. I like you. A lot. But I have to go."

More heavy silence and her nerves screamed for relief. Josie had to make him understand.

"From where I'm standing I'm not seeing why you have to go. Unless, of course, you just want to. I'm going to take a chance here, Lisa. It's one of the things I said I was going to do when I left the Marshals. I was going to do what I wanted and stop doing what people expected. Seems to me that you expect me to smile politely and drive you to the bus station. Fuck that. I like you too, honey. A hell of a lot. I'd like to see where that takes us. There. I said it. But maybe you already knew that. Maybe that's why you want to leave. Am I running you off? Am I being too forward?"

Shit and hell, she wasn't in the right frame of mind to deal with this. At any other moment in her life, his words would be pure heaven and she would have thrown herself into his arms and kissed him until they both fainted from pleasure. But she was in deep shit and didn't have the luxury. How did one let down the man of their dreams? Had any woman ever been that stupid before?

She opened her mouth to reply but the words kept getting stuck in her throat. "I–It's just–You don't understand."

He pulled the desk chair out and lowered himself into it, stretching out his long legs as if settling in for the duration. He wasn't going anywhere until he was satisfied with her answer. "You're right, I don't. Help me understand. I want to."

Defeated, Josie hung her head and stared at her bare feet. "I can't stay. I wish I could."

"Honey, you don't sound happy about it. In fact, I'd go as far as to say you sound mighty sad to be leaving. What can I do to fix things so you can stay?"

Everything that had happened in the last week welled up inside of her, stealing her ability to even draw breath. It was too much. Way too much for any one person to handle and although Amy had pleaded at the end not to trust anyone, the pressure of being alone and on the run and scared was simply too much for Josie. She hiccupped as a sob escaped from her lips and tears welled, spilling onto her cheeks.

"Can you turn back time, Evan? Because that's the only thing that can help me." She finally looked up into the kindest eyes she'd ever seen, eyes that practically begged to help her. "I am so fucked, I don't know which way is up and I don't know what to do. There are people that want me dead and they'll do anything, even burn down a motel with innocent people in it to kill me. If you had any brains whatsoever you'd save yourself and drive me to the nearest bus station, drop me there, and never look back. I could only get you killed or injured."

CHAPTER THIRTEEN

"I've never been all that smart, so I think you're staying right here. Talk to me, Lisa. Tell me what's going on and why you're so scared. Let's start with why you think someone wants you dead."

Holy hell, Evan was finally getting somewhere with Lisa but she wasn't making it easy. She had some delusion that the fire was set to kill her. She seemed so levelheaded most of the time, so being hysterical like this didn't make sense.

Lisa hopped up from the bed and began to pace back and forth. "I don't think someone wants me dead, I know it. I've been on the run since leaving D.C. Hell, they set fire to the motel last night, Evan. I don't want them to do that - or worse - to you."

The color in her cheeks was high and she was getting herself all riled up. He'd never get a coherent explanation out of her at this rate. She was working herself up into stroke territory.

"Calm down, honey. You need to stay calm."

She rounded on him then and leaned down until they were nose to nose, her finger poking him in the chest.

"Never in the history of calming down has anyone actually calmed down when told to calm down." She straightened, her jaw jutting out stubbornly. "And I am calm. At least compared to that night. Believe me, after everything I've gone through this is calm."

Fighting to suppress a grin, Evan nodded, keeping his expression neutral. Or as neutral as he was capable of.

"I'm sorry. You're right, that wasn't helping. How about we go downstairs, have some coffee, and you start from the very beginning? How does that sound?"

For a moment he thought she was going to argue, but instead she nodded and padded on bare feet out of the bedroom and downstairs, leading the way into the kitchen. He waved her to a chair while he poured them both a cup of coffee, the pot still fairly fresh from when he'd made it late in the morning.

"Now," he said, sliding a cup in front of her and settling into the chair opposite at the tiny kitchen table. "Why don't you go all the way back to the beginning? Pretend I don't know anything at all about anything. No detail is too small."

Waiting wasn't easy, but Evan sipped his coffee while Lisa added cream and sugar and gathered her thoughts. She had a few false starts but eventually put down her mug and spoke.

"First of all, my real name isn't Lisa. It's Josephine Eleanor Carlton. My friends call me Josie. I'm sorry for lying to you about that but I had my reasons for wanting to remain under the radar."

She kind of looked like a Josie. More than a Lisa. But he was still hurt she hadn't trusted him with the truth, although at the time he'd done nothing to earn that trust.

"Okay, Josie." He tried the name out on his tongue, careful to keep his own emotions from derailing her story. This wasn't about him. "You're not Lisa. I guess that's what I get for not asking for references and paying you in cash."

Her eyes widened and she took another gulp of her coffee. "I wouldn't have taken the job if you wanted those things. I would have left town, I guess."

That would have been a shame. Despite all this drama, she was the best thing to happen to him in recent memory.

"So Josie, you were telling me why people want you dead," he reminded her, watching her expressions and body language closely. He'd participated in hundreds of interrogations but this one might be the most important.

Her fingers twisted around the handle of the cup, her knuckles white. "I was coming home from work. I was working as a waitress after getting laid off and my shift ended late, after the restaurant closed. It was almost one in the morning."

"You lived in Washington D.C.?"

Lisa—no, Josie—nodded. "Like I told you before, I moved there to be closer to a friend from college - Amy. She helped me find a place to live and get a job."

Tears glistened in Josie's eyes and Evan reached out to place his hand over one of hers, squeezing lightly. He had a feeling there were going to be many more tears before this story was told.

"She sounds like a good friend. Does she know you're on the run?"

More tears. Shit, he'd hit a nerve.

"She does. I mean, did. She died that night." Josie released the mug and her hand flew over her mouth to cover a sob. "When I got out of my car I could see two men running from Amy's car. She lived in the same apartment complex I did. Anyway, they jumped in a car and drove away. I walked over to Amy's vehicle and she was lying on the pavement next to it. She was still alive but bleeding from her stomach. There was blood everywhere. I pulled out my cell phone to call 911 but Amy grabbed my arm. I remember being shocked that she still had that much strength. Anyway, she told me there was a thumb drive hidden in the covered saucepan in her apartment. She told me to take it and get away from there, to hide. I wasn't to trust anyone because they would kill for it."

Evan was struggling to wrap his mind around Josie's words. It sounded like something out of a Bond film. Thumb drives and deathbed warnings. However, he'd been in law enforcement long enough to realize that some things were more complicated than anything Hollywood could come up with.

Josie had pulled her legs to her chest, her arms wrapped around her knees as she'd recounted her friend's last moments. She appeared alone and lost and more than a little frightened. He hoped he could reassure her that he could and would protect her. He hadn't lost anyone under protection yet and this woman wasn't going to be his first.

"Honey," he said gently, walking a fine line between allowing her to wallow in her misery and needing to hear the rest of the story. There had to be more than what she'd told him. "How about a drink? I think you could use one."

She scrubbed at her damp cheeks and nodded, sniffling as he dug into his pocket for a handkerchief.

He reached into the cabinet over the refrigerator, far out of Josie's reach, and pulled down the hidden bottle of whiskey he hadn't touched in weeks plus two glasses. She shouldn't drink alone and he had a feeling he'd need one himself before her story was over.

He poured two shots and pushed one closer to her, watching as she knocked it back, a gasp coming from deep in her gut as it slid down, warming her stomach as it was heating his own. She wiped off her mouth with her hand and licked her lips nervously.

"I called 911 but it was too late. Amy died right then and I knew that I had to help her. She'd been frantic with worry so I had to get the thumb drive and get out of there. I just didn't know where I was going or what I was going to do. She didn't have time to tell me what was on it. And then–"

Josie broke off and reached for the bottle, pouring herself another generous measure. "I'm not sure about the rest of this, Evan. You were a cop before, right? Isn't there a saying…'once a cop, always a cop'? I need you to be on my side here. I need you to believe in me because some of the stuff I'm saying is going to sound pretty far out."

Josie had been watching too much television.

"In all my years in law enforcement I've never heard that once I'm a cop I'm always a cop. Never. I was a cop and now I'm not. That doesn't mean I still don't often think like one or still have the instincts, but I am not an officer of the law. Actually, I'm an out of work loser right now. And I am on your side."

"You're not a loser."

"Thank you. Before you go further, can I ask a few questions?" He was struggling to picture the scene in his mind and he needed it to be clear.

"Sure." Josie shrugged and took another sip of whiskey. "I'm not all that keen on telling the next part anyway."

"You said your friend Amy was lying on the ground, right? Next to her car? How far was that from her apartment and did she…well…pass on before you went to her place to retrieve the thumb drive?"

"Yes, she was lying on the ground next to her car. The apartment building was maybe twenty feet or so. Not far. And I did stay with her until she was gone. I didn't leave her. I wouldn't do that. She was my best friend. But even that came back to bite me in the ass."

This must be the part Josie didn't want to tell. From experience, he knew to ask open-ended questions and simply wait for the answers. Let her talk her way through a difficult situation.

"How so?"

Her head fell back with a long groan, her gaze on the ceiling and decidedly away from him. "I held her as she told me about the thumb drive and not to trust anyone. Then she…you know…left. In real time it must have all happened very fast, although it felt like it was all in slow motion. But our neighbor must have heard Amy screaming or something when the men were running away. She came to the door and turned on her porch light so she could see. And what she could see was me hovering over a bleeding Amy as she passed away. She started yelling that I was a murderer and she was getting her gun and calling the police. I realized I didn't have much time. I had to grab a few things and get out of there or I was going to be arrested for killing Amy."

Fuck. Evan felt like he'd taken a punch to the gut. No wonder Josie was terrified. Not only had she seen her friend murdered but she was a suspect.

"The neighbor had a good view of your face? You said the building was twenty feet away and it was the middle of the night."

"Good enough, apparently. She always hated me and Amy. Said we were bad for the building because we were out late at night. Of course I was out late at night. I was at work."

"So you ran, but you retrieved the thumb drive first. It must not have taken you long to find it."

Josie lifted her head and took another drink, her eyes watery and red-rimmed from crying. "Amy and I had exchanged keys so getting into her apartment wasn't an issue. She never cooked so her saucepan was in the same spot in the cabinet that it always was, and the drive was just where she'd said it would be. I grabbed it and shoved it in my pocket, then went to my place for my backpack. I didn't have time to take much as you can see but I got the hell out of there before the cops arrived. Headed to a cheap motel outside of the city to spend the night and figure out what I was going to do. But that didn't turn out like I thought it would. I ended up leaving in the middle of the night."

If she'd taken her own car, it wouldn't take long for the police to catch up with her.

"I assume the cops showed up and you had to run again?"

Leaning forward, she buried her face in her hands and took several deep breaths as if trying to steady herself. Evan wanted to reach out and comfort her but her body language was too forbidding at the moment. She didn't look as if she'd appreciate being touched while she was recounting her story.

"That would have been bad enough, but no, they didn't show up. Although I guess they might have later after I left. No, it was the guys who ran from the scene. The ones who killed Amy. I couldn't sleep and I heard some noises from the parking lot. I peeked out of the curtain and saw them getting out of their car, guns drawn. I didn't know what to do so I called the front desk yelling about men outside with guns. The manager ran out there with his shotgun and threatened to call the cops. It gave me a few minutes of cover to run. I left my car there and caught a city bus a few blocks over and it took me to the bus station. From there I emptied my checking account from a nearby ATM and boarded the next bus that was leaving fifteen minutes later. And here I am."

Evan's brain was putting the puzzle pieces together and a few were missing. "Wait. How did they find you? They didn't even know your name, did they?"

Josie sighed and shook her head. "Not originally, but when I got to the motel room I turned on the television. My name and picture were on the news. There was a hunt for a person of interest - me - and so my identity was blown. Stupidly I'd used my own car as a getaway vehicle and even paid the motel with a credit card. I'm not the brightest fugitive on the block. If it weren't for the dumb luck of exiting the bus here in town and meeting you, well, I'd have no luck at all."

Thank heavens that she had. Who knew what someone else might do with this information? Evan was absolutely going to help and protect her, his mind already working on all the possibilities. But he needed to make sure of one thing.

"Is that everything? Do I know it all?"

CHAPTER FOURTEEN

Josie wished with all her heart she could answer Evan's question in the affirmative. She wanted that to be the whole story but sadly, it was only the beginning of a very sordid tale. One she herself didn't know all the details to.

"There is more."

He quirked an eyebrow and lifted up the bottle. "Like *let's have another drink* more or *it's just a little thing* more?"

"I think we better have another drink."

This time both brows flew up but he did as she'd suggested, pouring his own quite generously since she was already one drink ahead of him.

"I want to help and protect you, Josie, if you'll let me. But I do need to know everything. So what else is there?"

Josie rubbed her forehead and temples, the pounding becoming intensely painful. "Sex."

"Sex," Evan repeated dutifully. "Can you be more specific?"

"Until last night I didn't have access to a computer. After you fell asleep, I used your laptop to see what was on the thumb drive. Thank you for not password protecting it, by the way. I was of two minds about seeing what was on it, thinking that maybe if I knew I would be in more danger, but hell, they want me dead and there isn't much more danger than that."

"And they want the thumb drive, I assume?"

"Probably, but perhaps they think killing anyone who knows about it is good enough."

Evan rubbed his chin and nodded. "Okay, who is having sex?"

"I don't know who specifically, actually," Josie sighed. "It's former Senator Lydell and an unidentified female doing some very raunchy things to one another. I don't think his wife would approve."

Rearing back, his mouth fell open and his eyes went wide with shock. Despite not having a television it appeared he was keeping up with current events.

"The guy that's rumored to be the next Secretary of Defense? Isn't he married with like four kids or something? Are you sure it was him?"

She heartily wished she was wrong. "You can watch it yourself but yes, I am sure. It's him. And it looks like he'll do anything to keep that video from going public. A video like that could ruin him completely, not to mention hurt his family who are innocent in all this."

Taking a big gulp of whiskey, Evan scraped his hand down his face before he spoke. "How did Amy come into possession of this?"

She took her own fortifying drink, letting the heat burn all the way to her belly, the pain distracting her from the equal hurt in her heart when she thought about her friend. Amy had been such a good person and she didn't deserve to have an end that violent and ugly. Josie was just glad she'd been there those last few moments even if she couldn't have stayed to see that a proper burial was planned.

"I'm not sure," Josie admitted. "Amy worked as an administrative assistant for the Department of the Interior. I can't imagine how she would get something like this in her possession.

She was so sweet and a really good person. When she convinced me to come down here she said she was going to help me find a new job as a designer. She said she had contacts with important people who had money."

"So that part was true? You were a designer?"

Josie curled up on the chair, pulling her knees to her chest and resting her chin on top. "I tried to be as honest as possible so I wouldn't have to keep track of the lies."

Evan played with his now empty glass and she waited quietly until he was ready to speak. She could practically see the wheels turning in his head as he took in everything she'd told him tonight.

"Why did you end up staying with me? What made you trust me?"

She had to be honest even if it was scary.

"First of all, I wouldn't say I trusted you. I didn't *not* trust you. I was open to trying to trust you. Second, it helped that you didn't have a television and you seemed to have no interest in the news. That was a big plus. You lived way out here all by yourself and you were willing to pay me cash. Something I desperately needed because I wasn't exactly flush with it when I fled."

"What was your plan when you were done here? Where were you going and what were you going to do with the recording?"

Grimacing, she hid her face again, hating to admit just how clueless she was about all this. "Honestly? I have no idea. None. Until last night I hadn't even seen what was on the thumb drive. I was thinking about heading to Dallas where I have an old college friend in journalism there. I was hoping he could help me but I hadn't decided to go for sure. The fact is nothing in life has prepared me to be on the run from bad guys and the law, Evan. I don't know what to do. I only knew I couldn't go to jail for a crime I didn't commit and that I needed to keep a low profile to stay away from the people who want me dead. Oh, and I needed money and a roof over my head. That's about as far I've gotten in the last week. I know that sounds pathetic but there it is. I'm not a good felon and I don't think well on my feet."

He seemed to ponder her words, rubbing his chin as several expressions flitted across his features - none of them anger and disgust, although one of them looked a great deal like frustration. But then he wasn't the first person to feel that way around her. Not in the least.

"Actually, for a civilian I think you've done pretty well. You did the right thing coming here to Cypress Corner, which is out of the way, and then getting a job to make more money while you figured things out. You told me just enough truth not to be tripped up by your own story. You kept yourself safe and that's the most important thing. But now I'm here to help you and that means we do what I say and follow my rules. I can help and protect you, Josie, but you have to help me. From now on you have to be one hundred percent honest with me no matter what. Can you do that?"

It kind of sounded like he didn't think she had been honest. She'd told him the awful truth and every bit of it.

"Of course I can," she said a bit defensively. "I just did. Do you not believe me? I didn't kill my friend, Evan. I would never do that to Amy. She was my best friend in the whole world. I didn't hurt her no matter what the police think. I'm innocent."

If he didn't believe this one fact then she would have to leave right then. Because if he thought she was guilty there would be no doubt he'd call his old law enforcement cop buddies and her ass would be sitting in some dank cell somewhere while she waited for her court-appointed lawyer who wouldn't believe her either.

Because she looked guilty. She'd been there when Amy died and even the thumb drive didn't clear her. A good attorney could make it look like a reason to kill.

"I believe you. I don't think you could murder anyone, honey. But I can't help you if you don't trust me."

"I wouldn't have told you the truth if I didn't trust you." Josie hopped up from her chair and the room spun, making her grab onto the table for support. The whiskey had done its job quite well. "I want your help, Evan. I don't know what to do or where to go. And I'm scared all the damn time."

Evan stood and pulled her into his arms, pressing her cheek to his chest where she could hear the steady beat of his heart under her ear. It was oddly reassuring and she relaxed in his embrace despite all the worries on her shoulders.

Or maybe it was the booze.

Either way it felt good to have someone hold her and tell her everything was going to be okay. Except...wait...he hadn't said that. Shit, he'd said he would help her but he hadn't said he could keep her out of jail. She probably should have brought that up first thing.

"Hey...are you going to turn me in?" she asked, the words sticking in her throat and a shudder running through her body. She wasn't prison yard material. She was more the My Little Pony and Strawberry Shortcake type.

His hand rubbed her back in circles, drawing a small sigh from her lips that she couldn't hold back. "No, honey, I'm not going to turn you in. I don't think the greater good would be served by doing that. But we do need to be careful because I can't speak for everyone else we might come into contact with."

"Thank you," she said, her words muffled by the cotton of his t-shirt. "I don't want to go to jail."

"We'll do everything we can to keep that from happening. Now first things first. I need to see that recording. We also need to investigate this Lydell guy. Find out if he has any weaknesses other than pretty young women. If I were a betting man I'd say that he does."

Almost dizzy with relief, she finally allowed herself to lean on someone else, even if only for a few minutes. Evan was always solid and dependable but now he was also smart and resourceful. He knew what to do and she would follow him anywhere.

Just not to prison.

CHAPTER FIFTEEN

Watching a sex tape never had the potential to be the most comfortable and enjoyable thing Evan had ever done and he'd dragged his feet about doing it, instead spending his time on the laptop digging up anything he could find about the former senator. Eventually he couldn't put it off any longer and he'd popped the thumb drive into the port and sat back and cringed, grimaced, and winced as the smarmy senator seduced the pretty young girl into the sack. Apparently, Josie had watched no farther because the last five minutes of the recording showed the kinky asshole smacking the crap out of the young woman when she wanted to leave and he wanted her to stay when it was all over.

What a slimebag.

Evan would admit to having a kink or two in the bedroom but his encounters with females were strictly consensual. If a woman even hesitated then the answer was a firm no.

In his career he'd spent more time than he liked to remember with low-life assholes who abused females. He liked this situation even less because Lydell was pretending to be an upstanding family man who was a good person, someone the public could trust. The lack of genuine emotion on the man's face in the video turned Evan's stomach. It was as if the girl was a *thing*, not a human being. Evan had seen it before in the eyes of the suspects that had paraded through the Marshal Service and this one was no different. Except that his suits and shoes were more expensive along with a well-practiced veneer of civilization.

After Lisa - no, Josie, he'd need to remember that - spilled her guts he'd had so many questions, none of them answered by watching the recording. If anything, it only spurred him on even more.

How did Josie's friend Amy get the recording?

Why did she have it?

What had she been planning to do with it?

How did Lydell find out she had it?

How in the hell did Evan get pulled back into the life of an investigator and cop?

Honestly, he'd thought that was all behind him but now here he was digging into people's backgrounds and planning protection details. Like he had never left the job.

Reaching for the phone, he did his best to ignore the troubling voice inside of his head that kept repeating the same thing over and over.

You're getting pulled in again. Run while you can. You don't want to do this, do you?

His head was saying no but his heart...His heart was a whole other deal. He couldn't leave Josie to the tender mercies of a man like Lydell who would kill to keep this video under wraps, nor could he hand her over to the authorities and let her take her chances with their protection. It had to be him. It was the only way he could be sure to keep Josie safe.

"Mitchell."

Reed Mitchell's usual terse greeting came through the phone loud and clear. Just as the sheriff had intended, Evan was sure. Reed was a member of the group of lawmen that Evan had been a part of before he quit. They banded together and shared knowledge as much as possible, making their jobs much easier.

"It's Evan. How are things in the cold north?"

"It's a chilly spring if that's what you're asking," Reed replied with a chuckle. "How the hell are you, man? How's Florida? And most importantly, when are you coming back?"

The last one was a doozy of a question that Evan had no answer for.

"It's hot and humid but other than that it's good. It's a nice change, if you know what I mean. How's Kaylee?"

Kaylee was Reed's wife and a bestselling erotic romance writer. Boy, did Reed take a lot of shit because of that but he smiled through it all, probably because he loved his wife and worshipped the ground she walked on.

"Kaylee's good. Busy, actually. She's on a deadline and that means we eat a lot of frozen pizza but I don't mind." Reed cleared his throat. "It's great to hear from you but I'm guessing you didn't call to catch up. If you're looking for a job, I actually know of one. The guy who took over Logan's town is stepping down due to family issues back east. The mayor is looking for a replacement. I think you'd be just the man for the job. I know Logan would recommend you in a heartbeat."

The mere thought of going back to small town law enforcement made Evan shudder. He wasn't ready to give up his freedom. Not yet, anyway. Of course, that all might change when the money ran out and he had to support himself somehow.

"That's really generous of all of you," Evan hedged, hoping to find a polite way to say thanks but no thanks without pissing off a good friend. "I'm actually not looking at the moment, although it sounds like a wonderful opportunity. Logan had good support from the town, which is important."

"He has excellent things to say about the job. Are you sure you're not interested? I could make a call to Logan. Just say the word."

"Not right now. I'm still working on that project for my family."

"Well, let me know if you change your mind. So if you didn't call to catch up and you didn't call for a job..."

The sheriff let his voice trail off so that Evan could fill in the blanks.

"I've got trouble here, Reed. Big trouble. A friend of mine is in real hot water and I need some help. She's in danger and you should also know that she's wanted for questioning by the police for a crime she says she didn't commit. I believe her. If you're not comfortable helping me because of that I'll understand."

He had to give credit to Reed; the man didn't hesitate for a minute. "If you say she's innocent that's good enough for me. I get that she's wanted by the cops but how is she in danger?"

Evan sighed and sat back in the chair, glancing over his shoulder to make sure that Josie was still downstairs.

"I should probably start at the very beginning. Do you have a few minutes?"

"For you? Absolutely. Shoot."

There were several stops and starts along with a handful of questions, although Reed tried not to interrupt if he didn't have to. When Evan was done, he waited in the silence to hear what the lawman had to say and whether he was truly willing to help now that he knew everything.

"That's a hell of a story. You've seen the video?"

"I have. It would definitely put a crimp in Lydell's future political ambitions. The asshole. If you saw it, you'd know what a worm he is."

"First things first then," Reed responded. "We need to protect that video. It may be the only thing that can convince a judge or jury that your girlfriend isn't guilty. Can you send me the file? I can save it on separate servers to keep it safe."

"She's not my–"

Reed snorted and laughed. "Don't even bother denying it. You like her. I bet she likes you too, although this seems like a bad time in her life to be starting a relationship. But once you get past this bump in the road everything else will seem minor."

"Bump in the road? You've lost your mind." Evan pulled the thumb drive from the port on the laptop. "I just loaded the video on that secure shared drive we used on the Mammoth case."

"Got it. I'm going to take a look at this before I store it. Any objections?"

It wasn't something Evan would wish on his friends but he understood their curiosity. "Go ahead but keep a barf bag close at hand. The guy's a sleaze."

"Makes figuring out who the bad guy is a simple task. Now I'll also look into the girl's background, run some facial recognition and see if we can figure out who she is. I know you're worried about her so I'll try and see where she might be. Look for credit card transactions. Stuff like that. I'll also look into Lydell as well. Maybe get Jason looking into it too. The asshole might have a few other skeletons in his closet if he's willing to kill over a sex tape."

Lydell craved power. He'd wanted power over that girl and now he wanted power over the country.

"At some point we have to release this recording," Evan pointed out. "As someone who spent most of their law enforcement career trying to avoid press and cameras I'm sorely lacking connections there. I don't suppose you have any that we can trust implicitly."

"I don't but I bet Jason does. I'll reach out to him and see what he can dig up. Now let's talk about protecting Josie. What do you have in place?"

"So far no one has found her. She thinks the fire last night was the men after her but I just saw a local bulletin on the Internet and it was just a couple of guys drinking too much and smoking in their room. They accidentally set fire to the mattress and drapes and it spread quickly. So that means they still haven't found her."

"Yet."

Evan was determined that it would stay that way. "She's using an alias and paying cash. She dumped her car and cell back in D.C. She's going to be tough to find. In the meantime, I'm keeping her with me here at the house. And I'm loaded for bear. They'll need to come through me to get to her."

The setup here at the house wasn't ideal but it would have to do.

"Security system? Cameras?"

Wincing, Evan shook his head and then remembered Reed couldn't see him. "Not on this old house. Hell, I don't even have a television. But I've protected dozens if not hundreds of witnesses. I've got this, so don't worry. It's the one thing I've been trained to do if you think about it."

"If you say so." Reed sounded reluctant but didn't push the subject. "I'll get on this and give you a call in a few hours to check in. Let me know if you need anything else."

"I'm just damn grateful for what you're doing. I really appreciate this. I can't even tell you how much."

"I think I have an idea. Take care of Josie and we'll talk soon."

Keeping Josie protected and safe was Evan's number one priority and he had a few ideas as to how he could make that happen.

CHAPTER SIXTEEN

Evan had forbidden Josie to work today but when he was done with his phone call, he found her in the half-cleaned out kitchen, up to her elbows in suds, washing the dusty dishes that had been sitting in the cabinets for who-knows-how-many years. Once again…stubborn. It was going to get her seriously hurt or killed if she wasn't careful. He'd do anything and everything to protect her but she had to cooperate and do her part.

By obeying his every command.

It didn't seem like much to ask.

"I thought I told you to relax. Do you call this relaxing?"

The little miss didn't even flinch at his scolding tone; instead she had the gall to smile and toss her auburn ponytail over her shoulder. She shouldn't look so damn cute being contrary but he couldn't help but notice the smattering of freckles on her nose and cheekbones. He had an almost overwhelming urge to kiss each and every one but luckily he didn't give in. This time, at least.

"Actually, I do call this relaxing. It gave me something to do with my hands and it calmed my mind. I can't just sit around here and wait to be murdered, Evan. Those men want me dead and last night's fire was only a preview of things to come."

About that fire…At least this was one way he could ease her fears.

"I saw on the local news site that it was just two guys drinking too much and smoking. They set fire to a mattress and the drapes. Nothing nefarious, honey. Just a couple of guys out of hand. They haven't found you."

The way Josie sagged against the kitchen counter with relief tore at Evan's heart. She was terrified and he needed to find a way to ease her mind. She wasn't as helpless as she believed.

"Not yet," she whispered. "It's only a matter of time though."

"Not necessarily. You were smart. You dumped your car and cell phone, haven't used your credit cards or your real name, and lived on cash. It's going to make it tough for them, if not impossible. But I'm not advocating sitting around here and waiting for them to find us. I think we need to be slightly more proactive."

Her brows pulled together as she pondered his words. "Proactive? Are we going after them? That doesn't sound like the best idea."

"I was thinking we might work on some of your self-defense skills and also your shooting skills. Have you ever fired a gun, honey?"

Josie pulled the plug from the sink and dried her hands on the kitchen towel. "Yes, but I wouldn't say I'm a great shot or anything. I've only done it once at a friend's bachelorette party. She didn't want to go see strippers—she wanted to shoot at the rifle range."

Interesting friend. Evan bet her husband to be was probably just as happy that there weren't any naked men involved in her celebrating.

"You don't need to be great. Let's see if we can make you a halfway decent shot. How about we head to the range before trying some hand to hand combat?"

"I thought you wanted me to relax? This doesn't sound relaxing."

"You had your chance. Now it's time to work."

There was much to do and not long to do it in.

◈ ◈ ◈

Every bone and muscle in Josie's body ached but she wasn't going to give up. After a few hours at the shooting range where she'd managed to do fairly well for a newbie they were now in the backyard of Evan's home, circling each other like a couple of sumo wrestlers. He was trying to teach her to defend herself in case someone tried to come after her and she was simply trying to survive the lesson. So far, if the attacks had been real she would have been screwed. And dead. Oh so dead.

"Let's try if I come at you from the front," Evan suggested, wiping his sweaty brow with the hem of his t-shirt and showing off ridiculously ridged abs that were sprinkled with a dark treasure trail to the waistband of his cargo shorts. The skin was smooth and golden and her fingers itched to run themselves up and down the flesh, eliciting a moan or groan of pleasure.

Except that she could barely move, let alone run her hands over his impressive physique.

"Because coming at me from behind worked so well," Josie muttered, bracing herself for the attack. "Clearly I'm a lover, not a fighter. I should be playing the guitar and singing folk songs somewhere with flowers in my hair."

Evan threw back his head and laughed, the sound rich, deep, and more than pleasant. He made happiness look good. "I didn't know you played guitar. I do too. I'd love to hear you sometime."

That was only one of her problems.

"I don't, actually. Can't carry a tune in a bucket either but I'm better at that than this. I suck at this. Are you ready to give up on me?"

"I am not," Evan replied promptly. "You're retaining more than you think. The fact is you shouldn't be able to win a struggle with me because I've been trained in the military and then in law enforcement. If you could whip my ass I would be a piss poor example of my former profession, so it's all right that you're struggling. I expected it and it's okay."

"What if they've been trained too?"

"It won't be like this in reality. I have the advantage of knowing you're going to fight back so I'm thinking ahead of countermeasures. These guys? They probably think you'll struggle a little bit and then give up. They won't expect you to kick them in the nuts or break their nose. That will be a surprise. And that's all you need, honey. Just surprise them and then run like hell."

Another issue.

"I'm out of shape," she admitted, feeling completely useless. "Running for exercise has never been high on my list of activities to do for fun. I've tried and usually give up before the first mile."

"What you lacked was a powerful motivator. Someone chasing you who wants to injure or kill you can be that motivator. I guarantee you will run farther and faster than you ever have in the past."

Part of her wanted to smack that smirk right off Evan's handsome face and the other part of her wanted to hug him for making her laugh when all she wanted to do was cry. Anyone else would have turned her ass in, but not only had he believed her when she said she was innocent he'd decided to protect her. Totally above the call of duty and she was more than grateful. She was humbled. She had friends back in D.C. who probably wouldn't have done all that he had.

It made him that much more attractive and he didn't really need the help. In the middle of all this chaos, he was constantly on her mind when she should be thinking about other things. Like staying alive.

"Are you speaking from experience?" she teased. "Is there a story behind this?"

"Baby, there's always a story. Maybe I'll tell you a few when we're done here. Now are you ready?"

As ready as she'd ever be. She was no badass but she'd try. For him.

"Bring it on. I'm feeling exceptionally macho right now."

Josie didn't feel that way for long. A half hour later she had melted into a puddle of sweat and grime, only wanting a bath and a strong shot of whiskey. He'd taught her about all the weak spots on the human body and how to exploit them. The only thing she had to worry about now was if the bad guys knew them as well.

Sprawled on her belly in the grass, she moaned softly at the aches and pains she'd garnered today. Dirt stuck to her skin and she needed an IV to replace the fluids she'd lost, but at the moment she didn't care enough to move. Dying right here seemed like a good plan. It was a good place to leave the world.

Of course, Evan simply wouldn't give her a moment's peace. All the wonderful fuzzy thoughts she'd had about him earlier in the day were gone and instead she wanted to rip his throat out. He was keeping her from shutting out the world and she was fucking annoyed. If she could even lift her pinkie finger she'd punch him but she was in too much pain. Between the horse-back riding and now the fighting she was done for.

"Josie? Josie?" His hand shook her shoulder and she lifted one eyelid about halfway to see him standing over her with a shit-eating grin. He didn't even have the grace to feel sorry for her. Asshole. "You need to get up and drink some fluids. I have some of that sports replacement drink from the cooler."

She managed to move her arm to wave him away but the effort drew another pained groan from her lips.

"Moving is not on the agenda. Just bring it to me and pour it over my face and hands. I'll lick at my skin. I don't even have the energy to suck at a straw."

Chuckling, Evan didn't listen but then she hadn't expected him to. Damn the man, he was as stubborn as an old mule. More stubborn than she was and that was saying something.

"This is no place to sleep, honey. Up and at 'em."

Before she could answer and without so much as a by-your-leave she found his arm wound around her waist and Evan lifting her bodily from the ground to stand on her own two feet. She was as wobbly as a newborn foal but she locked her knees so she wouldn't fall into a heap of indignity. Damn the man. Why couldn't he let her lie there for an hour or two?

"I hate you, you know. A lot."

"I know and I expected it. Just so you know, I don't hate you. I think you're brave and wonderful." He smacked her bottom and she yelped in response, almost tripping over her own feet and falling down again. "You've got a nice-looking caboose too. Now move into the kitchen. We need to get you out of this heat and rehydrated."

With legs like lead she climbed the few steps into the house before falling into the nearest kitchen chair. She wanted to be mad at him but she simply couldn't when he was being so nice.

And he liked her ass. She'd always thought it was too big but she wouldn't argue with him if he thought it was okay. Luckily, she didn't have enough energy to ask him if he liked anything else on her body.

Two bottles of sport drink and two ibuprofen later, she was feeling a little more human and less like dying. Evan had propped her in front of the air conditioner while he quickly showered, promising her a long soak in the tub when she was done. She'd thanked him and then promptly fallen asleep, dreaming convoluted images that she thankfully didn't remember when he shook her awake sometime later.

"I've run you a bath and you can soak as long as you want. Then we'll need to go into town to pick up dinner. I don't know about you but I'm starved."

She blinked the sleep from her eyes and sighed. "That sounds like too much work. I'll just waste away to nothing right here. Go…live your life. Remember me often and fondly."

A warm breath fanned out over her shoulder and she gasped in surprise when he simply lifted her, bridal style, into his arms and carried her into the bathroom. "You need to get clean and you need to eat. I promise you will feel a hundred percent better when you're done."

He was untying her tennis shoes and pulling them off along with her thick athletic socks and she inwardly cringed, wanting to dig a hole and hide for a month. Those feet were awash in sweat and had to stink to high heaven but bless his heart, he didn't even flinch.

"You start taking any of my other clothes off you might pull back a stump."

Still kneeling at her now bare feet, Evan simply laughed at her and helped pull her to a standing position.

"That's big talk from someone who asked me to let her die a few minutes ago. Just so you know, I'll remember you more often and fondly if I help you strip."

She lifted her startled gaze to his blue eyes that had those crinkles at the corners when he chuckled or smiled. He was flirting with her. Openly. Insistently. Sure, he'd played at it a little in the past week, but this was something else. Something more.

"What's gotten in to you?" she blurted, her cheeks growing warm. "You've never acted this way before."

His gaze skittered away before coming back and this time his cheeks were a ruddy shade. "I was pussyfooting around all last week when I really wanted to let you know how I felt. Now that I know that you're in danger I want to make sure you know how I feel. With everything going on I just don't think we should waste any time. I like you, Josie. A hell of a lot. Do you like me? If so, let's do something about it."

She wasn't sure what to think about it but his urgency fired up her own. The one thing she'd learned since that fateful night was that life was short. It could be over before she knew it and she didn't want to have a pile of regrets, things undone.

"Are you suggesting we fuck just in case we - or I - die?"

"Hell, no." His hands slid down her arms to hold onto her grimy hands. "I'm suggesting that we both let down our guards a little. I haven't had the best luck with women and I've put my career first for too long. I'd like to change that and I'd like to change that with you. Is that too forward or scary? Tell me to back off and I will."

Gathering every ounce of courage she could muster in her exhausted state, she looked up at him, brazen and bold. "Do you really like my ass?"

A smile bloomed on his face, showing off a small dimple in his cheek. "Honey, I think it's spectacular. But please note that I don't think it's your only charm. Honest to God, I think you're gorgeous. Flat out beautiful."

She rolled her eyes, knowing flattery when she heard it. "That's going a bit far. I know I'm not. There are mirrors in this house."

He tugged her closer, pressing her disgustingly foul body to his clean-smelling torso. "Then you need to take a second look because you slay me with how sexy you are. When you're dusty, when you're clean, when you're in cutoffs and a t-shirt. Fuck, especially when you're in those hot little cutoffs. You're the first thing I think about when I wake up and the last thing I think about before I go to sleep."

She'd never been that to anyone. At least that she knew of.

"I haven't had much luck with relationships," she admitted as he came closer, their lips inches apart. "I'm sort of backwards in that respect. Sex hasn't been anything to write home about, either. I've never seen what the big deal was."

His grin was predatory, almost feral, and a shiver of anticipation ran down her spine. "Then get a pen and paper, honey, because I intend to rectify that. Maybe not tonight or tomorrow night, but eventually."

Then his lips were on hers and all rational thought fled from her mind. The kiss was tender but demanding, his tongue sweeping her mouth with a mastery and expertise she'd never known before and had a feeling never would again with anyone else. He knew his way around her mouth and body, his hands stroking up and down her spine, eventually coming to rest at the curve of her bottom. By the time he raised his head she was a quivering mass of sensation, her knees turned to jelly. This man ought to be outlawed in all fifty states and the European Union. He was lethal but she loved it.

"Soak as long as you want, honey. I'll be downstairs waiting for you." He turned to leave the bathroom but stopped in the doorway. "I'll always wait for you."

He shut the door behind him and she sank down to sit on the edge of the tub, her entire body shaking with emotions she hadn't felt in a long time. She liked Evan, respected him, cared about him, and admired him. He was a good man to help her and dammit, he was sexy as hell too. She'd be crazy to turn away from him and crazier to get involved, considering all that was happening in her life.

One thing he'd said had caught her attention. He'd lived his life for a long time based on other people's rules and wants. Now he wanted to live by his own. It sounded like good advice and it was time to take it.

Time to live instead of simply exist. Time to…maybe…love.

CHAPTER SEVENTEEN

Josie did feel a thousand percent better after her bath and the pain medication kicked in. She'd assumed when Evan spoke about dinner they'd end up at the diner but he had other ideas. They were currently pulling into a parking space of a well-known chain restaurant in Ocala. At first she'd balked when she realized what direction they were heading but he'd assured her that no one knew where she was and that even if they did, a crowded eatery wasn't a place they were going to try and get her.

A warm glow took up residence in her chest when he caught her hand in his as they entered the restaurant and even when they followed the hostess to their table. It made the entire evening more date-like and it also made her stomach flutter with nerves. He slid into the booth opposite her and opened the menu.

"I don't know about you but I'm dying for something different than pizza and diner fare. I'm glad you were okay with coming here."

Josie opened her own menu and saw several things that looked delicious. After a hard afternoon, she had the appetite of a lumberjack.

"My memory must have been affected by the sun today because I don't remember being given a choice as you were barreling down the highway to get here. Unless I wanted to hurl myself from a vehicle going over sixty miles per hour, of course, but I was too sore to reach for the door handle."

Evan gave her a quick sideways glance and grinned. "You get sassy when you're not feeling your best. I like it."

Rolling her eyes, Josie groaned as she shifted in her seat, moving her legs experimentally. "Then you're going to worship me by the time this evening is over. I'm stiffening up like an eighty-year-old woman. Really, they've shot horses for less."

She was being dramatic but it was kind of fun.

"I'll keep that in mind. Do you know what you're going to have?"

"One of everything," Josie sighed. "And then dessert. I'm so hungry."

"You might want to pace yourself, honey. They have excellent cheesecake here and you won't want to miss it."

"I'm eyeing the lemon bread pudding."

All day they'd worked but had fun too so she was fairly relaxed and happy. So it was a shock to her system when two police officers came through the doors, their uniforms and weapons capturing her attention and setting her heart into an uneven rhythm. She should never have left Cypress Corner or Evan's house.

She buried her face in the menu, her hands shaking with fear and her mouth cotton ball dry. Despite how wonderful Evan was, her life kind of sucked right now. She'd be a fool to forget that for even a moment.

"Hey, it's okay." Evan's fingers tugged the menu out of her hands and placed it on the table. "You're fine. They're not here for you, just for dinner. They sat way on the other side. Let me repeat that. They don't have any interest in you and they can't even see us from where they're sitting."

Josie took several deep breaths to calm herself, hating to show this much weakness in front of Evan. He must think she was some sort of nervous Nellie but the thought of going to jail was more than she could deal with.

"I panicked for a minute."

"That's normal. Just remember that I'm here to help you. If I thought this wasn't a good idea or that you were in any danger, I'd take you right out of here. Can you trust me?"

She already had.

"Yes, and as soon as my heart starts beating normally I'll say thank you again. I needed to tell someone and you were there. You could have judged me or kicked me out but you didn't."

"That never would have happened." He closed his own menu and took a sip of his water. "I'm proud of you today. You stuck with it and didn't give up. I was hard on you, there's no doubt about that, but you came through with flying colors."

Josie rubbed her sore shoulder as the waitress came to take their order. "And those colors are black and blue."

They ordered - a steak and potato for him and a grilled chicken breast and fries for her. The bread basket was filled along with yummy honey butter and Josie held off just until the waitress was a few feet away before tearing into it, sighing as the warm goodness hit her taste buds. She might have been embarrassed to relish her meal so fully but Evan was doing the same, a big smile on his face as he chewed.

"It's nice to be out with a woman who enjoys her food. So many just pick at it and I feel like such a pig when I eat in front of them."

She swallowed the last bite of her dinner roll and reached for a second. "Glad I could assuage your guilt. I've never understood those females that live on kale and water. I like to eat. I can cook too when I'm in the mood."

"I'm going to test that theory when we're done with the kitchen. It's been a long time since I had a home-cooked meal."

She really was a decent cook, although she tended to make pastas and non-fancy comfort food. Gourmet anything wasn't really her style. Despite her jobs in the design world, Josie was a regular girl. She liked jeans and t-shirts, she liked spaghetti and meatballs and pot roast, she liked going to the movies, and hanging out with friends having a few drinks. She wasn't difficult to entertain and she could spend time by herself without going crazy. She'd spent time at high-class cocktail parties in New York City but she'd never fit in, and she'd finally come to the realization that she didn't want to.

Which only made her wonder what kind of women Evan had been with in the past. Was his style glamorous and sexy? He'd said he thought she was beautiful when she was sweaty and dirty but perhaps because it was a novelty?

"I bet women cook for you all the time."

Two glasses of wine were placed in front of them and then the waitress silently slipped away, only pausing their conversation for a moment, but it felt like an eternity as Josie waited for his answer. Evan was handsome, sexy, and funny. He'd probably had lots of girlfriends and she was afraid she couldn't compete. She'd been so busy working she hadn't dated much. One serious boyfriend and a smattering of casual dates was the sum total of her love life so far. She hadn't minded until now when some sophistication and experience with romance would certainly help.

"Hardly." Evan laughed before taking a sip of his wine. "My career and relationships didn't mix well. I traveled quite a bit and worked very long hours. Most women don't want a man that's never there and breaks dates at the last minute, and I know that because they told me so. In vivid detail. I was a lousy boyfriend so eventually I…"

His voice trailed off and he was shifting uncomfortably in his seat as if he'd said more than he intended.

"Eventually?" Josie prompted, hoping he would finish his sentence. She wanted to know more about this man. She wanted to know the name of his first dog and what his favorite ice cream flavor was. She wanted to know everything because they might not have much time to learn about each other. There was a large part of her that felt like she needed to rush.

His lips twisted and he rubbed his chin, clearly not comfortable with what he was about to reveal, which only made her want to know what he had been going to say even more.

"I eventually tried the friends with benefits thing. It seemed like a smart idea at the time."

His tone made it sound like it hadn't turned out that way.

"I've never done anything like that," she admitted, twirling her wine glass by its stem. "It seems kind of, I don't know, cold-blooded. But I can see why you would though. If your career is so crazy and all."

"You don't have to be polite. It didn't turn out like I thought it would. It was empty and cold. Maybe when I was younger it would have been okay, but at my age sex without emotion just doesn't do it for me anymore."

"Not many men would admit that."

"I think you might be surprised."

"I'm willing to keep an open mind about it." Josie dug into the salad that had been placed in front of her. "So tell me something else about yourself. You said that you were in the military. How did that come about?"

His eyebrow quirked in question. "Do you really want to know or are you just being polite?

"I really want to know."

He heaved a large sigh and took a long drink of his wine. "You asked for it. But the story starts much earlier. It's really all about my childhood."

◈ ◈ ◈

Evan didn't really want to do a post-mortem on his upbringing. His parents were wonderful people who had raised their children well. There wasn't a juvenile delinquent in the bunch and they'd all grown to have responsible careers but there had been a price for that as far as he was concerned.

Individuality.

His parents had come from the generation where conformity was prized and considered a virtue, and they had passed that belief down to their progeny. Evan and his siblings had grown up with certain expectations and questioning those was not something that was encouraged.

"I had a normal upbringing. My dad was an electrician and owned his own company and my mom did the books while raising us kids. It was pretty typical, I would guess. We had enough money to go on a vacation in the summer but not enough that we were rolling in it. Strictly middle class. With four kids, they had their hands full and dinner was an event. Back then we were all expected to sit down at the table as a family. I kind of miss that. They'd ask us about our day. They really cared. Hell, my dad was the Little League coach when I was growing up and my mom was a member of the PTA."

"Sounds very 'Leave it to Beaver'," Josie teased. "Very different than my own childhood."

"It was…comfortable…and secure." Evan struggled to put his feelings into words. "At least it felt that way. I thought my parents were perfect and our life seemed so ordinary. In a good way. They had barbecues in the summer and invited their friends. In the winter, they had parties and played bridge. As kids we played outside and got dirty, sneaking cigarettes and girly magazines behind the barn. It was all innocence and naïveté, and to be honest it didn't prepare us for the real world in the least."

Josie reached for his hand, tangling their fingers together but not saying anything, content to let him gather his thoughts and speak when he was ready.

"My mom and dad were big on responsibility and service. For as long as I can remember, my old man talked about military service being the making of a man. He talked about his own Army days constantly, all his buddies and the fun things they'd done. He made it sound like the most wonderful thing in the world. It was expected that me and my brother would enlist."

Josie's expression had dimmed considerably as if she could foresee what he was going to say.

"And you did enlist."

Evan nodded, his own thoughts back in that time so long ago. "I never even questioned it and looking back that shocks me. It was as if I didn't have a mind of my own. Dad wanted me to play football, baseball, and play the guitar. So that's what I did. Then he wanted me to go into the military. So I did that too. I guess I just wanted to please them, you know? Make them happy. We all did, looking back on it. Not one of the four of us rebelled in any way until my younger sister did in college. She got pregnant and then she married the father. They're happy and still together but the very idea that Carli had sex sent my mother to her bed for days."

It all seemed so incredibly dramatic, looking back on it. Carli had been twenty-two and girls that age had sex even if a parent was in deep denial. Evan and his siblings had a running joke that they still thought the two unmarried kids were virgins despite being over thirty.

"I'm guessing the Army wasn't as fun as your father made it sound."

Evan didn't speak much about his time in the military. He'd had a love-hate relationship with the Army. He'd loved the feeling of accomplishment and the camaraderie but he'd hated the bureaucracy.

"I will say he was right about one thing. It did make me grow up and take on real responsibility. Of course, one could make the argument I could have learned that as a civilian as well. But there's something about having the lives of others dependent on you doing your job. It will grow your ass up in a hurry."

"And all that fun your father had? Do you think he was making it up?"

Evan could tell Josie a few stories that would horrify her. In his younger days, he and his buddies had been hellions when they were on leave.

"No, he was telling the truth, although he might have embellished here and there. I had fun too. But Dad was in the Army during peace time and he wasn't in as long as I was. It was different."

The waitress slid their steaming hot meals in front of them and the smell of charred meat and spices wafted up from the plate. Evan's stomach growled in approval.

"This looks delicious," Josie hummed in anticipation as she took her first bite of chicken. "And it tastes even better. Or maybe I'm just starved."

"Do you want to try a piece of my steak?" Evan offered.

Josie laughed and shook her head. "I know you want every bite just as I want all of mine. Keep your paws off my dinner, buster."

One of the things he liked so much about her was that she enjoyed her food and didn't make any bones about it. She had a strong indulgent side that boded well for how she would be between the sheets.

"I know better than to put any fingers within a foot of your plate."

"Maybe I'll share dessert with you."

Snorting, Evan slathered butter on his baked potato. "I think that's a big *maybe*. Seriously, how is your dinner? You're making yummy noises so I'm guessing it was worth the drive out here?"

"It's heavenly and yes, it was worth it. Thank you for bringing me here." Josie took a sip of her wine. "You said you were going to explain what made you become a cop but so far all I've heard about is your Army days."

"The two are inextricably entwined. I never intended on staying in the military as long as I did but with everything going on in the Middle East, I felt they needed me. Once I did get out I was thirty years old, no college degree, and no job. One of my Army buddies talked about how the Marshal Service was recruiting. When I mentioned it to my parents they were thrilled. A steady job with the government plus I would still be serving my country, only in a different way. Needless to say I got the job and I worked there while finishing up my degree until I was shot in the leg."

He stopped there, formulating what to say about his life when he wasn't sure he even understood it. Many things didn't make sense right now.

"They wanted you to go to a desk job? Be a supervisor?"

"They offered me my own team but it didn't appeal to me. Still doesn't. My family and friends - well, a few friends - think I've lost my mind. Marisa, my former partner, has even started calling some of my cop pals trying to get them to talk to me about going back."

That reminded him that he needed to call her and tell her to back the hell off. She'd crossed a line talking to Seth and she needed to understand his life decisions were not up for discussion just because they'd slept together for a few months.

"Then you became a sheriff."

"And then I quit," he completed the story. "I did that because once again it was expected of me. But I'm damn tired of doing what everyone else wants me to do. I want to do what I want to do. Does it make me sound weak that I spent all these years doing things for the wrong reasons?"

"No, not at all." Josie shook her head, her green eyes soft in the dim lighting. "You weren't miserable and there were aspects of the job you enjoyed. I'm betting there are many people doing jobs they absolutely hate for worse reasons. I'm kind of in the same boat. I grew to hate design because it was so competitive and catty. Very dog eat dog. My waitress job sucked too. I'm not sure what I'm supposed to be when I'm grown up, to be frank. So I'm not much different than you, Evan. My big fear right now is that I won't get a chance to make any changes to my life. That I'll end up in prison or dead first."

"I'm not going to let that happen," Evan declared, reaching across the table to grab her hand with his. "Believe me when I say that because I mean it."

She placed her fork on the edge of her plate, her hand shaking. "I'm dragging you back into a life you didn't want anymore. You don't want to be a cop, remember? Now you're in a position where you have to protect me. Don't you resent me for that? Just a little?"

"Not a bit," he replied quickly because it was true. "I won't lie that I'm not conflicted slightly but the one thing I know, honey, is that I was a good cop. I can protect you. I know what to do to make sure you're safe and I'd be a piss poor human being if I didn't do it. Add in the fact that I think you're amazing and wonderful and there's no doubt that I'd take care of you. This doesn't mean I have to be a marshal again, or a sheriff. This is not a permanent situation."

"If you ever change your mind–"

"I won't."

"But you might–"

"Don't even go there. Not going to happen."

"You interrupt a lot."

That made Evan smile. "It's part of my charm. Now let's get that waitress over here and order some dessert. I'm still hungry."

"I want my own dessert."

He'd known she would.

"I'm not surprised. Let's decide what we're going to order. I vote for the chocolate fudge cake and the bread pudding. We can share a little."

He was fine as long as he didn't have to make any decisions too far into the future. But he had figured out one thing and that was a step forward.

Evan wanted to be a man that Josie could respect and admire.

Maybe even love.

CHAPTER EIGHTEEN

The wine had done its job.

Josie was relaxed and serene as they entered the house after driving back from dinner. All in all it had been a wonderful evening. She'd learned so much about Evan and it only made her care about him more than she already did. The one thing she hated was that her situation was forcing him into a role he'd been happy to leave behind.

All the way home, the awareness between them had built to a frightening level, punctuated by little glances and touches. A hand on her thigh, her fingers stroking his arm. Her body was hyper-aware of his as he closed the front door behind him, leaving them alone in their private world. They'd created a cocoon of sorts, free from worrying about prison or rogue killers. It was as if they were the only two people in the world.

If only they could stay that way forever.

They had tonight.

If she were being completely honest, Josie didn't know where they'd be days or weeks from now. While Evan swore he could protect her, the fact was he was one man against many. There were no guarantees of a tomorrow. No one had any, although until now she'd carried the illusion that the future was a sure thing.

Evan said he wanted to do what he wanted to, not what was expected of him. She did too.

He would expect her to climb the stairs, slip into her pajamas, and go to sleep. But in her mind she'd already crossed over that line, the one keeping them strictly friends. She wanted to be with him and he'd left no doubt that he felt the same. What was she waiting for?

For him to make the first move, that was what.

It wasn't in her nature to be the aggressor in a relationship, especially when it came to sex. The fear of rejection along with that nagging little voice in the back of her head that said good girls don't initiate lovemaking were both powerful forces and she found herself simply standing in the middle of the living room as he snapped on the lights one by one, illuminating the darkened space.

"I don't have a television or anything." Evan grimaced as he dropped his keys into the bowl on the table by the door. "It's still early but if you want to go to bed that's fine. I'm sure you're tired after the long day. I just need to get something out of my room and it's all yours."

That was one thing that needed fixing. It wasn't right that she'd kicked him out of his own bedroom. The camp bed he was sleeping on in the living room was too short and uncomfortable for a grown man to get a good night's sleep.

"About that," Josie began, her fingers twisting in the straps of her backpack. "I can't in good conscious take over your bedroom. It's your house and you worked just as hard as I did today. You just did it better because you're in good shape and I'm a blob that sits on the couch most of the time."

That scowl she knew so well was currently directed right at her but she stood her ground.

"It's no hardship, honey. I've slept on the cold dirt many times so having any sort of bed is a plus in my book. While you're here for me to protect, you'll sleep in the bed."

Scraping up every bit of courage she could muster, she took a deep breath and plunged in. "It's king size. There's plenty of room for both of us."

If she thought she was going to shock Evan Davis she was sorely mistaken. Instead of his mouth falling open, his lips curved into a smile. A smile that could only be described as wolfish and seductive. Heat curled in her belly in response and she had to remind herself to breathe even as her pulse began to pound in her ears.

"Well, you do have a point there," he drawled, looking quite pleased with himself. "The bed is very large and you're just a tiny scrap of a thing. You can't take up much space."

She liked to sprawl in the middle of the mattress, arms and legs flung to each corner but she wasn't about to admit that to him at this moment. Nor did she want to point out that no one in her life ever had described her as *bitty* or a *scrap*. She had heard the words curvy and zaftig. In other words, she had some junk in the trunk.

"So...if you want to share, I'm fine with it."

Whirling on her heel she didn't wait for him to respond, instead flying up the staircase, paying no attention to her sore bones and muscles that screamed in rabid protest. Quickly she stripped out of her clothes and into a pair of pajama shorts and a t-shirt. She slipped between the sheets and resolutely squeezed her eyes shut, covers to her chin, while her heart pounded waiting for him to join her. Or not.

He didn't make her wait long. The door opened slowly, creaking on its ancient hinges, and she let her lids flutter open to watch his deft fingers working on the buttons of his shirt. He didn't say a word or make eye contact as he shrugged out of his shirt, jeans, and socks, leaving on a pair of dark blue boxer shorts.

Josie had to grit her teeth to keep from making a noise as she surveyed every inch of exposed flesh on display. Evan was in amazing shape and had nothing to be ashamed of. She allowed her gaze to caress his wide shoulders, flat abdomen, and powerful thighs, skipping over the more intimate bulge between his legs.

I won't look. I won't look. I won't– Oops! I looked.

Swallowing hard, she realized she was panting and probably drooling down her chin as if she hadn't seen a half-naked man in decades. He was no more bare than if they'd gone to the beach but the mere sight of his gorgeous body had worked her up into a rare lather. Her arousal was humming and he hadn't even touched her and she didn't have any idea if he intended to. He might lie next to her and fall asleep, leaving her awake and aching.

Cruel bastard.

Josie felt the bed move and the blanket pull back so that Evan could get in beside her. He kept his distance, however, respecting her personal space. She reached up to snap off the bedside light, bathing them in moonlight from the windows.

Trying to scrunch into the smallest ball possible at the very edge of the bed, Josie turned her back to Evan and tried to relax enough to fall asleep. What a joke. There was no way she was going to simply drift off to sleep easily when Evan's fine self was lying only a foot away.

"Josie, if you're not okay with this, I can go downstairs and sleep in the living room."

"No!" Forcefully relaxing her rigid spine, she turned so she was facing him, his body half illuminated but his expression shrouded in shadow. "No, please don't. It's–it's just been a long time since I've shared a bed with anyone. Now that you're here I'm wondering if maybe I snore."

His shoulders moved in a shrug and a soft chuckle escaped from his lips. "That wouldn't bother me. I snore too."

"You never said that," she accused playfully, her palm pushing at his chest and finding bare skin over hard muscle. She froze, her fingers still pressed against his warm flesh, her teasing words dying as heat spread from her hand all the way to her toes. He felt wonderful and she wanted to continue her exploration of his body.

But she was a big chicken that wasn't going to do anything. A coward. A fraidy-cat.

Whatever one wanted to call her she'd willingly accept the title. She was terrified that her advances would be rejected despite Evan's copious hints that he was completely on board with the idea of them being together. After all, he might have changed his mind somewhere between the drive home and the climb up the stairs. Maybe he'd decided she was too much trouble or he was too exhausted.

A wave of self-consciousness hit her hard and Josie had to fight the urge to sniff at her underarms.

He, on the other hand, smelled amazing. A little like body wash and a lot like warmth as if he was the softest, cuddliest blanket on a chilly, rain-soaked afternoon. He represented everything that was good and solid in her upside down, crazy world. She trusted him with everything she was.

She trusted him with her life. It didn't seem much of a stretch to trust him with her body too. In fact, the more she pondered the point, the more it made sense. No man had ever taken care of her the way Evan had.

Flattening her palm against his chest, she allowed her fingers to run up and over his shoulders, down his arms, and then back up, only to travel down his torso and over his ridged abs, lingering at the waistband of his boxer shorts. Evan hadn't remained still and silent during her sensual foray; he'd reached out his own hands and clamped them down on her hips, tugging her closer until her nose was pressed against the hollow of his neck.

His masculine scent flooded her senses and her suddenly heavy eyelids drifted closed as he captured her lips in a soul-searing kiss that seemed to reach down into the heart of her, letting thousands of butterflies free in her belly. Her heart raced and blood whipped through her veins as his lips explored her jaw, all the way to a sensitive spot behind her ear. She jerked and moaned as his teeth nipped at the flesh, drawing a chuckle of pure male satisfaction from him while his long fingers splayed out as if to claim as much territory for himself as he could.

"Are you sure, honey? We don't have to do this."

His voice was low and husky, like a glass of aged whiskey and a fine cigar. She didn't answer for a moment, instead letting her hands reply by running up and down his chest, lingering on his flat nipples and pulling a tortured groan from somewhere deep inside of him.

"I think I do have to do this," she finally answered. "If I stop now, I'd never forgive myself. I want this. You. But I'm nervous as hell. It's been a long time since…"

She didn't think she needed to finish the sentence. He already knew she'd had lousy luck in love in the past. Funny, she had a feeling things might be looking up in that department.

"We can take this as slow as we need to. I'm not going anywhere."

Leaning down, he captured her lips with his own, nibbling on her bottom lip and sending frissons of pleasure through every vein and pore. She couldn't remember ever being this affected by a man while still wearing clothes.

"I don't think slow is going to do it this time. I think I need you now."

CHAPTER NINETEEN

Steadying his trembling hands, Evan rolled Josie onto her back and he hovered above her, his face buried in the fragrant curve of her neck while his hands were busily sliding under her cotton top to the silky skin begging to be stroked and explored. Her own fingers were testing his resolve by tracing a line on the flesh above the waistband of his boxers, causing his cock to harden even further and jump with each teasing touch of her fingernails.

He sucked in a breath when she scraped those nails over his fabric-covered erection and he bit her earlobe in retaliation, loving the way she shivered in response.

"Naughty girl. If you keep doing that this might be all over before it even starts."

Her hands slid up his torso to his shoulders, brushing his sensitive flesh on the way. "But I want to play. And touch. Just a little won't hurt."

Right now, it was very painful indeed. His balls were already drawn up tight and his cock was throbbing with every beat of his heart. Sinking into her hot, wet center was about all he could think about but there was a small part of his brain still functioning on a non-primitive level that was making sense.

Make this good for her. Then she'll want to do it again. Don't be an asshole.

His hands slid up her arms to gently hold her wrists, one on each side of her head. Josie could easily pull away if she wanted to or if she panicked, but hopefully she'd allow herself to be adored and worshipped without interruption. "I have a better idea. Why don't you just lie back and relax? Let me do the driving. I promise you won't regret it."

Her kiss-swollen lips curved into a smile and she gave him a small sigh, her lids half-closed. Grateful for her trust, he didn't hesitate to begin exploring her with his tongue, lips and teeth, cataloging all the spots that seemed to bring her the greatest pleasure.

Her clothes were in the way. They would have to go.

Sitting back on his haunches, he insinuated his hands under her top and slipped it over her head, Josie cooperating by lifting up slightly. Her bare breasts were magnificent, soft, round, generous, with dusky pink tips, but if he stopped to give them attention he'd be sidetracked for quite a while. Better to stay focused and come back when he could take his time.

He tossed it aside before hooking his thumbs in the top of her sleep shorts and slid them down her tanned legs, taking his time and admiring every lush line and curve he revealed. Josie might not have the athletic slim figure that was so in vogue these days but as far as he was concerned she had something far better.

A body that was luscious, abundant, sumptuous, and very delicious. She reminded him of those pinup girls from World War II like Rita Heyworth or Betty Grable. Everything about her screamed sin and sex and it was all he could do not to fall on her like a starving dog on a juicy steak.

The scrap of lace she called panties followed quickly after and he allowed his gaze to travel head to toe, drinking in the bounty laid out before him. Her legs moved restlessly and her fingers dug into his shoulders slightly as if to get his attention.

"Are you just going to stare or are you maybe going to do something? You got me naked and I figured you had a plan."

If his arousal-fogged mind had any plan at all it was to kiss every single inch of flesh he had exposed.

That seemed like a good place to start. He could decide what step two was while he was executing step one.

His tongue slid over the curve of her breast to circle a hardened peak and he delighted in her indrawn breath and moan of pleasure. Drawing it into his mouth, he scraped his teeth along the sides and her nails cut into the skin of his back as her legs fell naturally open as if in supplication. He situated himself between them, pushing them farther apart with his knees.

"I want you to scream my name when you come. That's the plan."

◈ ◈ ◈

As far as plans went, it was a good one.

Josie was completely on board, every part of her. Honey dampened her thighs and a bar of arousal had formed in her belly. Her limbs were heavy and white-hot heat licked at her flesh as his incredibly talented mouth kissed a wet trail down her abdomen, over her mound, and onto her inner thighs. His tongue swirled on the sensitive skin and she hissed in approval when he nipped and licked at the juncture where hip met thigh.

His hands had abandoned her wrists and she found her fingers tangled in his silky dark hair, the short scruff of his beard scraping ticklish spots and sending shivers of pleasure straight to her clit. Licking at her slit, he parted the drenched flesh and ran a callused finger around her swollen button, drawing a tortured moan from her lips. She canted her hips in desperation as his tongue sought out every nook and cranny but the one place she needed him the most.

"Please."

The word came out raw and barely intelligible but he must have understood because he immediately took pity on her, closing his mouth over the sensitive pearl and sucking softly while his tongue rubbed each side in turn. The wave of pleasure hit her like a barreling freight train and she froze, her spine stiffening and her toes and fingers curled into the sheets. Throwing her head back, Josie called out his name as she trembled and quaked with each crest and surge. Before she could catch her breath, she heard the rustle of foil and the snap of latex.

It was about damn time.

She should have known that making love with Evan Davis wouldn't be the same as any other lover she'd had in the past. There was no hesitation, no tentative, fumbling touches. Only a sure alpha male between her quivering thighs. Evan hooked one of his arms under each of her knees and pushed them up and apart, spreading her wide open to his hot, avid gaze. Every shred of decency and ladylike behavior must have fled at some point because instead of feeling embarrassed or ashamed she felt aroused at the pleasure he was displaying as he looked her up and down, clearly enjoying what he was seeing. He made her feel like the sexiest, most desired woman on the planet and she could only hope she made him feel the same.

God, she wanted this man. So much. And more.

She didn't just want this, the physical and carnal incarnation of Evan Davis. She wanted it all. The way he lost patience with bad drivers on the road, and the way he enjoyed a good steak cooked medium rare. How his Adam's apple bobbed up and down when he tipped his head back to drink down a cold beer after a long, hot day, and how intense his expression could turn when he really gave a damn about something. She wanted the whole package and would gladly take the good with the bad. Heaven knew she wasn't perfect either.

His cock nudged at her slick entrance and for a moment she tensed up as she got an eyeful of Evan's impressive equipment. Not only had she not had sex in quite a while but also she'd never had one that big.

This might hurt a bit.

"Easy, honey." He seemed to sense her trepidation, and his hand softly stroked the side of her face until she relaxed. "We'll take this as slow as you like. You're the boss. You tell me what you want."

"I need you," she whispered, her heart squeezing in her chest. "Don't make me wait."

He didn't bother to reply, intent on pushing into her even as her body resisted, clamping down on the head of his cock. Instead of becoming frustrated, he bent his head and took an already hard nipple into his mouth, suckling until she could feel it all the way to her clit. She cried out at the intensity of the sensation only to realize he'd used the distraction to enter her another few inches. Sneaky man. He chuckled as he turned his debauched attentions to her other breast, teasing it with his tongue before nipping at it with his teeth.

The breath was knocked from her lungs as he seated himself deeply inside of her, all the way to the hilt. His groin rubbed at her clit with every movement of his hips and she lifted her own to try and get more contact, resulting in Evan beginning a slow but steady rhythm of strokes. He'd pull almost all of the way out and then piston back in, rubbing all sorts of crazy spots inside that sent tingles to her already over-sensitized clit. Her nails dug into the muscles of his shoulders and she sucked oxygen into her starved lungs even as her orgasm began to build, stronger than the first.

His hips snapped and his breathing grew ragged as his thrusts sped up, each one sending her higher into the stratosphere until she was standing on the edge of a cliff, the air around her shimmering with heat. Their bodies were slicked with sweat and she lifted up her head to swipe her tongue against his chest, the skin damp and salty. His groan of approval only served to ramp up her arousal and she heard herself urging him on, begging him to fuck her harder and faster until they both exploded into tiny pieces.

When that explosion finally came, it was as if they were caught in a maelstrom of bliss. Lights blinked behind her lids as waves coursed through her limbs leaving her languorous, sleepy, and euphoric all at the same time.

Evan reached his own peak, his jaw tight and his head thrown back, showing off the muscles and tendons of his neck. Eventually he slumped against her before rolling onto his back and tucking her into his side, his hand petting her hair and stroking her back. Always touching her gently, almost reverently.

She lay in his arms feeling incredibly safe and protected while he pressed kisses to the top of her head and whispered how beautiful she was and how lucky he felt.

She could listen to that all night long.

Except she was exhausted and a series of yawns escaped from her lips although she tried to muffle them with her hand. Evan chuckled and pulled the covers over the both of them as she turned on her side, her head pillowed on his bicep. She liked being the little spoon.

"Sleep, honey." His voice was soft and his breath warm against her cheek. "Tomorrow is another day. I'm here and I'll make sure nothing happens to you."

Trusting him implicitly, she allowed her heavy lids to flutter closed as she drifted on a cloud. Tonight was about Evan, love, and pleasure. She'd deal with the mess of her life in the light of day.

She didn't have a choice.

◈ ◈ ◈

Once Evan heard Josie's even breathing, he eased his arm from under her head and slid out of bed, grabbing his boxers and blue jeans that had been strewn on the floor in the midst of their undeniable passion. He quickly tugged them on along with his tennis shoes and headed to the wall behind the door to the bedroom closet, leaving the lights off so as not to disturb his sleeping lover.

He located the number pad on the wall and quietly pressed in the code number that would release the lock on the gun safe. Installing it had been the first thing he'd done when moving into the home since he didn't want to leave his personal guns and rifles where they could be found.

With a click, the heavy door swung open and Evan wasted no time selecting his favorite firearm, which was ready and loaded. He tucked it into the back of his waistband and locked the safe, taking one more glance at the still sleeping form of Josie before padding downstairs.

His training flooded back as he walked from window to window, checking that each one was secure. When he arrived at the front door, he opened it slowly, checking the perimeter of his home before stepping out onto the front porch. The air had cooled slightly from earlier in the day but the humidity hung heavily in the air along with the pungent aroma of hibiscus and fresh cut grass. He needed to check around the house and then upstairs before he would allow himself to sleep.

Descending the steps, Evan's gaze skittered left and then right, taking in the expanse of his property although the exterior lights that he'd left on tonight didn't illuminate much past twenty feet. He paused at the foot of the steps, listening closely for anything or anyone out of place but nothing seemed to be amiss.

Good news in the middle of so much bad. He would have his hands full keeping Josie out of jail and off the radar of whomever wanted her dead. He'd promised but his word wasn't the only reason he wouldn't waver from his mission; it was how he felt about Josie. She'd become so important - so much - in such a short time. In the past it would have scared the hell out of him but this time was different. Josie was different. Their relationship was more than he'd ever had or hoped to.

He was falling in love.

And it felt better than anything ever had.

It wasn't just the sex, although that had been pretty terrific. It was about how she made him feel. She didn't care that he was in this crazy transition part of his life because she was in one too. Maybe together they could figure out a future that included the two of them.

First, he had to keep her alive and out of prison. He had a feeling it sounded much easier than it was actually going to be.

CHAPTER TWENTY

Josie stretched her arms as the sun began to peek through the curtains and groaned as her muscles protested vehemently. Clearly, they were not happy about being asked do things like... move, but she was too happy to care about something so inconsequential. She was too busy focusing on the man lying right beside her.

Evan.

Last night he'd shown her what all the fuss was about and frankly, she couldn't wait to do it again. If the hardness poking into the back of her thigh were any indication, she wouldn't have to.

"Morning," she whispered, reaching back behind her to tangle her fingers in his hair. He leaned down to drop kisses on her shoulder and then began nipping at her ear.

"Morning, baby. I don't have to ask if you slept well. You barely moved all night."

She pressed her ass back, grinding against his hard cock and drawing a chuckle from him while his hands wandered up her belly to cup her breasts and brush at the hard tips.

"Did I snore? Or talk?"

Laughing, he slipped his hand down her abdomen and between her legs, parting them so he could toy with her swollen clit. Already wet with anticipation, his fingers easily circled the button until she was a panting mess.

"I couldn't shut you up," Even declared, teasing her to the edge of climax. "You kept muttering all night long and when you weren't doing that you were snoring like a buzz saw. I didn't get a wink of sleep."

Her leg was thrown back over his and her arm was curled around his neck as he peppered kisses on her jaw and ear. Pleasure ricocheted through her body and she moaned her approval with a deep kiss to his lips.

"You're a liar. I don't snore or talk. You don't look like a man who didn't get any sleep."

"You'll never know what the truth is. Now relax and enjoy, honey."

He pressed forward, sliding in easily this time, pumping in and out lazily as if they had all the time in the world despite her impending orgasm. She'd whimpered and wriggle, trying to get him to speed up but his hold on her simply firmed as his steady rhythm began to drive her ever closer to the goal.

The fingers of one hand pinched at a nipple while his other fingers stroked over her clit and that gorgeous cock of his rubbed all Josie's sensitive spots deep inside. It was all too much and she went into sensory overload, her breathing heavy and her body on auto-pilot. Her brain had melted down into a puddle and coherent thought was impossible. Consumed by flames, she heard herself call Evan's name a few times before tumbling over that cliff, awash in pleasure.

He groaned his own completion as she clamped down on his cock, his last thrust going deeper than she'd ever thought possible. A couple of expletives fell from his lips and then he was kissing her again until all the breath in her lungs was gone and she was a clinging mess.

A happy clinging mess.

They were both smiling as he pulled her close, her head nestled on his chest and her hand curled around his jaw, those whiskers she'd grown to love under her palm. There was something so inherently masculine about this man and she allowed herself to revel in it for a few minutes while she felt very feminine indeed. It wasn't a feeling she'd had in any other relationships and while the modern woman in her balked slightly, she couldn't deny how safe and adored he made her feel.

His tongue traced the swirls in her ear. "We have to get up and go into Ocala. I need to get some things to make the house more secure."

Was he saying they weren't secure now? She didn't have the guts to ask and decided to leave his remark alone. The bottom line was she trusted him to take care of her.

"I need a shower and breakfast. In that order."

"I think we both worked up an appetite. Let's get cleaned up and head to the diner. I'm planning to eat my weight in bacon."

That sounded like an excellent idea although she'd add on a stack of fluffy pancakes and syrup on the side.

Despite all the shit she had going on in her life, she had this good thing. Evan was the kind of man she'd wanted in her life but never thought she'd be lucky enough to find.

Somehow there had to be a future for them together, but she had a feeling it wasn't going to be easy.

◈ ◈ ◈

Evan snagged his keys from the table by the front door and cast his gaze up the staircase. Normally Josie didn't take long to get ready but she'd been messing with her hair this morning, muttering under her breath that she needed a haircut or some hedge clippers. When he'd made a hasty retreat from the bathroom, she'd been yanking her hair into a ponytail and he'd inwardly sighed at the crime of restraining her gorgeous tresses. He had vivid memories from last night of her long, messy auburn curls against the stark white of the pillowcases.

Breathtaking.

"Honey, are you almost ready?"

"Just a minute," she called down. "I'm trying to find my backpack."

Quickly he scanned the living room and saw it sitting on the floor by the couch. She must have left it there last night when they'd come home from dinner.

"It's down here."

The roar of an engine diverted his attention from the stairs and the beautiful woman getting dressed to the front door where a dark SUV was pulling up in front of the house. Frowning, he reached for the Glock 22 tucked under his light jacket, his fingers brushing the leather holster and his body on high alert. Any vehicle that wasn't familiar was automatically suspect in Evan's current world.

The three passengers spilled out of the truck and Evan's face split into a grin when he realized just who his visitors were. They all had better things to be doing and yet these guys had taken the time to come down here and help him. Money couldn't buy loyalty and friendship like that. Throwing open the door, he was down the steps and shaking their hands within seconds. He hadn't known how tense he was until they had showed up. It was like the weight of the world was off his shoulders. He didn't have to face this all alone.

"Jesus, Mary, and Joseph, what are you doing here? How did you even find me?"

Three of his best friends in the whole world and possibly the finest lawmen he knew stood in his driveway with mischievous grins on their faces. They'd intended to surprise him and had managed it spectacularly. Evan hadn't a clue they were on their way. They must have taken a red-eye flight.

Sheriff Reed Mitchell.

Sheriff Dare Turner.

Sheriff Seth Reilly.

There were handshakes, hugs, and some back slapping as Evan greeted men he hadn't seen in months. Although he knew he'd done the right thing quitting his job as a small town lawman, he'd missed the camaraderie he'd found in their tightknit group.

"We wouldn't be much of a cop if we couldn't find you," Seth shrugged carelessly, his gaze sweeping the property. "Besides, you told me your location. As for what we're doing here, well, that seems self-explanatory. Reed says you've got yourself into quite the pickle with a girl wanted for murder. You sure know how to pick 'em, my friend. You've got taste in the ladies a lot like mine."

"I didn't kill Amy. I didn't kill anyone."

Evan whirled around to see Josie standing there, hands on her hips, sporting an unwelcome expression. In direct contrast to his reaction, she didn't look happy to see his friends in the least.

◈ ◈ ◈

Josie stood on the top step, trembling with a combination of fear and anger. She wasn't guilty and Evan believed her. But it didn't appear that his friends felt the same way. If they were here to convince Evan to turn her in? She was screwed.

From the greeting the three men had received they were close friends. Josie had seen less warm hellos between family members. Evan had a prior relationship with these guys and he'd known her a week and a half. She'd be behind bars before nightfall.

The man with the sandy blond hair who had spoken stepped forward. "No one here is saying you did. Evan says you're innocent and that's good enough for us." His face broke into a grin and she felt herself relax slightly. "Besides, I've got no room to talk. I was on the run with Presley from arms dealers and the federal government. No one here is going to judge you."

She descended the steps but stayed a few feet away. "You ran from the government?"

The man slapped Evan on the back. "Specifically I ran from Evan here but we don't talk about that much." He moved closer and stuck out his hand. "I'm Seth and you must be Josie. I'm pleased to meet you. We've come to help."

She didn't extend her arm. Not yet. "Help? By help do you mean put me in jail?"

A dark haired man stepped forward, leaving the scowling man near the vehicle with his massive arms crossed over his chest. If Seth believed in her, that unhappy guy looked like he wanted her executed.

"No one is going to jail," the handsome man with dark hair replied. "We saw the recording and we believe your story. In fact, we have a few things to tell you about Lydell. He's no saint, that's for sure. I'm Reed Mitchell, by the way. Glad to meet you."

"What about him?" Josie pointed to the mountain of a man with an unhappy expression. "Did the airline lose his luggage? He doesn't look like he believes anybody is innocent."

To her surprise everyone burst into laughter, including the sour giant. Evan stepped closer to her and wrapped an arm around her shoulders, pulling her to his side. "Honey, that's Dare Turner and he's an ornery son of a bitch with a permanent scowl on his face. But I promise you he's a good guy. Christ, get over here, man, and say hello. And wipe that pissed expression off your face. You've got nothing to be unhappy about since Rayne took pity on you."

Dare had to easily be six-foot-four in his stocking feet with shoulders wider that a yardstick. He shook her hand but held it gently as if he was aware that he could crush the fingers without a second thought. Josie didn't know who Rayne was but hopefully the poor woman was an Amazon. If this giant rolled over in his sleep, he'd squash his bed partner.

"It's nice to meet you, ma'am, and no they didn't lose my luggage but the flight was delayed. We'd planned to be here much earlier this morning." He gave Evan a hopeful look. "I don't suppose there's some place to get some breakfast? We haven't eaten in hours and the peanuts on the plane was just enough to piss a body off."

"That's where we were headed actually. Why don't we go to the diner and then we can get some food while you get to know Josie."

"We have a lot to tell you," Seth replied, opening the car door for Josie. She hesitated for only a moment before murmuring her thanks and sliding into the back seat. Before he could turn around she held out her hand.

"I think I forgot to do this," she said. "It's nice to meet you."

He smiled and took her much smaller hand in his. "It's a pleasure, Josie."

Reed slid into the seat on her other side and she shook hands with him too. If Evan said these guys were the real deal then she had to trust him...and them.

CHAPTER TWENTY-ONE

Josie popped the last bite of bacon into her mouth before sitting back into her chair and patting her pleasantly full stomach. She'd decided to avoid making herself miserable in front of Evan's friends and had ordered a manageable size breakfast. Evan, on the other hand, had ordered practically one of everything on the menu and his friends had followed suit. She'd never seen this amount of food inhaled in one sitting. Every square inch of the table was covered in dirty dishes. Where were the Guinness World Record book people when you needed them?

Evan pushed his plate of biscuits and honey closer to Josie. "You're welcome to some if you're still hungry."

"Are you sure? Because I'd hate to lose a finger or two reaching for one. You boys are hungry this morning."

Dare took another bite of his hash browns. "You've got that right. But we'd never snap at a lady. Each other? That's a different story. Reed or Seth reaches for my food? They're gonna need a doctor."

Patting her stomach, Josie shook her head. "Thank you but I'm full." She glanced at Evan who was still demolishing his link sausage. "Actually I'd love to hear what you've found out. That is, if you can talk about it."

Reed leaned forward after checking out the neighboring diners. The restaurant was particularly loud this morning with the sounds of clanking dishes and the raised voices of the patrons trying to be heard. No one was paying any attention to their group at the back corner table.

"We can talk but please understand that what I've found out is preliminary. I've got a friend who is working more on this and he'll call if or when he finds something new."

"Jared?" Evan asked in surprise. "You called him in?"

Reed nodded. "A guy who has this much money and political clout is beyond my skill set. We needed the master to come in for a search like that and he was happy to. But I did get a few interesting tidbits. You were right—Lydell is a grade A asshole."

Josie rolled her eyes. "I could have told you that. He marches around our state like he owns it."

"What Reed found out was interesting," Seth piped up after swallowing a mouthful of waffles. "The guy has business and political connections that are extremely powerful. I made a point to watch a few of his speeches from when he was in the Senate and I'll be damned if I can figure out what the guy is for or against. He says a lot of words but never actually says anything of substance."

That sounded like every politician she'd ever seen.

"That's how he was elected to the Senate in the first place," Dare observed. "He's known for taking both liberal and conservative positions so people think he can work across the aisle. From what we could find, he simply votes how the person or group with the most money wants him to."

"Welcome to the current state of politics." Josie wrinkled her nose in distaste. "I lived in a city that was drowning in it."

Seth leaned forward, his hands wrapped around his coffee mug. "Do you have any idea why Amy was in possession of that tape, Josie? Or how she came to have it?" He sighed and rubbed his chin. "I know this is going to sound bad so feel free to reach across the table and smack me. Did Amy have money troubles? Might she have been trying to blackmail Lydell?"

Josie didn't want to think that about her friend but she didn't take offense. Now that she'd spent a little time with these guys she could see they were good people who only wanted to help Evan, and that meant helping her by extension. Nobody was giving her the side-eye as if they thought she was secretly guilty.

"I can't be angry at you for something that crossed my mind as well. Until that night, I had no idea my friend had possession of anything like this. The only thing I can think of is her boyfriend was a reporter and he may have somehow gotten his hands on it. How it ended up with her though would be a mystery."

"Did she know Lydell or his family?" Reed asked as he pulled out a notebook from his shirt pocket. "Maybe someone that worked for him?"

"Not that I know of," Josie replied, trying to remember any details that Amy might have divulged other than that people in politics often had giant egos. The only political people that Amy liked hanging out and talking to were the ones lower in the ranks. "She had some sort of assistant job to the accountant guy for a government entity. Amy had a finance degree."

Evan tapped his pencil on the table. "Maybe she knew something about the financial records?"

Perhaps but that didn't explain the video.

"But that's not why they..."

Josie voice drifted off, not wanting to say the word. She was still in some weird state of denial about what happened that night. A part of her expected Amy to send her a text or call. Maybe post a funny status and photo on social media.

Seth patted her hand. "We'd like to get any phone numbers and email addresses she might have had so we can look into who she was communicating with. Can you do that?"

"Yes, although I don't know how much help they might be."

Reed slid the notebook across the table along with a pen. "You never know what might give us just the lead we need. Is there anything else you can tell us about Amy or her job?"

Painstakingly, Josie tried to draw a picture of her gregarious friend who always had a smile and a friendly word for everyone. Nothing about Amy had been unusual, right down to her middle class upbringing, her two siblings, and her divorced parents. She'd been a normal girl who liked to have fun with her man and friends and dreamed of settling down and getting married. Sometimes Amy and her boyfriend Billy had talked about getting a cat.

Her job hadn't been any more interesting. Amy complained about the bigwigs that threw their weight around and disrupted the office when they were in town, which luckily wasn't often. She liked her boss though and they worked well together.

Josie finished scribbling down every number and email address for Amy that she knew along with all her social media profiles. "Were you able to find out who the girl was in the video? Is she okay?"

Seth grimaced and shook his head. "Jared and Jason have some contacts and they're running some facial recognition software. Hopefully we'll know something soon. I've been checking the recent missing persons reports and haven't found anything, so we're hoping she's alive and healthy."

The image of watching the light go out in Amy's eyes had tears gathering in Josie's eyes. "From what you've found out so far, do you think Lydell killed that poor girl?"

Reed sighed and rubbed the back of his neck. "No, I don't think he did. From what I've been able to dig up so far Lydell is the kind of guy to get other people to do his dirty work. He doesn't like to be on the front lines if you know what I mean. So I think there is a pretty decent chance she's alive and well, but sporting a black eye and bruised ribs. He's still lower than a rattlesnake's belly, make no mistake. I'm just saying he doesn't seem to have a lot of balls."

"I kind of got that impression just seeing him on television," Josie murmured, her thoughts on that night. She wanted desperately to remember something that might help these men who had volunteered to help her.

"Even the media doesn't care," Dare shrugged. "A retired politician that's a total jerk. No one would be shocked. If anything, they'd be surprised if he wasn't. We don't ask much of our public servants these days. Sad, really."

Josie glanced down at the sea of plates and bowls on the table. Empty. These boys could put away some chow.

"I just want to thank you guys for coming." She linked her arm with Evan's and gave his hand a grateful squeeze. "You dropped everything at a moment's notice and here you are. I'm overwhelmed. I know you're really here for Evan but I'm also going to be the recipient of your hard work and I don't want there to be any confusion about this. I'm incredibly grateful. I didn't kill Amy and I don't want to go to jail. It scares the hell out of me. And those men that want me dead? They terrify me too. Basically I'm a lily-livered shit."

Reed shook his head and smiled. "Lily-livered? I don't think so. You managed to run and hide all this time, plus find someone you instinctually knew you could trust. That's damn brave if you ask me."

All four men were grinning and Evan was even tugging on her ponytail playfully. She was going to like having all of them around. She hadn't felt this safe in a long time. These three men were like the big brothers she'd never had.

"Awww, you guys are so sweet," she teased. "How about a group hug?"

Laughter, warm and rich, filled the air and caused several heads to turn, if only to take a closer look at the newcomers. Strangers were always news in this town and this morning wasn't an exception. Add in the fact that four gorgeous, strapping men sat at the table with her and she was the envy of every female in Cypress Corner.

"I have a better idea." Evan slapped the table lightly to get everyone's attention. "How about a group meeting? We need to talk about what the plan is to keep Josie safe. Actually, I was planning to head into Ocala to the hardware store and pick up some items to make the house more secure. Maybe we should all go."

The other three men exchanged glances but Dare was the one who spoke up. "We already stopped and picked up some things we thought you might need on the way here from the airport. We didn't want to waste any time. We were the first through the doors of the hardware store this morning."

Josie didn't know which one of them to hug first.

"I know we got off to a rocky start but I really like you guys."

Seth winked at Evan. "She's a keeper, bro. She's got damn good taste in bodyguards."

Josie wasn't sure about that but she was sure that her taste in men was improving. Evan Davis was a keeper indeed.

CHAPTER TWENTY-TWO

The drive back to the house only took a few minutes and Evan took the opportunity to watch Josie interact with his friends. She'd been scared and prickly at first but now she'd fully embraced them, confident that they weren't here to extricate Evan from a sticky situation he wanted out of. Frankly, the last thing he wanted was for Josie to go. After last night, he needed her to stay. What they had deserved a chance to grow and flourish.

Seth pulled the SUV into the driveway and Evan climbed out, followed by Josie, Dare, and then Reed. The stack of hardware supplies stowed in the back of the vehicle meant a busy day ahead but Evan was damn grateful his friends were here to help.

"Should we get all these boxes and bags unloaded?" he asked, heading for the rear of the truck. "All my tools are in the garage. I'll open it up."

Reed opened the back and began to sort through the supplies. "We have some cameras to place around the house and property, plus some exterior lighting. In one of those bags over there are some motion sensors to place on the doors and windows."

Seth stood on the other side of Evan. "There is one thing we don't have. To get here quickly we had to fly which means–"

"I understand," Evan nodded, getting their meaning immediately. "No firearms or ammunition. Don't worry, Granddad was a collector. We'd be fine for the zombie apocalypse if it came to that."

Josie shuddered and peered over his shoulder to see what was in the boxes. "Wow, that's a lot of stuff. Do you really think we'll need it all?"

Evan didn't have a chance to answer before a car appeared on his long driveway, pulling up behind the SUV.

The unexpected visitor drove a nondescript sedan that made Evan instantly suspicious. Cars like that were driven by government people.

He ought to know. He'd driven every American made four-door, boring as hell vehicle in his career. Supposedly it made him blend in to the surroundings, but the cars were so plain it was almost a calling card.

"Go inside the house, honey." Evan put a hand on her arm. "Upstairs in the bedroom where it's cool. We have company."

He felt a tremble run down her arm and he dropped a reassuring kiss on her temple. Even before reinforcements had arrived, he wasn't planning to let anyone near her but now he knew he could actually keep her safe. These were three of the best cops he'd ever had the pleasure to work with. They knew their business and he'd trust them with his life.

"Who is it?" she whispered, trying to see through the windshield even as he blocked her view.

"I don't know and that's why you're going upstairs."

"I'll stay there with her," Dare offered, placing his hand on Josie's arm. She allowed herself to be led into the house and hopefully upstairs.

But she was far from safe as only Evan was currently armed.

Seth, Evan, and Reed stood shoulder to shoulder as if a wall between their visitor and the house. The driver's door of the sedan opened and a long leg clad in skinny jeans and ankle boots appeared and then a second. Evan knew those legs and the person they were attached to. He inwardly groaned and stepped forward, giving his friends a put-upon look that told them they could stand down.

But Josie needed to stay in the house.

"Marisa, I had no idea you were coming today."

Evan greeted his former partner as she climbed out of the car. Along with her dark jeans and boots, she was wearing a white blouse with sleeves that were rolled up almost to the elbows. An oversized brown leather handbag that matched those boots was thrown over her shoulder, finishing off the ensemble. To this day, Evan had no clue how Marisa could stay so unwrinkled. She'd probably been in the vehicle for hours but she looked like she'd just pulled on her clothes.

"That's because I didn't tell you. I was afraid you'd have a million excuses as to why I shouldn't come. So give me a hug and tell me all about your handsome friends. Oh hello, Seth. It's been a long time."

Of course Marisa would notice them. Evan quickly introduced her although she'd already spoken to them on the phone about trying to convince him to return to the Marshal Service. She gave Seth a hug and he looked quite uncomfortable about the whole thing. Presley and Seth had never warmed to Marisa.

Tugging at her collar, Marisa nodded toward the house. "I'll never get used to the heat down here. How about we go inside and catch up?"

Evan had a feeling *catch up* meant something very different to each of them.

"And you always overdressed for the climate," Evan observed, pointing to her boots. "Sandals probably would have been a better choice. Shorts too, for that matter. You're off duty, after all."

"Shorts and sandals? I don't think so."

Some things never changed and Marisa was one of them. She loved her blue jeans and would probably be buried in her favorite pair.

"It won't be much better in the house, I'm afraid. No air conditioning."

Evan almost laughed at Marisa's appalled expression. It spoke volumes about how close their friendship was that she didn't bother to hide it. After all, they knew some awfully intimate things about each other after working together almost daily for two years.

Her eyes went wide and she seemed to gaze at the house in a whole new light. Not a good one. "How can you live there without air conditioning? It's going to be absolutely miserable in a couple of months."

Evan laughed and pointed to the upstairs. "I have a window unit in the bedroom but I don't think all of us would fit on the mattress. How about we head back into town? We can sit in the air conditioned diner and have a cool drink."

He'd whisk Marisa off to the diner and the other men could keep Josie safe while he was gone. The last thing he needed was for his former partner to get a close look at Josie and start asking uncomfortable questions. Hopefully Marisa would simply think Josie was Reed's woman.

"That sounds like a perfectly wonderful idea. Is everyone going?"

Evan glanced back at his two friends but they'd already figured out the plan. Seth and Reed shook their heads and mumbled something about calling their wives and checking in with the office. It sounded plausible enough and Marisa seemed happy with the explanation.

"Let's just take your car." Evan moved toward the passenger door and elbowed Reed on the way, the other man giving him a grin of understanding. "I'll even let you drive."

It was a running joke that Evan liked to drive everywhere but today he simply wanted her out of his driveway and he didn't care how that happened. He'd listen to her sales pitch about returning to the marshals and then nudge her home to Tampa. He had no intention of going back and he was going to make that crystal clear this morning and stop all this nonsense. She was sticking her nose into his personal life and dragging his friends along with her.

CHAPTER TWENTY-THREE

"They're gone," Reed, or maybe Seth, called up the stairs. Josie didn't know their voices well enough yet to tell them apart through a closed door. "You can come down if you want."

Dare shrugged and grinned. "Up to you. It's awful nice in this cool air. We didn't sleep much last night between the flights and the drive so I could curl up on this floor and nap."

A knock and then the door opened, Reed sticking his head in. "I heard that, Dare. No way are you taking a nap. Just because Evan left doesn't mean we don't have work to do. We can get started on those lights and cameras but if you want to stay in the cool a little longer, you can install those motion detectors on the windows."

Giving her a wink, Dare lumbered to his feet, seemingly unconcerned about being scolded by his friend. "Sounds like a plan. Josie, have you ever wanted to learn how to install motion detectors and cameras?"

Sitting by herself didn't sound like fun but asking these men all sorts of questions about Evan? That was tempting.

"How did you know? I've always wanted to learn how to do that. It's on my bucket list."

"Then it's your lucky day," Reed laughed, turning back to the stairs. "Let's see how much of this we can get done before Evan gets back. Hopefully he'll be able to shake Marisa off after a coffee and a piece of pie."

That's how Josie found herself handing tools and supplies up to Seth who was perched on a ladder leaning on the side of the house. He was installing some lighting and a camera that could be remotely accessed from a laptop or even a phone.

"So how long have you known Evan?" Josie asked casually as she held the Phillips screwdriver up for him to grab. Apparently she wasn't acting all that sly because his lips curved into a knowing smile.

"You can just ask me, you know. What do you want to know about Evan? I'll tell you what's common knowledge. But deep dark secrets are off limits. Not that I think I know any, actually."

Josie fidgeted, shuffling her feet before speaking. "Who is this Marisa and why is she here?"

Grimacing as he tightened a screw, Seth didn't answer immediately, appearing to formulate his answer. That only served to make her feel more nervous about the woman who had shown up unexpectedly today. Marisa must be someone important if Evan's whisking her away from the house was any indication. Clearly he didn't want her and Josie to meet.

Finally Seth stopped and leaned against the metal railing of the ladder. "Marisa is Evan's former partner at the Marshal Service. And his friend too."

"A good friend?"

"If you're asking if they're friends with benefits, I don't know the answer," Seth chuckled. "That's a question for Evan himself. I do know they worked closely together for a few years and that she's been trying to get him to go back to the marshals. She even called me to try and convince me to talk to him. She called Reed too."

This Marisa sounded like a real busybody.

"Evan doesn't want to go back."

"That's true but from what I can tell, he doesn't know what he wants instead. I think Marisa believes that it's better that he does something than nothing."

Josie could honestly say she didn't care what Marisa believed or wanted.

"He's not doing nothing," Josie protested. "He works hard every day. It's not like he's kicking back at the beach or lounging around the pool. He does things. Lots of things."

She didn't mention the writing Evan had been doing, not sure that he wanted anyone else to know about it.

"I'm sure he does," Seth laughed, turning back to the camera he was mounting under the eaves. "Marisa is an ambitious person and sometimes she doesn't see that other people aren't as driven as she is. Evan will let her blow off some steam and then tell her how it is. They have that type of relationship. He's not going to let her continue this line of thinking."

"You don't like her."

Seth sighed and stopped working again. "I never said that."

"You didn't have to. Your body language said it all."

"She's a nice person, she really is. It's just that she can be a little...what's the word I want? By the book. When she was helping Presley, she didn't convey much sympathy or emotion. It was as if Presley was just another assignment. Just another case file."

Josie was liking this woman less and less.

"What happened with your wife?"

"Her stepsister tried to frame her for arms dealing and then murder her with a car bomb. Evan put her in witness protection with me. That's how we met."

Holy shit. And I thought I had it bad.

Seth's lips were curved into a smile and whatever memories he was thinking about obviously made him quite happy. These sheriffs had a strange idea of fun.

Wait…car bomb? Arms dealing? That was the second story that Evan had written. Either Seth was leaving out a whole bunch or Evan had embellished a whole heck of a lot.

"Sounds romantic, but I bet there's more to the story."

"There is but that's for another time. If we're here long enough I'm betting you'll hear a bunch of stories with and without Evan. You'll be screaming for mercy in a few days, mark my words."

She doubted that. Evan was a fascinating man and he had very interesting friends.

"I'm not clear as to why this Marisa is bugging Evan about going back. Is she lonely or something? She doesn't like her current partner?"

Seth cursed softly as he tried to position the camera but it kept veering to the right. "If he went back they wouldn't even be partners. He'd be riding a desk and she's a field agent. From what I've been able to gather, he'd have a team of agents under him but he doesn't want to deal with the unending government bureaucracy."

Josie remembered a particularly dicey interaction with the DMV a few years ago so she couldn't disagree with Evan's sentiments. Dealing with that day in and day out would drive even a calm, laidback guy like Evan around the bend.

"So what does she get out of it then if he comes back?"

Seth shrugged and then grunted in satisfaction. The camera had been successfully installed. Only a half a dozen more to go.

"Maybe she just wants to see him happy."

Wrinkling her nose, Josie took the tools from his hands so he could climb down the ladder. "Maybe. Or perhaps I'm a cynical woman. I've simply found that if someone is so persistent about something there's usually a reason. And that reason is that they benefit somehow."

Wiping his hands on a small towel, Seth chuckled at her assessment. "You are cynical for someone so young but you might have a point. Although I can't imagine what the benefit would be. Hell, maybe she is lonely."

Or Marisa was looking to deepen her relationship with Evan. What better way than to have work in common again? Was she in love with him?

"I'm not all that young. I'm thirty."

"And I'm pushing forty. Trust me. Thirty looks young from here." Reaching down into one of the boxes, Seth held up another camera. "Are you ready to do this again? We've got one on every corner of the house—now we need to place them around the perimeter of the property and at the end of the driveway to see anyone who might drive by."

At the thought of what these men were doing to keep her safe, Josie's mood immediately sobered. For a short while she'd let herself forget why they were here and what a monumental fiasco she'd made of her life.

"I hope we never need any of this," she replied, her voice tremulous with suppressed emotion. If any of them were hurt because of this she'd never forgive herself. These men had wives and families that needed them. "I hope this is all for nothing and that they never find me."

"Better to be safe than sorry, Josie. These people that are after you? They're serious. They went after your friend and I guess we could conjecture all day long as to whether her death was an accident or deliberate, but it doesn't change the fact that she's dead. That means that you now possess something they want. Badly. I don't think we can overdo this. If anything, I hope the four of us are enough."

Josie threw up her hands as tears filled her eyes. "I don't even consider myself a Democrat or a Republican. I hate politics."

"This isn't about choosing sides. This is about truth and about whether some people are above the law. Personally, I don't think anyone is but to some that's an old-fashioned notion. No,

Josie, this isn't about which political party to vote for. This is about a man who says one thing and then does something else. This is about a man who will do anything to gain power. Right now, you're the person standing in his way."

If she wasn't careful she'd end up as roadkill.

CHAPTER TWENTY-FOUR

Evan didn't waste any time beating around the bush.

As soon as the puzzled waitress - who had already seen him once before in the same morning - scuttled away to fill their order, he went straight to the point.

"What are you doing here, Marisa? I mean, really? I'm not going back so if that's why you're here you are wasting your valuable time."

A flush creeped onto her cheeks and she gave a huff as her coffee was placed in front of her along with Evan's iced tea. "Can't a friend come visit another friend?"

"They can and you have but this is more. This isn't about checking to see how far I am on my projects. So spill it so we can move on."

Stirring cream and sugar into her coffee, Marisa sighed and rolled her eyes. "Fine. I'm here because you are wasting your life and your talents. You are a great lawman and you are letting it all go to hell by sticking yourself in this backwater town and cleaning up a house you know you don't want to live in. What you're doing is a travesty, Evan. You need to be back on the job and I don't mean going back to be a small town sheriff. That was almost as much of a waste of time as what you're doing now."

Evan wasn't a big fan of people telling him how to live his life. Since the day he'd slapped his badge down on the mayor's desk he'd swore he was going to do only the things he wanted to do. Other people's expectations weren't needed or wanted.

Schooling his features, he kept his voice even despite his irritation. "I don't think it's your place to decide what is or isn't a waste of my time and talent. Last I checked you weren't my mother or my wife and hell, they wouldn't even get a vote at this point in my life. You're my friend, Marisa, but you are skating on thin ice here. Watch yourself."

Flushing a deeper shade of red, she shifted uncomfortably in her chair. "I'm just trying to help you. You're not thinking straight since the shooting. You've thrown everything you worked for away but it doesn't have to be this way."

"Not thinking straight?" Evan repeated, an amused smile on his face. "Is that a polite way to say that I'm crazy? Or stupid? I just want to be sure of what you're saying to me."

Marisa slapped her cup down on the table so loudly heads turned all the way in the kitchen. "Now you're just being a jerk. I never said any of that."

He was enjoying this more than he should but she'd brought this on herself by interfering in something that wasn't any of her business. "So now I'm crazy and a jerk? Honestly, I don't know why you're friends with me then. And it sounds like I shouldn't be a marshal either if my judgment is so fucked up. You should run back to Tampa while you have the chance."

"Just stop it," she hissed, leaning forward so only he could hear her. "I'm trying to help you and you're trying to be an ass-hole. I care about you, Evan. It's killing me to see you waste away doing nothing with your life. You have so much to give the service but you refuse to even consider it. You could have your own team."

She didn't understand and probably never would.

"I don't want my own team," Evan said as gently as he could. She was right; he was being unnecessarily cruel. Her intentions were good although she needed to realize when to give up and move on. "I've never wanted that. Sitting at a desk, going to boring-ass meetings, and filling out paperwork is not my idea of fun. If it's yours I worry about your sanity, frankly. And before you say anything, no, I don't care that I would be the boss."

Marisa sipped her coffee as if formulating her next plan of attack. He knew her too well to think she'd give up so easily.

"Okay, let's try something different. What do you want to do then? You can't stay here the rest of your life. You must have a plan of some sort."

Evan thought about the stories he'd written and how Josie had raved over them. She'd given him some excellent suggestions and had encouraged him to expand them into a full-length thriller novel.

"I have plans," he replied, choosing not to go into detail. "They just aren't the kind of plans that you'd want. But - and I hate to state the obvious - I'm not you. I'm older and a hell of a lot more tired, Marisa. I don't want to climb the ladder anymore. I'll leave that to you."

"You're not that old."

Evan shrugged and dug into the apple pie the waitress placed in front of him. Thankfully he was always hungry and a second trip to the diner didn't faze his appetite.

"I'm not that young either," he countered with a laugh. "Talk to me in ten years and we'll see if you still feel the same. I'll give you the preview now. Your job won't keep you warm at night or give a shit when you've been shot off the top of an armored truck. It won't help you when the road is rough nor celebrate when times are good. In other words, the only thing a job does is pay the bills. And honey, lots of things can do that."

The fork with her coconut cream pie paused halfway to her mouth. She was looking at him like he'd lost his mind, which didn't surprise him. She thought the Marshal Service was everything.

"I'm not talking about a job, I'm talking about a career. A job is flipping burgers. This is about building something that's bigger than yourself."

"And you want the thing you create to be in some god-awful government entity? No, thank you. I'll build a legacy another way and in another place." He set his fork down, levity gone from his features. He needed to make sure she heard him loud and clear. "The decision has been made. There is no more discussion or debate to be had. It's a done deal. Please respect my wishes on this."

Marisa's gaze fell to the table and she fiddle with her napkin. "Is she supportive of your decision?"

She? His mother?

"What are you talking about? Who are you talking about?"

Tossing the napkin to the side, she picked up her fork. "You know who I'm talking about. Her. I saw you hustling a woman into the house when I drove up. How long have you been together? Is it serious?"

Protecting someone from being killed or wrongfully imprisoned was about as serious as one could get.

"What makes you think she's my girlfriend?" Instead of answering, Evan threw back another question at Marisa. For obvious reasons he wasn't going to discuss Josie with her. Hopefully, she'd only caught a quick glimpse but it had obviously made an impression. Another sign that Marisa had been more emotionally involved than he had. "She could be Reed's wife Kaylee."

"Is she?"

Once again Evan found his patience with Marisa running thin. His life wasn't any of her business.

"Where are you going with this line of questioning and what do you hope to gain from it? I don't ask you about who you might be dating. My opinions on your career and love life don't matter in the least and I'm sure you'd tell me that too, so I'm not sure what you want me to say."

Marisa's fingers ran up and down the side of her coffee cup. "We had a good thing going. Is it so unheard of that I might be wondering if you want to pick up where we left off?"

He didn't even know what to do with that question. They hadn't "left off" anywhere.

"We had some fun," Evan agreed carefully, watching her expression closely. He didn't want to hurt Marisa but he'd never had an emotional attachment to her other than friendship. "But I don't think we were ever in love or anything. Am I wrong here?"

"No, but who knows what could happen. We understood each other and the job. It could be like that again."

After making love to Josie Evan couldn't go backward. He wanted so much more than he'd ever had with Marisa and he was sorry she didn't see that what they'd shared was a piss poor substitute to a real honest to God relationship.

Evan shook his head but reached out to pat Marisa's hand. "We're not in that place anymore. Besides, a friends with benefits relationship has no future. It simply exists for a time. If everyone is happy, it's great. But I wouldn't be happy with it. Not anymore. I know you don't like things to change but it's inevitable."

Marisa's eyes had gone wide and her mouth hung open. "Are you saying you want…to get married and have kids? Like that white picket fence shit? Jesus, Evan, what's happened to you? I think the Florida sun has turned your brain into mush. You never used to be so sentimental. Now you say you want a family? Next thing you'll tell me you want a dog and you're going to name it Fluffy."

He drained his iced tea and laughed at her horrified expression. The same look was on her face as when he told her he didn't have any air conditioning. "I like dogs and kids. As to whether I want to get married and start a family, hell, I don't know. But I didn't really have a choice before, the job consumed almost every waking moment. But now I can decide. And that's what this is all about - me making the decisions. I'm the captain of this ship and dammit, I decide. It's all about control and I'm not giving it up."

Shoving her plate away, she dabbed her napkin on her lips. "So that woman…is she Reed's wife? Or is she your girlfriend?"

They weren't going to continue this conversation. Evan's patience with Marisa had run out.

"Maybe. Or maybe she's the housekeeper. Or my secret love child from my high school sweetheart. Or maybe she's a headhunter for a multi-billion dollar corporation and they want me to be their new CEO. It doesn't matter who she is. She's not a part of our discussion."

Marisa slumped down into the booth, her lower lip stuck out slightly like a child who didn't get ice cream.

"I think you're being stubborn. I also think that eventually you'll regret not going back. Maybe not now and not tomorrow, but sooner or later. And it will be too late."

"Then that's on me," Evan replied, using his most no-nonsense tone. "If I make a mistake I will own it. Now can we drop this subject? I'd like to hear all about you. What's going on in Marisa-land?"

She clearly didn't want to let go but she did, nodding and launching into a tale of how incompetent her new partner was and how she had to train him to do every little thing. Evan only half-listened, instead watching her body language and facial expressions as she spoke. She was upset. Angry, even. Frustrated too.

He might have ruined a good friendship this morning, and that made him sad. But he wouldn't allow anyone to push him into decisions that he knew were wrong. He hated the wall of tension that had sprung up between them but she had built it herself with her insistence on forcing her opinion regarding matters that were personal.

It was what separated Josie from so many others. She only wanted what made him happy. No agenda.

He was a lucky man, and he intended to stay that way.

CHAPTER TWENTY-FIVE

"You've done a hell of a lot of work in the last two hours," Evan observed with a grin. Cameras were perched on all four corners of the house. "Is there anything left to be done?"

Seth chuckled and handed him a screwdriver. "Don't worry, there's still work left to do. We still need to get the cameras around the perimeter."

"The motion detectors?"

Dare stomped out of the house just then with a smiling Josie on his heels. Evan couldn't stop the twinge of jealousy that ran through him when he saw the two of them together. It was stupid and he knew good and well that Dare was head over heels for Rayne, but maybe Josie was seeing that there were other men out there that could not only keep her safe but were also gainfully employed.

He needn't have worried because she headed straight for him, brushing her lips across his cheek shyly. Clearly she wasn't much for public displays of affection and frankly, neither was he but…He might make an exception this time. She looked so damn cute with a bit of sweat on her face and chest, giving her a youthful glow that he could barely drag his gaze away from.

"Josie and I finished the motion detectors just moments ago. They work, too. I hope your neighbors didn't hear them go off," Dare grimaced. "At least it's not the middle of the night."

Seth rolled his eyes and shook a hammer in Dare's direction. "I can attest that they are indeed functioning. Damn near broke my eardrums."

"No one will be sneaking up on us and that's the point," Dare laughed, grabbing a bottle of water from the cooler on the porch steps. "I see Marisa dropped you at the door and high-tailed it out of here. Was it something we said?"

"No, but it was definitely something I said," Evan replied with a grin. "I don't think she liked me pointing out to her that my life was none of her damn business. She got a little huffy and basically told me I was an idiot. Of course, she's not the first to say that. Luckily it's not a trend."

"I don't think you're all that bright," Seth deadpanned. "In fact, I've never thought you were smart at all. Or funny."

"But I'm good-looking and that's all that matters." Evan slapped his friend on the back while keeping an arm around Josie. He leaned down and dropped a kiss on her freckled nose. "Let's get those cameras up and then we can relax a little."

Reed stepped out onto the porch, a notebook and pencil in his hand. "How about we all take a break? I just got off the phone with Jared, Logan, and Ava. There's a lot to tell and I think you'll want to hear this."

Hopefully it was something they could use.

◈ ◈ ◈

They were all settled into the only room that was air conditioned.

The bedroom.

Josie sat on the edge of the mattress cross-legged while Evan lounged on the floor with his head against her knee. Dare and Seth reclined against the wall, their long legs stretched out and a cool drink in their hands. Reed was perched on the chair at the desk, tapping away at his laptop. He cleared his throat before he began.

"I just got off the phone with Logan and Ava."

"I thought you talked to Jared–" Seth began but Reed held up his hand as if anticipating the question.

"I did, before I spoke to Logan and Ava. But I'm going to start with my conversation with her. You know she's a writer and she has quite a few contacts in the press. When I filled her and Logan in on what's going on, she made a call and found a journalist we can trust. Ava says she went to college with this woman and she's on our side. She works for a major newspaper in Chicago and she'd love to break a story about Lydell. Plus, she won't turn Josie in to the cops. A win-win all around."

Relief ebbed through Josie's limbs, letting her breathe much easier. The weight of being wanted by the police was beginning to wear her down.

"Chicago?" Evan replied, sitting up a little straighter. "When do we leave?"

Evan looked like a man who wanted to take action. Any action. Sitting around waiting for something to happen was obviously not his style. She felt badly that he was stuck protecting her when he wanted to be out vanquishing the enemy.

Whoever that was. Even she wasn't truly sure.

Reed laughed and shook his head. "We don't. After a long talk with Logan, he and I decided there was no way we could guarantee Josie's safety if we left here. We'd also be taking a chance that someone might recognize her. Her face has been out on the news in the Washington D.C. area and maybe more, for all we know. No, we need to keep things on a lockdown here where we have some control over the situation. I talked to the reporter and she'll come to us. She's going to grab the next flight and should be here by tomorrow."

Then maybe this will all be over. Once the video is public, they won't want me anymore.

Dare nodded as he rubbed his chin in thought. "That makes sense. Once we're out in the open, anything can happen."

"And usually does," finished Seth with a grin. "I'm happy to stay here. Especially now that we're almost set up with the security equipment. A fly couldn't get into this house without us knowing about it."

Reed tapped on the laptop keys. "Now for my discussion with Jared. He and Jason used some government contacts and got access to the facial recognition software. Don't ask me how. Just be glad they did. They found the girl in the video. She's one Kelly Martin, originally from Roanoke, Virginia. She works on Lydell's staff in public relations. Or should I say she did, past tense. She's now unemployed."

Josie slapped the bed, anger beginning to bubble in her gut. This guy was a real creep. If he didn't have money he would have been thrown in jail years ago. "He has sex with her, beats her up, and then fires her? What a total asshole."

Reed's brows shot up at her display but he simply appeared amused at her vehemence. "Actually, he didn't fire her. It looks like she left of her own accord. It also appears that she won't have to work for a while. Her bank account is now two hundred thousand dollars richer."

Dare whistled and climbed to his feet so he could peer over Reed's shoulder and see the laptop screen.

"Sounds like she had a lot of vacation pay saved up."

Seth rubbed his chin and chuckled. "How many years of vacation would that be for some poor sheriff? Like maybe ten or twenty years' worth? More? Math never was my strong suit."

"It's a shitload," Evan said flatly. "The rat bastard paid her off so she wouldn't tell on him."

Her body trembling with fury, Josie had to clench her fists to keep from springing up from the bed and starting a rant. But screaming and complaining wouldn't do a damn bit of good. She had to be patient. Lydell was going to get what he deserved.

Reed nodded and clicked a few things on the screen. "Seems like the former senator has a bad habit of this. He does something illegal and despicable and then has to pay them off. So far, Jason and Jared have found over a dozen payments to ex-employees, from his administrative assistant to one of his household staff. He doesn't even restrict himself to pissing off the fairer sex. There are payments to males as well. But that's not the most interesting thing they found."

"I'm afraid to ask," Josie growled. "Let me guess. Human trafficking? Drugs? Weapons?"

Reed stood and pulled a paper from the printer, handing it to her. "Lydell helps run a super PAC for his favorite candidates. This super PAC is getting loads of cash from Wall Street firms. But there's one in particular that Jared found. They've given millions under the guise of their shadow holding companies. It took Jared hours to wade through the paperwork of all these shell corporations. When it came down to it, Lydell's single biggest contributor - by far - is this company."

The realization jolted Josie like a light being snapped on in a pitch black room. "That's what the muffled talking in the background of the recording is about at the end when the girl leaves and those other men come in. They were talking about the SEC and the Treasury. This isn't about him beating up that girl at all."

Evan groaned and ran his fingers through his hair. "Jesus, Lydell is a real tool."

Reed nodded in agreement. "My guess would be that many of those Wall Street bankers are hoping that they're buying some political influence."

"And without this recording he just might get away with it," Josie sighed, anger tightening her chest. Such a waste for something that truly didn't matter in the long run. That senator couldn't take the money and prestige with him. "That's why they want me. That's why they killed Amy. God, what have we come to as a country that our fellow man is willing to sell us out to make a buck?"

Dare jumped to his feet and paced the small space. "This is about more than money. This is about power. Lots of it."

"The power to make lots more money," Seth snorted. "Guys like Lydell don't care who they screw. It's not just the regular citizen that gets hurt. He'll fuck over anyone in his way, millionaire or ditch digger."

Something inside of Josie became stronger…more resolute. This was bigger than Amy or herself. This was about so much more.

"If anything happens to me–" she began softly, her mind already running miles ahead.

"Nothing is going to happen to you, honey. No one and nothing is going to touch you," Evan interrupted, jumping to his feet and pulling her up so she was in his arms. "If anyone wants to get to you, they're going to have to go through me."

That didn't make her feel any better. The last thing she wanted was for Evan or his friends to get hurt.

She reached up and placed her fingers on his lips. "Wait. Listen. If anything happens to me, I want you to promise to get that recording to the journalist. I don't want Lydell to get away with treating people like garbage, all that Wall Street bullshit aside. He shouldn't be able to use good people and then pay them off. It's not right. Promise me, Evan."

Evan looked away and groaned in frustration but Josie didn't give in. He needed to understand that this was more important than her life. Amy had trusted Josie. She'd died for this. Josie couldn't allow her friend to die for nothing.

"Promise me."

Finally nodding, Evan raised his head to look in her eyes, his own dark with emotion. "But nothing is going to happen to you."

"Just in case."

He sighed in defeat. "Just in case. I promise."

She hoped he wouldn't find himself in the position of having to keep that promise.

CHAPTER TWENTY-SIX

They finished installing all of the security hardware and then Evan drove into town to get pizza for everyone. The boys were serious about keeping Josie close to home, which was a blessing and a curse. She loved hanging out with Evan's friends - they were funny and entertaining - but eventually she was going to get antsy and want to go somewhere. It was inevitable.

Over dinner, Seth had told his version of his wife's story and how Evan had been there to help them. Two things came through loud and clear when he was speaking. The first was that he adored his wife and thought she hung the moon. Second, he had a deep respect for Evan, which only confirmed Josie's feelings that he was one special man.

When they moved on to the story where Evan was shot, he clearly was uncomfortable, trying to shut down the discussion several times. He wasn't able to stop Seth and Reed from telling the tale but he did manage to change the subject a few times, veering them off course for a short while.

Until Dare would ask a question, putting them right back on the road. He hadn't been there as he wasn't a part of the group yet, so he took the job of asking questions about that particular night.

"So Tanner and Madison got married?" Josie asked, leaning back in the metal chair on the front porch. It was a cool evening and they were all enjoying the breeze and the tranquility. They didn't know how long the peace would last. "That's so romantic."

Seth's expression grew serious, almost troubled. "Actually she's pregnant with their first child right now and things aren't going well. That's why he's not here to help. He didn't want to leave her right now. She's on bedrest in the hospital."

Evan jerked in his chair, his brows pulling together. This was news he hadn't known until now and she could see he wasn't happy about that.

"Why is this the first I'm hearing of this? When was someone going to tell me? Are Madison and the baby okay?"

Reed scratched his chin and grimaced slightly. "They're fine. Listen, Tanner said not to mention it to you. You've got your own plate full and there's–"

"If he needs–"

"And there's nothing we can do," Dare finished, breaking into the conversation. "Not a damn thing. The ladies fix meals and stock his refrigerator, and we all try to visit Madison and keep her company so she doesn't get bored but ultimately there's nothing we can really do. It's a waiting game. The doctors want her far enough along so the baby won't have issues when it's born."

"He should have told me," Evan muttered, color high on his cheeks. "You're here when you should be there."

Seth snorted in derision. "Who do you think sent us here? Tanner wanted to come himself but he knew he couldn't. We volunteered. Hell, the entire town of Springwood is pulling together to take care of them, plus citizens from our towns as well. They're taken care of, Evan. You aren't. Tanner would never forgive himself if you were left hanging in the breeze because of what's going on. He was adamant that a few of us come down here and lend a hand. He's just disappointed that he couldn't come himself. You know how he loves the action."

The corners of Evan's lips turned up and he chuckled. "That he does. I'm going to call him and Madison tomorrow though, maybe send some flowers. Dammit, someone should have said something."

Josie hoped Evan would allow her to thank Tanner as well. But there was still one thing she needed to ask…

"What do you mean by *action*, exactly?"

The four men didn't answer right away, giving each other funny looks as if silently saying, *What should we say? Should we tell her the truth?*

Evan eventually cleared his throat and manned up. "When we say action, we mean the suspense. The chase or the mystery. Finding and getting to the bottom of something."

Josie rolled her eyes and slapped her soda can down onto the iron table. "Perhaps you should have been a politician too. I'll try again. When you say action do you mean things like shooting? Or car chases? Or dodging bullets and fists?"

The silence again. These boys weren't fooling anybody.

"I'll take that as a yes," she sighed. "And on that disturbing note, I think I'll head to bed. I'm exhausted and we have a big day tomorrow if that journalist makes it here. I can't wait to hand over this recording and get all of this cleared up."

Dare lifted his beer bottle. "Here, here. I think we all are in favor of that."

The others nodded in agreement, even smiling after their serious exchange regarding their friend Tanner. Josie stood and reached for her soda can but Evan shook his head. "I'll take all the trash to the bin in the garage. Head on up and I'll be there in a few minutes to say goodnight."

Tomorrow would be a better day. There was light at the end of the tunnel and all she had to do was survive a few more hours. She could do this. For herself and for Amy.

◆ ◆ ◆

Evan tried to crawl into bed as quietly as possible so as not to wake Josie. She was lying on her side, her face turned toward the windows so her skin was bathed in moonlight and the freckles sprinkled across her nose looked like fairy dust. He'd never known a woman as beautiful as this one.

He and the boys had ended up talking deep into the night about different scenarios they might encounter protecting Josie. He felt better that they had concrete plans but he hoped like hell they'd never have to use them. He'd feel better when that footage was turned over to the reporter and the cops were off Josie's tail.

Speaking of…

Her cute little caboose looked quite fetching in her pink cotton panties that peeked out from under a fuchsia t-shirt. The covers had worked their way down around her knees, probably due to the warm temperature in the room. Josie was always reluctant to crank the air conditioning, always going on about power bills and the environment. She simply didn't want to cost him any money, which was sweet. She was always trying to do nice things for him which was something he wasn't used to. He'd rarely met a woman who would put him before herself.

This might be a good opportunity to put her first.

The first orgasm. She could thank him later.

Cuddling up to her back, playing the part of the big spoon, he pressed feather light kisses on her exposed neck and shoulders, her skin baby soft under his lips. He breathed in her scent that was part body wash, part vanilla lotion, part Josie. It never ceased to make him harder than a fencepost and painfully aroused. He hadn't felt this all-day and all-night horny since he was a callow youth and it both exhilarated and scared him. He wasn't a young man anymore but she certainly made him think he was.

Evan slid his mouth up to her ear, finding that sensitive spot just behind it and giving it a little nip with his teeth before soothing it with his tongue. Sighing in her sleep, she shifted slightly, brushing her shapely rear end against his already hard and ready cock, sending a bolt of lightning up his spine and down to his balls.

Sliding a hand around her body, he pulled her closer to his own and then cupped one of her round and tempting breasts. The nipple beaded immediately under his touch and, emboldened by her response, he moved his fingers over the softness of her bare belly to the juncture of her thighs, holding his breath at what he might find waiting for him there.

Feast or famine?

Despite her slumber, her body had clearly recognized his attentions. The crotch of those pretty pink panties were soaking wet and his heart accelerated as his fingers delved more deeply into the softness he found there, growing slick with her honey.

Josie fidgeted and moaned in her sleep, her movements becoming more agitated with every light stroke over her clit. Pressing a finger inside her, the tight walls clinging to his digit, he shifted her in his arms so she was lying on her back. It had required him ducking down almost to her ankles as he lifted her leg slightly and there was no way she wasn't going to wake up after that.

Her lids fluttered and another moan escaped her full, pink lips as he added a second finger, rubbing against that sweet spot that sent her to heaven.

"Evan," she sighed, her hands reaching for him and landing on his shoulders. "Evan, what…what's going on?"

"Baby, if you don't know then I'm not doing this right."

Her hips lifted off the mattress after he bent his head and gave her swollen clit a light kiss. "Oh God. Don't stop."

Her voice sounded like a cat scratching against a chalkboard and she was probably still half asleep, but Evan had every intention of doing exactly as she'd asked.

Lapping at the swollen button, he slid his hands under her bottom to nudge her closer while pushing her thighs farther apart with his shoulders. He ran his tongue in circles, teasing Josie until she was moaning underneath him, her eyes closed but her lips parted and panting. Her arms were thrown over her head and her auburn hair lay in a halo on the pillow as her chest rose and fell with every breath. She was fucking gorgeous and he couldn't wait to be as deeply inside her as possible.

Her legs began to shake and that's when he knew she was almost there. Closing his mouth over her clit, he gently sucked as his tongue rubbed back and forth over the top. Her body bowed and stilled for a moment before she came beautifully undone. She called his name as her fingers clutched at the pillow under her head and her thighs pressed against his ears. He didn't stop, allowing her to ride out her climax until she was a mass of jelly, limp and sated.

"Hell of a way to wake up," she said, her voice husky and filled with satisfaction. "Do I get to return the favor?"

Fuck yes.

◈ ◈ ◈

Evan crawled up her body, his gaze raking her from head to toe. Normally, she'd be shy and modest but something in the way he looked at her let her know without a doubt that he liked what he saw. Her t-shirt was pushed up to her armpits and her panties had somehow found their way down her legs so they were dangling off an ankle. She didn't remember any of that happening but she'd been happily asleep when he'd started his foreplay. Now they were going to finish it.

Pleasure began building again, humming through her veins and sending delicious quivers to every cell. She dug her ankles into the mattress in anticipation as he positioned himself between her legs, the head of his hot hard cock pressing against her entrance.

She was drenched with honey and he glided in, all the way to the hilt. A breath of air was pushed out of her as he filled her completely, stretching her pleasurably and making her wonder how she ever did without this. It felt so damn good.

"You okay, honey? Are you ready for me?"

His mouth was close to her ear, his breath warm on her cheek and the musk of sex heavy in the humid air. Arousal pooled in her belly and her nails dug into the muscles of his biceps, pushed by some unseen force she could neither deny nor identify. She only knew that it made her want desperately…need overflowing from every pore. She needed his complete possession.

"Take me," she breathed, running her fingers over his shoulders and into his silky hair. "Hard. Fast. So I don't know where I end and you begin. Make me forget my own name."

Any other man would have laughed or run from the bedroom, terrified or simply amused by the challenge she'd thrown down between them. Not Evan. She felt rather than heard his chuckle, his chest vibrating against her own. In the dim light, she could see his lips stretch into a grin of pure, devilish delight. Not only was he not scared, he obviously relished the opportunity. She'd finally found the right man after kissing too many frogs. And toads. And a few snakes. And one particular rat who had asked her for rent money before she showed him the door.

All Josie could do was hold on for dear life.

Evan slammed into her over and over, his groin rubbing her sensitive clit with every stroke while his cock caressed sweet spots inside that had her curling her toes and gasping in pleasure. He rode her hard and fast until all she could moan was his name over and over, her cries becoming more hoarse with each passing moment.

She teetered at the apex as he thrust into her, holding his weight on his hands, which were planted on either side of her shoulders. With every stroke, his expression grew more pained as he held off, delaying his own gratification for hers. Bending his head, he drew one pebbled nipple into his mouth, scraping it with his teeth so she had a bit of pain with her pleasure as he suckled the tip.

That was all it took.

Multi-colored explosions danced behind her lids and she trembled from the force of her completion even as Evan reached the peak himself, her name on his lips. He collapsed on top of her when he was done, dropping kisses on every inch of exposed skin he could find until he finally rolled onto his back, taking her with him. He tucked her into his side and tangled his fingers into her long hair, playing with the strands.

"Honey, I started this whole thing to do something nice for you but damn if you didn't turn the tables and do something nice for me. That was amazing."

"Amazing," she echoed, full sentences still beyond her. "Unbelievable. Hot."

He pulled away, sitting up in bed and reaching across her. "Are you hot, honey? Let me turn up the air conditioning. It is warm in here."

They were both covered in sweat but that's not what she'd been talking about. She shoved at his shoulder but he was so big he barely moved. It was like a mosquito slapping at a rhino.

"Idiot. I was talking about the sex, not the temperature. But now that you mention it…"

He flipped the switch higher and icy air streamed out, sending goosebumps over her damp flesh. It felt good but it also felt cold. She had a love-hate relationship with that thing. Pulling the sheet over them, he cuddled up to her, rubbing his hands over her chilled limbs, letting the quiet night surround them. For a few minutes she'd forgotten why there were three men sleeping downstairs and cameras attached to the house. She'd forgotten that her life would never be the same no matter how this situation turned out.

Her body must have stiffened because he seemed in tune with her thoughts.

"It's all going to be okay. You know that, right? I made a promise to you earlier but I'm going to make another one. Everything is going to be fine. Trust me to take care of you, Josie. I'm a man of my word."

She was counting on that.

CHAPTER TWENTY-SEVEN

Marisa hated mornings. She loved staying up at night, reading or binge-watching television with a reckless disregard for the next working day. She'd done it again last night, reading the latest best-seller until three when the alarm would go off at six. She'd hit the snooze several times but it hadn't made much of a difference. Hopefully, the giant mug of coffee she was currently sipping on along with the sugar-filled cinnamon bun would perk her right up.

It was early enough that the office wasn't buzzing yet. There would be the standard meeting at nine to update her team lead on the case she was currently working, but other than that she was in a lull, waiting for a break in another case. She hated these downtimes and preferred to be busy and on the go.

Opening her email, she quickly perused the usual digital flyers that were sent to every marshal regarding current fugitives on the run and those that were caught. Same old, same old. She recognized a few of the faces as men who had been on the run before. Once a runner, always a runner. They never learned.

She was just about to move to the next email when the last flyer caught her eye. Gasping, she studied the photo - obviously a driver's license picture - and the details provided.

Murder. Gunshot wound. Last seen in the Washington D.C. area. Josephine Elizabeth Carlton was on the run and wanted for questioning as a person of interest. Whereabouts unknown.

Well, well, well...this was very interesting.

Did Evan know that his pretty girl was wanted as a person of interest on a murder charge? Of course he did. That had to be why he'd hustled her into the house when Marisa had shown up unexpectedly. That's why he'd pushed for them to leave the house and go to the diner.

Miss Josephine Carlton must be mighty good in bed to make Evan break the law.

Was the jerk in love? He'd looked happy and content. Satisfied. Much happier than he had the last time she'd seen him.

Evan Davis - former US Marshal and sheriff - was harboring a fugitive, and with a lot of help from the looks of the guys that were there. Seth Reilly knew how to keep a girl safe from everyone, including the government.

This was business. And the law. The fact was she'd begged him to come back and he'd refused. If she hadn't bugged him she doubted she would have even heard from him these last months. He'd moved on and left her behind.

It wasn't supposed to happen that way.

He should have missed her.

It only took her a moment to make up her mind. She reached for the telephone and punched in an extension.

Sorry, Evan. Maybe someday you'll forgive me.

◈ ◈ ◈

Evan was on edge all day as they waited for the reporter. A phone call from Ava had let them know that the woman would show up mid- afternoon, probably around four, depending on traffic from Orlando International. The waiting sucked and he wanted to be done with it. Once that recording was public, Lydell wouldn't need to go after Josie. Then the only problem would be Amy's murder.

He inwardly groaned at the use of the word *only*. Getting her cleared of a murder charge wasn't going to be easy but he was determined to find her the best lawyer if the police pressed their case. He was hoping against hope once they saw the tape that they'd rethink their investigation and go after the senator.

He and Josie were spending the afternoon in the living room, going through the file on Lydell that Jared had emailed over. Every page revealed a man that definitely needed…help. Perhaps therapy. He treated the people around him like dirt, as if he were Louis the Sun King. His former employees were unanimous in saying the guy was a real prick.

Evan shook his head in disgust. He'd never understand some people. It was just as easy to be nice as it was to be an asshole. Hell, it might even be easier. It took effort to be a jerk.

Seth had been lounging on the floor, his back against the sofa, playing a game on the tablet computer when he sprung to his feet. "Three cars coming down the driveway very slowly. I don't think our reporter was planning to bring friends."

Evan didn't like the sound of this one bit. No, she wasn't supposed to bring friends. She was renting a car at the airport and from what Ava had said traveling alone, although Dare had agreed to accompany the journalist back to Chicago once she had the recording. Just in case. Although it wouldn't matter anyway. She'd said that the minute she got the file she'd transfer it to the news station where she worked. She wasn't taking any chances.

Evan kissed Josie's brow and helped her to her feet. "Honey, go upstairs. Stay in the bedroom."

Her face had gone white and he pulled her in for a reassuring hug, hopefully reminding her of last night and how he'd vowed not to let anything happen to her. He'd meant every word. If someone wanted to hurt her, they'd have to go through him.

Once she was upstairs and out of sight, Evan and the men checked their weapons, tucking them in their waistbands and huddling by the door and windows, out of sight. They watched on the tablet as the three dark vehicles, two sedans and one SUV, came to a halt at the front door. His muscles tensed and his heart skipped in his chest when the doors of the front car opened. He waited impatiently, his fingers flexed on the cool metal of his revolver as one leg and then another stepped out of the car.

Son of a fucking bitch.

"It's Marisa," he whispered right before she climbed out, standing on his driveway and staring up at the house. She was dressed in her usual work garb of black slacks, white blouse, and black blazer. Her gun was strapped to her waist along with her shield in plain sight. She was clearly here on official business.

Shit. Shit. Shit.

"She's back," Seth said unnecessarily. "Looks like she's brought company with her. Official company."

Several agents had exited the vehicles, all looking as if they were on duty, including a few faces he recognized. They weren't here to see how he was doing in retirement, that was for damn sure.

Marisa turned and said something to the other marshals and then climbed the porch steps to his front door.

"What's the plan?" Dare asked, keeping his voice low. "We'll follow your lead."

His mind racing a mile a minute and the blood rushing his ears, Evan tried to clear his head so he could think straight. He didn't want a shootout. Technically he was a law and order kind of guy and the idea of a showdown with his former co-workers didn't sit well with him. He didn't want anyone to get hurt and he didn't particularly want to go to jail, although he would if it meant keeping Josie protected. But he had a responsibility to his friends who had come here out of loyalty to him.

But he couldn't just throw up his hands and give in either. It was Josie's life at stake and he'd promised to do his best to keep her safe.

Marisa knocked and waited on the other side of the door. He could pretend no one was there but they probably had a warrant and could come busting in anyway.

"Let her in," he finally said with a sigh. "Let me talk to her. Maybe she'll listen."

CHAPTER TWENTY-EIGHT

Perched at the top of the stairs and hopefully hidden out of sight, Josie listened to the conversation between Evan and Marisa with increasing hopelessness. The police were here to bring her in and they didn't look in the mood to forget about it, turn around, and go home.

Josie had obeyed Evan in the beginning and gone into the bedroom, locking the door behind her. But curiosity had captured her attention and she'd peeked out of the window, seeing the line of vehicles and the armed and uniformed officers. They weren't here to sell tickets to the policemen's ball.

Scooting behind the corner wall, Josie didn't have to strain to hear the voices below. Both Marisa and Evan seemed to be unhappy with one another and of course, Josie was the cause of the rift between the friends and former partners.

"How did you know?" Evan asked.

Josie couldn't see their faces but she could hear the tension in their tone. At this point, anything could happen.

"Her fugitive flyer came in my email this morning. Why are you harboring her, Evan? Did you know she was on the run for murder? From the looks of things, I think you did."

"She didn't do it, okay? Amy was her friend. She found her dying in that parking lot. She would never hurt anyone."

Wrapping her arms around her legs, Josie drew them up to her chest and rested her chin on her knees as if protecting her own heart. Listening to Evan defend her was emotionally wrenching. She'd put him in this position and hated herself for it.

"There's a witness, Evan. A neighbor saw her with blood on her hands. That girl you're protecting? She's a stone cold killer. You're letting your dick overrule your common sense."

A stone cold killer? That's how I'm viewed?

"Are you saying that I'm whipped?" Evan growled, clearly offended by Marisa's statement. "Because I'm not letting my cock do any thinking for me. Josie couldn't kill anyone. She's as pacifist as they come. What that neighbor saw was Josie discovering the dying body of her best friend. She held her so there was blood. Tell me you wouldn't hold your dying friend as they gasped out their last words?"

"And what were her last words? *Why did you kill me*?" Marisa mocked. "There's a witness. Stop being so stubborn and listen to yourself."

Josie heard Evan snort and his footsteps pacing back and forth on the hardwood floors. "Eyewitness testimony is notoriously undependable. You and I both know that. Besides, Josie doesn't deny being there. She doesn't deny touching her friend. She does deny pulling the trigger."

"Then who killed Amy Dalton? Are you trying to say this was a random thing? A fluke? Because I'm not buying it."

"That's not what I'm saying. Listen, Josie is in danger and I'm protecting her. If you take her out of here, you can't guarantee her safety. Her death will be on your head."

There was a long silence before Marisa replied and Josie held her breath as blood pounded in her ears, sounding like a marching band in her head.

"You're being rather dramatic. Why would Josie be in danger? Is she mixed up in something?"

"I'd like to hear about that also."

Josie started at the sound of the unfamiliar voice and uncurled from the fetal position she was in to peer around the corner. A middle-aged woman with dark hair stood in the doorway, a huge messenger bag thrown over her shoulder. Wearing a navy blue suit and sensible shoes, she looked slightly rumpled as if she'd finished a long journey.

The reporter.

The woman held out her hand to Evan, glancing at Marisa standing nearby. "I'm Casey. Casey Melrose. I believe Ava let you know I was coming."

Evan's shoulders, which had been stiff and unyielding, seemed to relax slightly as he shook the woman's hand.

"She did and we're very glad to have you here. I was just about to explain the situation to Marisa. She's a US Marshal and is here to take Josie. I'm trying to explain why that would be a mistake. Josie is in grave danger."

Marisa was frowning and she stomped over to the door, looking outside. "How did you get in here? My men should have stopped you at your vehicle."

Casey smiled and chuckled, hefting her bag onto a clear spot on the couch. "I'm a reporter and I've slipped in and out of situations more dangerous and dire than this one. It's one of my superpowers. Don't be angry at your men. I'm sure they did their best but you can't stop what you don't see."

Marisa opened her mouth to speak but then must have thought better of it. Instead, she crossed her arms over her chest and tapped her foot impatiently. "I really don't have time for this. We need to get Josie back to Tampa before rush hour. She'll be held there overnight and tomorrow morning be transported back to Washington D.C. If she's innocent, Evan, you can hire her an attorney. My job is to return her for questioning. Whether she's guilty or not isn't my call and frankly, it isn't yours either. You've forgotten everything you learned on the job."

"Thank God," Dare muttered and Josie had to stifle the urge to fly down the stairs and give him a hug. "What you're talking about is shutting off his brain and not thinking. That sounds like a hell of a way to do your job. Is it working for you?"

Apparently Marisa didn't like being put on the spot or made fun of. She sputtered a few times as she tried to answer and eventually waved him off. "You don't know anything about me or this job. You're a small town sheriff in some backwater, piece of shit town that no one cares about. This is the big leagues, boys. Try to keep up."

Evan took a step forward, invading Marisa's personal space and causing the woman's face to turn white with fear when she caught a glimpse of his expression. "Do not talk to my friends that way. These are some of the best lawmen in the country and you will be respectful."

Swallowing hard, Marisa shrugged and took a step back. "Fine. Now send Josie down here so we can get on the road. I'm losing patience here."

Evan shook his head. "I won't let you take her. I told you. You're not the only ones that want her, Marisa. This could get very ugly very fast if you're not cautious."

"Are you threatening me?"

"No, just stating a fact. The people that want her aren't playing a game. They killed Amy and who knows how many others. They won't hesitate to do it again as they have a hell of a lot to lose."

Casey, who had been watching the play by play closely, took that opportunity to speak up. "I think this is my cue to ask that you start from the beginning and tell that story, Mr. Davis. And I'd like to see that recording too. If I think you have something,

I'll send it up to my paper's office so they can begin authentication of it. We have to make sure that you haven't altered it in any way."

"It's as real as it gets," Evan assured her. "But yes, let's all sit down and I'll tell you what I know."

Marisa exhaled noisily. "I suppose you think that once I hear this I'm going to be all sympathetic? She's a killer, Evan. You can't hide her forever." She looked up the stairs and Josie crouched back behind the wall to hide herself, her pulse racing and sweat pooling at the back of her neck. "Is she up there?"

Yes, I'm up here and I'm not planning to come down, either.

"Give me fifteen minutes. That's all I'm asking. As a friend."

Tears pooled in Josie's eyes as she listened to the plea in Evan's voice. He shouldn't be having to do this at all.

"Fine. Fifteen minutes. This better dazzle me."

Only her entire future balanced on the next quarter hour.

No pressure at all.

◈ ◈ ◈

Evan patiently - or as patiently as he could - explained Josie's story, answered their questions, and then popped the thumb drive into the laptop so they could watch the recording. Both women had a nauseous expression when the video completed and that buoyed Evan's mood. Perhaps he had convinced Marisa that Josie needed protection from Lydell.

Casey held out her hand. "I'd like to transfer that file to my people in the newsroom so they can begin the authentication. We have a lot of work and research ahead of us to put this story together. It could take a few days."

Heart heavy with disappointment, he handed her the drive. He'd hope it would be on the evening news tonight. "The sooner it's made public the sooner Josie's life won't be in danger. Can't you release it now?"

Casey shook her head as she reached into her messenger bag, pulling out her own laptop. "We have to look it over first. I wouldn't be doing my job very well if I put this out there and then found out you had manipulated it in some way." She held up her hand when Evan huffed in anger. "Not that I'm saying you have. I do believe you but I have to do my due diligence. My bosses aren't going to just let me throw this out there."

"I should have just leaked it," Evan groaned. "I thought it would be better to have the press do it but now I think I should have just posted it online and let it go viral."

"That's one way," Casey agreed. "But this way we can put the recording in context."

Seth's brows shot up. "What other context is there? Lydell is slime."

Casey sighed and handed the thumb drive back to Evan after sending the file. "People aren't shocked anymore when politicians are jerks. They have to be shown that they're super jerks and that it affects them. If my leads pan out, I can show that not only is Lydell a man who assaults women but he's also for sale to the highest bidder. But I don't think you care as much about discrediting him as clearing your girlfriend. This should give him a strong motive for killing Amy Dalton."

"That's all I want. Josie didn't do this. As for his political aspirations, that will sort itself out."

Marisa reached for the drive but Evan snatched his hand back. "Get a warrant. Until then, it's mine."

"Don't you have copies?" she asked, her face scrunched up and her cheeks red. She wasn't happy with him at the moment but Evan didn't care much. "I can't help you if you don't help me."

Evan took a deep breath and appraised his former partner from head to toe and then back up again. He'd known her, worked with her, and even slept with her. She was all about the job and ate ambition for breakfast. Josie just might be her ticket up the ranks. Marisa would get a ton of attention for bringing in a woman who could possibly expose a bigwig like Lydell. There was murder and sex too. The press would eat this up and Marisa would be in the middle of all of it.

The thought of the relationship they'd once shared left a nasty taste in his mouth. He could truthfully say he didn't have a clue what he'd been thinking back then.

"Are you going to help me?" Evan finally asked Marisa. "Are you going to let me protect Josie? She didn't do this. She's innocent."

The shuttered look in his former partner and friend's eyes told him everything without her saying a word.

Fuck. Fuck. Fuck. Fuck you.

"You know I can't. What would I tell those men out there?"

"That she's not here," Evan retorted. "You questioned me and she wasn't here. Go back to Tampa and let Casey do her job. In a couple of days, things will look completely different."

"But she is here, isn't she?" Marisa challenged. "She's here and I can't leave without her. She has to be taken into custody, Evan, and right now you are obstructing justice. I can run you and your friends in as well. You need to step aside and let me do my job. I can keep her safe until you can get her free. There's no place safer for her than with us."

Evan didn't believe that for a minute. He knew for a fact that government agencies were rife with leaks. He couldn't take that chance with Josie's life.

Dammit, he loved her.

"I think she's safer here." Evan leaned forward trying to get Marisa to really listen to him. "She's not a danger to anyone. She's not going to go on a killing or robbing spree and knock over a half dozen liquor stores. She's a scared woman who doesn't want to die. Can you understand that? She's not going anywhere. You can keep tabs on her right here. With me."

For a split second, he thought he'd managed to get through to Marisa but then his heart plunged to his feet when she shook her head. "No, Evan. We do this by the book. She comes with me."

He wouldn't - couldn't - allow Marisa to take Josie. He stood and backed toward the staircase as he drew his weapon. He hadn't expected it but Reed, Seth, and Dare did the same until they'd created a very large and strong human wall in front of the stairs to the second floor.

"If you take her, you take me. Simple as that."

The reporter was watching this entire situation play out with great interest. He was sure she was already formulating her headline.

Marisa stood, her entire body tensed and her lips in a flat line. "Stand down, Evan. I can bring in more firepower than you can imagine. Do you want to end up dead? You won't be any help to her in a body bag. Do you want to be responsible for your friends' deaths as well? They've got wives and kids to think about. Do you want to be responsible for that? I'll take good care of her if they actually arrest her after they question her. I'll make sure she eats okay and that she's not near any of the other prisoners. You can trust me with her. You trusted me with your life but you won't trust me with hers?"

Evan was gritting his teeth so tightly he thought his jaw might snap. He could barely breathe as his chest squeezed painfully at the mere thought of Josie out of his sight.

No, that couldn't happen.

"I trusted you with my life…but hers? Fuck, her life is way more important than mine. She stays here."

"You're not thinking clearly. Best case scenario is that you and your friends end up doing some time for this little stunt. The decision is simple."

She had no idea. None at all.

"My decision hasn't changed. You have to go through me."

"Then I will."

Marisa turned on her heel but then there was a noise from the top of the stairs. Evan didn't dare turn around but he had a terrible feeling as to what or whom it was.

No. No, Josie. Don't do this. Baby, don't.

"Wait. Actually, this is my decision. And I'm deciding to turn myself in."

CHAPTER TWENTY-NINE

Josie had never been in handcuffs before and it felt strange to not be able to move her arms. Marisa hadn't placed them all that tightly on Josie's wrists but the cold metal against her skin was a constant reminder that she was headed to jail.

For a crime she didn't commit.

Evan's face was red and he didn't bother to hide his anger and frustration with her decision to turn herself in. What he didn't seem to comprehend was that as much as he cared for her and wanted to keep her safe, she cared just as much. She didn't want anything to happen to him or his friends. She didn't want them to go to jail or get in some crazy shootout with the cops. It wasn't worth their freedom. She'd have to fight this head on. Hopefully one day he would understand.

Marisa stood off to the side letting them say goodbye.

He gently grabbed Josie's arms and pulled her close, pressing a kiss onto her lips. A tight pain began in her chest and tears to well in her eyes. She was terrified of going but she couldn't allow him to suffer because of her. "You don't have to do this. Let me talk to Marisa some more."

They both knew it was a wasted effort. The marshal wasn't going to suddenly change her mind and walk away. She had way too much to lose.

Her vision glazed with tears, Josie swallowed the lump that had taken residence in her throat. Even worse than going to jail was leaving this man. How she ever thought she'd leave, she had no idea.

"I have to go and we both know it," she said quietly, not wanting Marisa to overhear. Josie had a feeling privacy had just become a thing of the past and she wanted to hold onto at least a shred of it for one more minute if she could. "I can't let you get hurt or arrested. Your friends either. She said she'd make sure I'm okay and I think we have to believe her. I'll be all right."

His own eyes were bright with tears and he crushed her body against his, lips near her ear. "I love you, honey. Stay strong. I'll get you out of there as soon as I can."

It was the absolute worst thing he could have said and yet it was amazingly wonderful too. She'd finally found a man she could love and trust with her whole heart and they were being torn apart by terrible circumstance.

"I love you too," she whispered, her heart shattering into a million pieces in her chest. This was so incredibly unfair. "I love you and we're both going to be okay. I'll be home before you know it."

Home. She hadn't had a real one in a long time but it was definitely here with Evan. Or rather wherever he was. She'd follow him to the ends of the earth and back just to be with him. All she wanted was the opportunity.

"I know some good lawyers, honey. Dare's already on the phone to one right now. With any luck he'll meet you in Tampa, plus we'll be right behind you. I may not be with you every step of the way but know that I'm close by."

Tears slid down her cheeks and he swiped them away with his thumbs. "Just knowing that you won't give up helps."

"I won't give up. Ever."

He reached into his pocket and pulled out a handkerchief, telling her to blow. Smoothing her hair behind her ear, he kissed her a few more times before finally stepping back.

It was time.

A few more words were spoken but Josie barely heard or acknowledged them. Her fate had suddenly become more real than she'd ever bargained for. People thought she was a murderer and they wanted her to answer to those charges. She was going to be questioned at the very least and possibly arrested. She might go to jail and then maybe prison. All she had done was try to help a friend and then everything had gone so very wrong. How had she come to be here?

Marisa took Josie by the arm and led her out of the house and down the front porch steps to the vehicle. It was all Josie could do not to wrench away and run as far and fast as she could. She wanted to scream at the top of her lungs that she was a good person and hadn't done anything wrong. Words clogged in her sore and swollen throat along with a maelstrom of emotions from sadness to fury to flat-out terror. She wasn't anyone special. Why would anyone believe her?

Josie kept her head down, not wanting to look any of the officers in the eye. She didn't want to see the scorn or pity there. They'd probably seen and heard it all. One more person crying out their innocence meant nothing to them anymore.

Somehow Evan had insinuated himself on her other side. She doubted anyone else would have been allowed but Marisa must have been feeling generous today. "We're right behind you, honey. Don't answer any questions until your attorney gets there."

Nodding wordlessly, Josie allowed herself to be placed in the back of the SUV while Marisa climbed into the driver's seat. She and Evan spoke for a moment but Josie couldn't hear what they were saying as much as she tried. Was Evan extracting one more promise to take care of Josie? His fingers trailed over the closed window and he gave her an encouraging smile, or what passed as one. Reed, Seth, and Dare all stood in a row behind him, their arms crossed over their chests and extremely pissed off expressions on their faces. At least after she was gone, they'd be there for Evan. He was going to need someone too.

The motorcade pulled away from the house and glided soundlessly down the driveway and onto the road. There was nothing but silence in the vehicle until they hit the interstate. It was at that point Marisa decided to speak.

"You did a good thing back there. I didn't want to have to take Evan and his friends in but I would have done it."

Of course you would have. You're a total bitch.

Josie didn't know if Marisa expected a reply but talking kept her mind off where this car was headed.

"I would never let any harm come to Evan," Josie finally answered.

"Because you love him."

It wasn't phrased as a question.

It also wasn't any of Marisa's business. Josie had only admitted it to Evan moments ago. She wasn't about to start spilling girlish secrets with the woman who had a warrant to bring Josie in for questioning as a person of interest in a murder case. She was dumb but she wasn't stupid.

"You do, don't you?" Marisa prompted when Josie didn't answer.

"I think I did what any decent human being would do," Josie countered instead. "I don't think anyone could watch someone get hurt or go to jail just to protect them."

"And you're innocent, after all."

The way the woman drawled through the syllables spoke volumes as to her opinion on Josie's guilt.

"I am." Josie spoke firmly despite the fact she wouldn't be believed. "Amy was a good friend and I loved her like a sister. I miss her every day. I want to see whomever did this brought to justice probably more than you do."

"I'm sure."

They didn't speak for several minutes and Josie watched out the window as the scenery whipped by. It wouldn't take long to get to Tampa.

"When we get there you'll be taken to a conference room and questioned. I assume you'll invoke your right to remain silent until an attorney arrives?"

Just like on television, Josie had been advised of her rights when she'd been handcuffed. She wasn't officially arrested per se according to Marisa. She was wanted for questioning and they could hold her for twenty-four hours without charging her with anything.

"I will," Josie agreed. "Evan is working on that."

"I'm going to do Evan a favor and not process you in any way. You can hang out in the interrogation room until the District Attorney decides what he wants to do with you. I just wanted you to know that I'm doing this for Evan as a friend."

It hadn't crossed Josie's mind that it would be done for her. "He'll be grateful. I'll let him know that you did it for him."

"You won't have to tell him. He'll know. He knows procedures backwards and forwards. He was a great marshal and he should come back."

The certainty in Marisa's tone took Josie aback. The woman was acting as if she knew what Evan wanted and needed better than he did.

"He doesn't want to. He wants to do something else."

Marisa didn't turn around but Josie could see her knuckles turn white on the steering wheel. "He's confused right now but the one thing he's good at is being a lawman. He'll come back as long as people don't encourage this mid-life crisis bullshit. You're not doing him any good, you know, by promoting this bum life he's been living lately."

This woman didn't have a clue. She'd spent years as his partner and Josie had spent less than two weeks with Evan but she already knew he wasn't going back. He'd moved on in his mind and heart. That part of his life was done and over.

Josie could go on and on about what a talented writer he was or how handy he was around the house but she didn't. Marisa was living in a fantasy of her own making and nothing Josie said was going to change her mind. Only time would tell the real truth.

The rest of the ride was silent and Marisa drove them into a parking garage somewhere in downtown Tampa. She put the SUV in park and twisted around in her seat to face Josie who was having a hard time breathing in and out now that they had arrived. She was going to be questioned, and based on that the DA would decide if she was telling the truth. Everything was at stake and the next few hours would be crucial to her future.

"Are you ready? The DA is upstairs waiting."

Josie simply nodded because it didn't matter if she was ready or not. It was happening.

Denial? Not an option.

CHAPTER THIRTY

Evan shifted impatiently in the passenger seat of the SUV. Seth was driving and Reed and Dare were in the back seat on the way to Tampa. Evan was hoping he'd be allowed to see Josie before she was questioned and maybe - just maybe, if he could swing it - he would sit in. He knew the men and the women in the District Attorney's office well although Washington D.C. had jurisdiction in reality. If it were locals he had a better than average chance to convince them it would be a good idea for him to be in the room when they talked to her. He'd be able to hold her hand and keep her calm.

But who was going to keep him calm? Frankly, since Josie had announced that she was turning herself in he'd been a mess. On one hand he was grateful that she loved him enough to sacrifice herself but dammit, his job was to protect her from just this situation. He'd failed spectacularly.

Whatever his former partners faults, he did trust Marisa to try to keep Josie safe while in custody so that was some comfort. It wouldn't be enough, however, until he could see the woman he loved with his own two eyes.

While he didn't have a clue what his future held he knew she had to be in it.

"We'll be there in about fifteen," Seth interrupted Evan's thoughts. "Do you want to go straight there or do we need to stop at the attorney's office?"

With his inside contacts, Evan had secured one of the best criminal lawyers in the state. On such short notice it had taken some doing but he'd called in every favor owed.

"He's meeting us there."

"She's not under arrest," Dare added, obviously trying to lighten the mood. The whole drive had been about as happy as a funeral. "Not really. It's just questioning. When she tells her story, they may just let her go, especially if she has some high-powered, high-priced lawyer by her side."

"It does help but there's so much I don't know," Evan sighed. "Who is going to do the questioning? Are the D.C. police here? Will they hold her until they are? Shit, will Marisa even get to be there to keep an eye on Josie? This is the one moment I hate being a civilian."

"Will she keep you informed?" Dare asked. "She seemed pretty frosty at the house. I kind of got the feeling she wasn't super fond of Josie. Maybe I'm crazy but she appeared to be jealous."

Evan shook his head. "No way. It was always casual between us."

But he'd been thinking that perhaps Marisa had been more involved than he'd given her credit for. At the very least, she didn't like change and Evan moving on to another woman wouldn't sit well.

Reed chuckled as he stared out of the window. "It was casual for you, but was it casual for her? Maybe she has more feelings for you than she let on. Seeing you loving up on another woman might just put her in a nasty mood. Remind her of the past."

"She said she'd take care of Josie."

Although now that Evan thought about it, Marisa had been acting strangely these last few months, constantly trying to talk him back to the Marshal Service.

"Yep, because every woman loves taking care of her ex-boyfriends girlfriend," Dare observed. "Even if she didn't have loving feelings for you she might not be all that thrilled about her babysitter role. Is Marisa the soft-hearted, caring type?"

"Fuck no," Evan admitted with a groan. What he knew about the fairer sex could fit on the head of a pin. Relationships weren't his forte. "She's all business and all about the job. Ambitious as hell too. Shit, I thought the whole friends with benefits thing was too good to be true."

Thank God, Josie had taken pity on him and loved him because he knew zero about females.

"It always is," Seth laughed. "It sounds like a great idea, doesn't it? Sex. No strings. No feelings. Except that there's another human being involved and you can't control them. They could end up hating you or loving you. Which one do you think fits here?"

Good question. Maybe a little of both. Neither one boded well for Marisa treating Josie well.

"Not sure but let's kick it up a notch. We need to get there and see if I can talk my way in. I need to make sure Josie is okay."

And that meant back home with him.

◈ ◈ ◈

The girl was terrified.

Marisa sat next to Josie and could almost feel the younger woman vibrating with pure terror. Her skin was pasty white and a sheen of sweat had broken out over her forehead when Marisa had cuffed her to the table. She had to give the girl credit, though. She'd been incredibly strong the entire way here but this was where the rubber met the road. She swore up and down she was innocent but now that she had to actually tell her story…

One thing had been a surprise and that was the DA wasn't present in the room. Instead, two FBI agents sat across the table looking decidedly tame, almost friendly, when Josie sat down. They'd asked her if she wanted a soda or if she was hungry. They had even inquired as to the temperature in the room. Looked like they were going for the "I'm your best friend" interrogation technique.

"Good afternoon, Miss Carlton." The older agent with salt and pepper hair spoke first while the younger man sorted through a stack of files. "My name is Agent Stokes and this is Agent Harrison. We're from the Federal Bureau of Investigation."

Finally the questioning would begin and Evan would find out that this little girl wasn't nearly as innocent and naive as she appeared to be. Where there was smoke, there was fire. She was involved in all of this somehow, someway. Marisa would relish telling Evan all the details.

"We're relieved to see that you're safe," Agent Stokes continued. "The people after you can be very dangerous. It looks like you know how to handle yourself in a crisis."

Wait. Something wasn't right. They were praising Josie? Was this more interrogation bullshit?

The younger woman also seemed shocked by the turn of events. She'd stopped shaking in her chair but tears had welled up in her eyes as she leaned across the table as far as the handcuffs would allow.

"I didn't kill Amy. She was my friend and like a sister to me. I would never hurt her."

Right. Sure. You're completely innocent.

Agent Harrison finally looked up and nodded. "We know. The ballistics came back days ago and matched a gun used in another murder from three years ago. We already had a suspect for that crime although we haven't been able to make the case. We're hoping you can help."

Marisa couldn't believe her ears. She must have misunderstood.

Josie, on the other hand, burst into tears, sobs wracking her body as what was probably pure relief coursed through her. Apparently she thought she was home free.

But she was still in cuffs.

Stokes stood and rounded the table, patting Josie on the shoulder while Harrison rushed out of the room bellowing to someone in the hall. When he came back in, he had a box of tissues and he pulled up several, pressing them into Josie's hands. When she tried to blow her nose, they realized she was cuffed to the table.

"Please get these cuffs off of Miss Carlton's wrists," Stokes barked impatiently, stepping aside as another FBI agent brought in a can of soda and some snacks. "Miss Carlton? Why don't you take a moment to gather yourself and then have a drink or a bite to eat."

Unlocking the cuffs, Marisa stepped back to survey the scene in front of her that had taken such a one hundred and eighty degree turn. "Why is the FBI involved? And why did the D.C. police have a warrant out for her if they didn't think she was guilty?"

Josie dabbed at her cheeks and sniffled loudly.

Disgusting.

"I'd like to know that too. I thought you wanted to put me behind bars and throw away the key."

Both agents sat back down but Harrison answered the question. "And we're sorry about that. Very sorry. We couldn't tip our hand to the real people we wanted that we were on to them. We were also concerned about your safety. If they killed your friend, they wouldn't hesitate to kill you, Miss Carlton."

"That's what I figured. That's why I ran."

"Very effectively," replied Stokes with a smile. "But we really do need to talk to you. You may have information that can help us put some bad men behind bars."

Marisa had had about all she could stand. She hated being completely ignored and these men had barely glanced at her. "You didn't answer my question. Why is the FBI involved?"

Before the agents could reply, the door swung open - again - and Harker Prentiss stood in the doorway. One of the preeminent attorneys in the area, he exuded money and confidence and both were on display today from his Armani suit to his Christian Louboutin black leather loafers. Despite the trappings of wealth and success, he resembled a surfer with his blond hair, blue eyes, and golden tan. She'd heard he owned a yacht out of Clearwater Marina.

"Sorry I'm late. Hi Josie, I'm your attorney." He shook Josie's hand, and then the agents' hands and then finally Marisa's, although his brow had quirked slightly when he saw her sitting in what would normally be his chair. He probably wanted her to move. Fuck him. "Traffic. I have the paperwork and I looked it over on the way. Seems straightforward."

"Paperwork?" Josie asked faintly, her fingers wringing together. "Do I have to sign something?"

"No, no, no," Prentiss said with a smile. "They just sent over the case file for me to review. They'd like to talk to you today to see what you know about your friend Amy and her business and personal dealings and then you can go. I'll be right by your side the entire time. How does that sound?"

Like crap. This entire day had gone to shit. Evan would be cuddling with his little princess by nightfall.

Josie buried her face in her hands and a few more sobs escaped before she wiped her nose again and smiled.

"That sounds amazingly wonderful. Does Evan know?"

Jesus, she's crying. Again.

"My assistant will be giving him a call. Now I'm sure you want to get this over with so you can leave. So let's get started, shall we?" Prentiss turned his attention to Marisa who was sitting there, her temper almost at a boil. "Do you mind? I think you're in my chair."

Swallowing down the bile that had gathered in her throat, Marisa stood on shaky legs and moved toward the door, not giving Josie even a glance. The little redhead led a charmed life, apparently. She was free and she'd managed to get the guy too.

Isn't she special?

"If you need me–" Marisa began but Stokes cut her off immediately.

"We won't. We've got this handled. If you see Mr. Davis just let him know that he can take Miss Carlton home when we're done here. We'll be sending along a few agents for her protection as well until this is over."

Thoroughly and humiliatingly dismissed, Marisa rounded on her heel and stalked off to her desk where she dug through a drawer looking for the cigarettes she only allowed herself to smoke every now and then. If today wasn't a candidate for at least two, she didn't know what was.

Getting Evan back into her career, life, and bed was further away than ever and Josie stood firmly in the way.

CHAPTER THIRTY-ONE

Josie was almost sick with relief and she sagged in the chair, her hands wrapped around the soda can so she had something - anything - to hold onto. This meeting had taken on a surreal quality that she still didn't quite believe but the men were so friendly and nice it didn't appear that they were trying to trap her into confessing or incriminating herself in any way. Plus she had her attorney right next to her and he seemed completely at ease.

She had questions. A bunch of them.

"So you knew that I didn't shoot Amy," she began, wanting to hear more. She'd watched enough true crime shows on cable to know what ballistics meant but how did they know she didn't kill that other person three years ago? "Because of the bullet."

Stokes nodded and pulled a file from the pile near his partner before sliding it in front of her. "I think we should start at the beginning. The FBI has had an active investigation open on former Senator Lydell for quite some time. William Connaught worked for us."

That name took Josie aback. "Billy? He's a freelance reporter for an online political magazine."

He was also Amy's boyfriend.

"That was his cover but he was actually investigating the senator. That's how he came into possession of the recording."

She was being slapped around by one surprise after another. "You know about the recording?"

It was Harrison who answered. "We do, although we haven't seen it yet. Billy sent us a message about it. Do you still have it?"

Josie shook her head, hoping she wasn't in trouble. "We gave it to a reporter hoping that its release would make them stop chasing me. Does that mess everything up?"

"It changes our strategy but we can deal with it. We thought you might release it to the press and honestly were surprised we hadn't seen it yet."

"She said she had to authenticate it," Josie said, her head still reeling as she took in the details. Billy was a Fed, not a reporter. "So Billy gave Amy the recording. Why? Was his life in danger too? Is he okay?"

Harrison rubbed at his temples, his naturally pale skin taking on a ruddy pallor. She instantly knew Billy wasn't fine. "Agent Connaught's body was found about a week ago in an alley in Washington D.C. He died from a close-range gunshot wound to the head. The same gun that killed your friend Amy, by the way. Another item that cleared your name. You weren't in D.C. at the time so you couldn't have done it. We think Connaught was meeting with his inside man and was made. He was extremely upset about his girlfriend and about you. He was trying to bring the case to a conclusion. He felt guilty that he'd stashed the jump drive with her thinking they'd never know, but he was being watched. You were just in the wrong place at the wrong time."

That sounded like the Billy she knew. A good hardworking guy who adored Amy with everything in him. But tragic that he was gone as well. He and Amy had had plans about the future-marriage, kids, a house. They weren't going to get to do anything like that. Tears pricked at her eyes again and she blinked to hold them back. She was damn sick and tired of crying and feeling like the world was falling in. She was tired of feeling like a victim.

"Although I have an idea as to why you were investigating the senator after seeing the recording, that doesn't seem like a case the FBI would be interested in. Is there something more?"

Harrison turned to a page in the file and pointed to a photograph of Lydell with several other men. "Actually, the recording has very little to do with our investigation. It just shows that he's not a nice, honest man. What we've been investigating him for is complex but to simplify it I'll say that Lydell is a suspect in several white collar crimes such as money laundering, which the FBI is always interested in. He has friends in Afghanistan who broker the poppy crops and he helps hook them up with people who can make the profits from the international drug trade clean, so to speak. The investigation became a much bigger deal when rumors began that he might be appointed to a cabinet position."

Josie took a calming sip of the soda before formulating her next question. Delicately. "So what happens now? The recording is going to be out there soon so I'm guessing his hopes for an appointment will be over, but then what? Are you going to arrest him? It sounds like you have evidence."

Harrison fiddled with the folder, closing it and added it back on the stack of files. "We can't comment on that either. What we can do is keep you safe until the recording is made public. We believe at that point they won't have any reason to come after you."

"You believe?" Josie echoed. "That sounds kind of wishy-washy. Do they know that I've given the recording to the press? Are you going to make some sort of announcement?"

"We don't announce the news before it is news," Stokes remarked with a shake of his head. "And as far as we know, they don't know anyone else has it. The chatter we've intercepted is focused solely on you."

Oh goody.

"And that chatter says they want to kill me?"

She might as well just state the obvious. They'd carefully skirted the subject but she knew how screwed she was.

Harrison exhaled slowly, scratching at his chin like he had a bug bite. She'd made him nervous. He must not like to talk about future assassinations. "We're not going to let that happen. You're already protected by a former US Marshal according to Mr. Prentiss. We'll add to that security detail a few agents of our own."

These men should have gone into politics themselves. The non-answer answer.

The questioning continued for what felt like forever but was probably only an hour or so. Stokes and Harrison were very interested in what Amy might have told her about Billy and his job but in the end Josie wasn't sure she'd helped the agents at all.

"How much longer do I need to hide? I've already been on the run almost two weeks and I bet my plants are dying in my apartment back home."

"Not long," Stokes said, rising from his chair. Apparently, they were done talking and answering her questions. "A few days at most. We just need to confirm that they've moved on from you once the video is released."

Harrison also rose, shoving the folders under his arm. "A couple of agents will be coming for you and will follow you and former Marshal Davis back home. They'll report directly to us. If you need anything else please give us a call."

Magically, a business card was placed in front of her and she tucked it in her pocket. She'd make use of it if she needed to, without hesitation. The two agents left the room leaving her with

Harker Prentiss. He too was packing up his things to go but he didn't seem to be in a hurry.

"That went very efficiently, don't you think?" he asked with a grin, showing off even white teeth in his freakishly tan face. He didn't look like a man who spent his days in an office. "I spoke with the reporter and she's already at the airport and headed back to Chicago. This should all be over soon. I'll just step out in the hall and call Evan, let him know where we are so he can come meet us. Just before I came in here I received a message that he's in Tampa."

Just the thought of Evan so close made her more serene. Her racing heart had slowed to normal and the sweat that had been pooling at the base of her neck was drying in the over air conditioned office. Even her appetite was beginning to come back. Perhaps she could convince the boys to stop for dinner once they were out of here.

Who was she kidding? Those men could eat twenty-four-seven and never get full. Especially the big one, Dare. She'd watched him really pack it away. He'd be hungry, she was sure of it.

Smiling - a real honest to God smile - for the first time in a long time, Josie sat back in her chair and looked around. The room looked brighter, more colorful. The air seemed sweeter and cleaner. Even the soda tasted better. She felt lighter and more carefree than she ever thought she'd feel again.

Life was good and she was in love.

Let the future begin.

◈ ◈ ◈

Marisa exhaled the cigarette smoke, hoping the tension and frustration of the day would exit with it. She'd come outside of the building to indulge in the guilty pleasure but there was very little happiness or contentment at the moment. She'd been summarily dismissed upstairs after finding out the Josie was in fact innocent and in danger. Now Evan would feel even more responsible and protective than he did before.

The unrelenting Florida sunshine beat down on her shoulders as she sat on the stone bench watching the passersby. The heat felt good after the cool, filtered air of the office but it failed to calm her agitated state like it normally did. She was too twisted around and pissed off. Nothing was going right today.

"Ms. Arbor? Do you have a moment?"

Raising her eyes, Marisa found a man who appeared to be about thirty-five or so, attired in blue dress slacks, a white button down shirt, and a blue and silver striped tie. He wore the usual regulation holster and firearm around his waist and she assumed he was another FBI agent. Or maybe DEA. All the Feds looked alike.

"I suppose," Marisa answered coolly and waved to the empty area on the bench. "I only have a minute. I need to get back upstairs."

She really didn't but she wanted to make sure she had a firm excuse in case the conversation grew tedious.

The man sat down and leaned forward, his elbows on his knees. She continued smoking her cigarette while he gathered his thoughts. He seemed to be having difficulty expressing himself.

"I'd like to offer you an opportunity, Ms. Arbor. An opportunity to make a great deal of money and perhaps help yourself in the bargain."

This was interesting. Federal agents didn't offer random people money making opportunities.

Which meant he wasn't an agent, even though he was dressed like one.

"Is this a job interview?" she asked, staring straight ahead, not ready to look at him. She needed to know what he wanted. "I don't have my resume."

The man chuckled and smoothed down his tie. "We know all about your resume, Ms. Arbor. Very impressive. But the Marshal Service doesn't appreciate or pay you well enough, now do they? I can help with that. Today you can make a quick twenty-five thousand and all you have to do is go upstairs, retrieve something that's ours, and bring it over to the parking garage across the street. That's it. Easy money."

She wasn't appreciated or paid well enough. But he didn't need to know much about her to know that. Most government jobs were the same. She was the cog in a very big wheel. A wheel she wanted to someday be in charge of. She had big dreams and plans. Evan had been a part of them.

"Something that belongs to you? Like a pair of sunglasses or a briefcase? Maybe a cell phone?" She blew out the smoke watching the gray-blue curls fade into the light wind. "The evidence locker isn't here. I can't help you fix your trial…I don't think I caught your name."

"That's because I didn't tell you," he answered smoothly. "But it's not really that important. I work for some powerful people in Washington, Ms. Arbor. The kind that remember who helps them and who doesn't. They're the kind of people that can help you climb the ranks and get you what you want. Power, if I'm not mistaken. We can help with that."

Marisa couldn't suppress the shiver of excitement that ran down her spine at his words. He must have done his research because he'd summed up her life's ambition very succinctly, although she would have put it slightly differently.

She wanted it all. Everything. The man, the sex, the job, the power, and the money. With every day of toiling in anonymity her goal had gone from fuzzy to clear, her resolve now as solid as granite. She'd started at the Marshal Service a wide-eyed ingénue with fantasies of helping people and making a difference.

She knew better now. The only person she could truly help was herself. She'd watched too many people work hard for nothing but a retirement party at the end. No way was that going to happen to her.

"Why should I believe you?"

"Senator Lydell has what you want, Ms. Arbor. He can open doors for you and make things happen. The kind of things that can change your life. And it all starts here and now. Can we count on your support?"

Stubbing out her cigarette with her high heel, she turned to the man with a smile.

"What do I have to do?"

CHAPTER THIRTY-TWO

Josie stretched her arms over her head as she stared out of the conference room window, watching people scurry by on the sidewalk down below. They all had somewhere to be and so did she. She wanted to go home with Evan and according to Agent Stokes that was going to happen very soon. She'd given them all the information she had regarding Amy and Billy but she didn't think it was going to help them much. She knew they liked to watch Netflix and that Billy was a Star Wars fanatic. They liked to eat cheese fries as an appetizer and drink craft beers together. She didn't know much more except that they were madly in love and they would have had a lovely future if given a chance.

The door swung open and Josie turned, hoping to see the agents that were going to escort her and Evan back to the house but Marisa stood there instead. The woman had never really smiled before and even now it seemed forced, but Josie doubted they were destined to become close friends. She had a feeling the other woman was more into Evan than he thought. He'd described them as friends with some benefits but Marisa looked like awfully possessive for just a friend, so it followed she wouldn't like Josie.

"Ready to see Evan?"

That's what Josie had been waiting to hear. She was more than ready. "I am. Is he downstairs? What about the agents that are supposed to go with us?"

"They're downstairs with Evan. They're working out protection details I believe. Let's go."

Josie trailed after Marisa who turned in a different direction than the one they'd come in, the hallways twisting and turning almost labyrinth-like. They stopped in front of what appeared to be a freight elevator and Josie hoped it would take her straight to Evan and the other men.

"I'm taking you out the back way," Marisa explained, obviously catching on to Josie's unspoken question. "The agents wanted to sneak you out of here quietly if possible. Lydell's men might be watching."

That made sense and Josie relaxed as the old elevator lumbered slowly to the first floor. The worst of the ordeal was over. She completely trusted Evan and his friends to protect her plus the other agents. She was as safe as a baby in its mother's arms.

"Thank you for taking care of me," Josie found herself saying as the doors slid open. She wasn't fond of the woman but Marisa had treated her well while she was in custody. "I appreciate your professionalism."

"It's my job."

Josie followed Marisa as they exited the elevator and crossed the empty street, moving away from the courthouse and cutting through another parking lot.

"Where are we going?" Josie asked, her gaze darting all around her. Although Marisa was a trained marshal, Josie still didn't like being in the open like this without Evan or one of his pals watching over her.

"Just over there." Marisa pointed to a parking garage. "Lydell's men might be watching the courthouse annex. When I gathered the resources to bring you in that meant revealing your whereabouts in the system. Anyone monitoring our communications could find you. We can't be too careful."

They entered the bottom floor of the parking garage, which was half empty and much cooler than outside without the early evening sun beating down on it. The lighting was bad but Josie could make out a black SUV with tinted windows that sat next to the stairwell, two men standing next to it. They were dressed very like Stokes and Harrison although their hair wasn't quite as short. Evan and the boys, however, were nowhere to be found.

"Where's Evan?" Josie asked, her gaze whipping from left to right and then back again. Marisa had said he was down here waiting for her. He wouldn't have left without her. No way. "And what about Reed, Seth, and Dare? They're supposed to be here."

A shove from behind sent Josie straight into the arms of one of the agents whose grip locked onto her arm like a vise, surely leaving bruises behind. The woman who had pushed her wore a triumphant smile, the first real happiness from Marisa that Josie had ever seen.

Adrenaline zipped through Josie's body and she tried to yank her arm away but she didn't have a prayer of getting free. And that bitch Marisa knew it.

Josie's heart stuttered in her chest as icy fear ran through her veins. She'd been sold out and turned over to the men who wanted her dead. These weren't agents. These were Lydell's men.

"Don't worry about Evan. I'll take care of him. I'll let him know that you changed your mind and decided to leave without him."

Struggling against the strong grip that held her immobile, Josie fought the rising panic that threatened to overcome any rational thought. If at any moment in her life she needed to think straight it was right then and now.

"He'll never believe you. He loves me and he won't let this go."

Marisa didn't bother to answer and Josie didn't care what the woman had to say. The man holding her lifted her bodily into the back seat of the SUV while the other man pulled a gun on Marisa.

Marisa's eyes went wide with fear and she held up her hands in a sign of surrender. "Now wait. I did you a favor and it's your turn. We agreed to twenty-five thousand in payment. You said Lydell could help me, my career."

"He could," the man smirked, clearly showing a love for his job that made Josie sick to her stomach. She didn't like the other woman but she didn't want her shot down in cold blood either. A quick perusal of the parking lot didn't help much. It was after five o'clock in the downtown area and most of the workers must have gone home. This little side street was deserted with only a few cars remaining in the parking lot across the street. There was no one who was going to intervene. "In fact, that was the original plan but the heat is on with the Feds and we can't afford any loose ends. You are a loose end."

There was no real warning and nothing to prepare Josie. Marisa didn't even have a chance to plead for her life before Josie heard the marshal scream and then slump to the concrete, her knees giving way and her hands cradling her abdomen where a bright red stain was rapidly spreading over her white blouse. Josie didn't have to be a doctor or a genius to know that Marisa was going to bleed out pretty fast from a bullet at such close range.

The man grabbed the dying woman by the arm and dragged her toward the stairwell. To hide the body? It wasn't much of a camouflage to anyone that might eschew the elevator to get to an upper level. They were going to notice a body covered in blood, for sure.

With the sound of the gunshot still ringing in Josie's ears, she realized it was now or never. One man was at least ten feet away and the other had loosened his grip on her arm where she knew she could get free. She'd always heard that if they took a person away from the abduction site the victim was as good as dead.

Besides, wasn't Evan out there? Somewhere? Prentiss had said so and so had Stokes and Harrison. He'd promised to be right behind her and right now she had to trust that he'd spoken the truth.

She had to trust him.

She also hoped he'd been right when he said that she could fight and run when she was motivated, because she sure as hell was at the moment. Death was not high on her to-do list and she needed to make a get away. Preferably now.

Josie had to give Marisa credit as she wasn't going quietly into any good night or whatever the saying was. She was struggling and Josie wasn't certain why the woman was rolling on her side but then it was all clear. Marisa had managed to reach across her body and grab her service revolver.

The rest happened so fast Josie almost missed it. Marisa shot at the burly man dragging her across the dirty garage floor, hitting him once in the chest and knocking him backward into a vehicle before sliding down, blood smudging on the rear panel of the car. His eyes were wide open and his face had gone pale. He looked dead or at least what passed for dead. Marisa looked the same, whatever energy she'd had gone. She was still and ghostly white, the blood in a pool under her body.

Suddenly Josie wasn't hating on Marisa quite as much. Whatever the woman's motives, she'd evened the odds although it still wasn't going to be any picnic getting free from one man.

"Mother fucking bitch!" The man next to Josie fumbled for his own gun, letting go of her arm and knocking her sideways in his haste to get to his friend. He was muttering curse words under his breath and blessedly distracted. This was her chance. Her only chance.

Taking a deep breath and with as much force, energy, and adrenaline as she could muster, Josie drove the heel of her hand up into her captor's nose just like Evan had taught her. She heard the crunch of bones and felt the warmth of blood spurting all over her t-shirt and jeans but this was no time to be persnickety. What had Evan said she should do next?

Move.

The man was cursing and howling, holding his nose and rocking back and forth, his gun forgotten, as Josie hopped out of the SUV. They'd carelessly left the back door open so she wasn't slowed down as she hit the pavement at a frantic pace, her heart banging against her ribs and her lungs begging for air. Thank goodness she didn't have any good clothes so she'd been taken into custody wearing her tennis shoes. She'd always hated when damsels ran in the movies wearing high heels and skirts. Josie didn't even have a purse to slow her down.

Run. Hide. Stay alive.

Josie was running on pure survival instinct. She didn't know where she was going but it was far away from these men.

And hopefully closer to Evan.

CHAPTER THIRTY-THREE

Josie was nowhere to be found and Evan was frantic with worry. The two FBI agents named Stokes and Harrison had grabbed a few other agents and were currently searching the courthouse annex floor by floor but it was slow going. Dare and Seth had gone outside to check the perimeter of the building while Evan, along with Reed, looked on the floor where they had been questioning her.

At his wit's end and terrified for Josie, Evan was ready to call in the cavalry. Lydell's men must have managed to get to her somehow although he didn't have a clue as to how they'd done it. Security was tight in a building like this with metal detectors and cops everywhere.

Evan was reaching for his phone when Reed turned, a grim expression on his face. "Listen, I hate to say this but have you noticed something out of place? Or should I say someone out of place?"

Shaking his head impatiently, Evan tamped down his growing fear and frustration. He didn't have time for guessing games. "Say what you mean or don't say anything at all. I need to call the police."

Reed nodded and hooked his thumbs in the belt loops of his jeans. "Fine, I'll say it straight out. Where is Marisa? I thought she was going to look after Josie but she's nowhere to be found and everyone I talk to has no idea where she is. I think that's a little too much of a coincidence."

Shock jolted Evan physically, making him grab onto a chair for balance. Did they have Marisa too? Jesus, now they had two women to save but at least Marisa was trained for something like this. Josie would be safer with her than without her.

"They took her too," Evan growled, now more pissed off than anything. He should never have left Josie alone no matter what anyone said. "I blame myself for this. I should have insisted on staying with Josie."

Reed's phone rang and he jerked it out of his pocket, growling his impatience. Scowling, he listened for only a moment then shoved the phone away. "Seth and Dare heard a shot coming from across the street."

His heart plummeting to his stomach, Evan and Reed didn't wait for the elevator, hitting the stairs at a flat out sprint. By the time they burst out of the back doors of the building Seth and Dare were waiting for them. Seth pointed across the street where there were a few small buildings, a small parking lot, and a parking garage on the far end.

"From what I could tell, the shots are being fired either from or near that parking garage. I called 911 and the police are on their way."

The four of them were crossing the street when one more shot was heard coming from the same direction. They all put on a burst of speed, only slowing down when they approached the parking garage. There were no people milling around the small buildings and parking lot. The garage had to be the place but it wouldn't do to go in guns blazing and no plan.

Evan pulled his revolver and pointed to the other side of the structure, lapsing into lawman mode. For the next few minutes, he needed to be the man he used to be. Josie needed it and

Marisa too. If they were going to come out of this alive, he had to draw on every bit of training and professionalism he had inside even when his heart was screaming so loudly it drowned out any other sounds.

He needed to think with his head and leave his emotions behind. He could fall apart later.

"Dare and Seth, head inside from the street entrance around the corner. Reed and I will go in here. Stay low and out of sight until we figure out what we're dealing with."

Evan and Reed creeped closer to the garage entrance, pausing at the entrance to peer around the corner. A black SUV was parked near the stairwell with the back passenger door wide open but no one around it. Moving toward the vehicle, his body stiffened and the breath caught in his chest when he spied two bodies near the door to the stairs lying in a pool of blood.

Marisa.

Relieved that it wasn't Josie, but furious that these assholes had hurt Marisa, Evan slowly knelt next to his ex-partner, her skin waxy and pale. A quick check of her pulse on her neck had him almost crying with relief and happiness. She wasn't dead. The pulse was faint and she'd lost a shitload of blood from what he could see but dammit, she was still alive.

Reed was kneeling by the other body, a man Evan had never seen before. He had a large hole in his chest and Evan doubted he'd survived. Marisa had always been a good shot.

"He's gone," Reed confirmed. "They're each holding a gun. Looks like they're might have been a shootout. Now the question is...are there more and where is your girl?"

Marisa must have protected Josie with her own life. Evan owed her.

Reed had a good point though. Just how many other men were here and did they already have Josie?

"Call an ambulance and stay with Marisa while I find Josie. I hope to God she's somewhere around here."

Nodding, Reed knelt next to the woman and spoke encouraging words as if to soothe the unconscious woman as he pulled his phone from his pocket. Her eyes opened for a moment but she simply moaned softly, her gaze unfocused, before her lids fluttered shut and she was quiet and limp again.

"I've got her," Reed assured him. "Go find Josie but for fuck's sake be careful. There have to be more of them. There's no way they would have sent one lone guy on this job."

Sucking in a breath, Evan inched along the outer wall of the parking structure, his gaze darting side to side and then up to the second level.

Up.

Checking the text that had come into his phone, Seth and Dare had already scoured the first floor and found nothing. That meant if Josie was still here, she was somewhere in an upper level. Quickly and quietly texting back that they should go to the top and work their way down, Evan headed back to the stairwell so he could make his way upwards.

He'd only gone up a half a flight when he heard two more gunshots.

CHAPTER THIRTY-FOUR

The bullets had come way too close to Josie for her to feel any sort of comfort.

After Marisa had shot one of the men and Josie had broken the nose of the other, she'd taken off running as fast as she could simply trying to put distance between herself and the guns. Unfortunately, the man with the bloodied nose had shaken off his injury rather quickly and managed to keep her from getting to the other side of the garage where the other large drive in entrance and exit was located. From there she could have run down the street screaming her head off but he'd made sure she didn't make it.

Her only choice had been to go up two levels, and she'd watched enough horror movies to know it wasn't the smartest move, but she was hoping to sneak back down the stairwell or even the elevator if she could get close to them.. She was pretty sure the other bad guy was dead and wouldn't be an impediment to escaping.

One guy. She only had to outsmart and outrun one man. She'd call it a fair fight except that he had a gun. And superior strength along with nothing to lose. Perhaps she could get him to shoot all of his bullets and then she'd only have to worry about getting manhandled and her ass kicked.

With the smell of urine and gasoline burning her nostrils, she'd stayed close to the inside wall, hiding behind vehicles. They were sparser on this upper level than down below and eventually she'd had to make a run from one to another, the distance at least twenty feet, tripping and falling along the way, ripping a hole in the knee of her jeans. She'd cursed under her breath as pain shot up her leg and warm blood trickled down her calf, mixing with the sweat on her skin.

That's when the unnamed asshole - she'd dubbed him Skippy - had gotten off a few rounds. If there was anyone nearby, hopefully they wouldn't think that was a car backfiring. She needed them to call the police.

Now she was wedged underneath an Escalade, near the front tires and the outer wall off the parking structure, but still at least fifty feet from the stairwell and elevator. She was sweaty, dirty, and breathing so ragged she was gulping oxygen into her aching lungs. Her knee throbbed in time with her heart, which was pounding so loudly in her ears she was sure they could hear it several miles away and she'd had to put her hand across her mouth to keep from whimpering. She had to be incredibly quiet. Skippy was out there, not far away, and he knew she was close too.

From her low vantage point, a pair of shoes came into view and she had to bite down into her lip, drawing blood to keep from screaming. She tried to take very small, shallow breaths as if he might be able to hear the air swooshing in and out of her chest if the environment were just quiet enough. The feet passed her by and she allowed herself a momentary inward sigh of relief before getting back to the original goal.

Going downstairs to the street level. Running. Getting away.

Finding Evan.

She was contemplating a run for the elevator when she heard the scrape of shoes on the filthy cement floor. Skippy must have worked his back to her location when he didn't find her on the other side. Crouching low to make herself even smaller, she held her breath as his shoes came into sight when he walked in back of the truck.

Wrong shoes.

Those weren't Skippy's shoes, the ugly brown lace ups that needed polished. She'd memorized those the last time he'd walked by and these were different.

It took her fear-laden brain a few moments to realize they belonged to the one man she'd wanted to see - Evan. Her knight in shining armor and sometime pain in the ass had pulled on those worn out cowboy boots he loved so much.

Now she was sorry she'd made fun of them because she was so damn happy that he was here, perhaps with Seth, Dare, and Reed as well. Just having him here tipped the odds in her favor. Suddenly breathing was much easier, although her heart was still racing and she was still dirty from head to toe.

Evan was here. He'd told her to trust him and here he was. For perhaps the first time in her adult life, she had someone she could truly believe in. A man for thick and thin, hard times and good.

For better or worse?

Shit, don't even think that right now. Too soon. Way too soon. Live in the now. Right now someone's trying to kill you.

So did she let him know she was hiding here or did she shut the hell up and let him hunt down Skippy?

The fates must have taken pity on her because she didn't have to decide at all. Sirens sounded, coming ever closer and then two more shots rang out, closer this time and she assumed they must be from Evan's gun. Not wanting to get killed in the crossfire, she prayed to whatever deity might be listening that the two men would keep their bullets far from her soft tissue and bone.

There was shouting and cursing, lots of running, a few more shots and then silence.

Silence.

Slowly exhaling, Josie realized she'd been holding her breath as the room seemed to whirl around her from lack of oxygen to the brain. She squeezed her eyes shut and then blinked three or four times as hot tears began to build behind her lids. She prayed it was over and that Evan and his friends were safe.

"Josie? Josie, are you here? Honey, you can come out. You're safe."

Evan's reassuring voice brought forth a sob of pure unadulterated relief and it must have been loud because before she could even respond he was looking under and around the cars where she was hiding.

"Here. I'm here."

She was shocked at how tiny her voice sounded, her throat scratchy and dry from running and sheer terror. Sliding on the dusty concrete, she peeked her head out from under the truck to find Evan and Dare standing a few feet away, looking everywhere but where she actually was.

"Here. Down here."

This time Evan honed in on her voice and he let loose a long string of expletives before firing off questions regarding her health but he didn't give her a chance to answer before asking another one.

Lifting her bodily onto her feet, he had to hold onto her when her trembling legs gave way and she almost tumbled right back down to the concrete floor. He crushed her to his chest and buried his face into her hair.

Nothing had ever felt so good and wonderful. He smelled good and his arms felt warm and safe. She allowed herself the luxury of leaning against his broad chest soaking in his strength and love, hoping it would somehow chase away the fear and despair she'd been feeling since Marisa had shown up.

Marisa...Did he know? Was she...?

"Are you okay? Are you hurt? Did they hurt you? Answer me, Josie. Jesus, you're bleeding."

Slapping her palm over her mouth to stifle a hysterical sound, she shook her head, still drinking in the handsome face she hoped she'd see every day for the rest of her life. "You didn't give me a chance to answer but yes, I'm okay. I'll have a few bruises and a scraped up knee but I'll live. Thanks to you."

Dare had a grip on Skippy's arm, the man slumped and woozy. It looked like he'd taken a few punches to the face and perhaps elsewhere as well. Good. "Don't thank me or anything. I just ambushed him from behind while your boyfriend shot a few times to distract him." Dare perused the disheveled man with blood on his face and shirt. "Who broke his nose? Did I do that?"

Laying her head against Evan's chest, she could hear the heavy thump of his heart and she sighed with happiness. If Dare was being a teasing little shit then things must be all right.

"Thank you, Dare, and your friends too, of course. We couldn't have done this without you and I'm forever grateful for your help. Evan has some good friends. Oh, and I broke his nose courtesy of the self-defense lessons Evan insisted giving me. They did come in handy."

His hold tightening on her until she almost couldn't breathe, Evan laid kisses on the top of her head. "I don't know about that. I could have taken the guy—it just might have taken a little longer."

"Right," Seth drawled, joining them, wiping his sweaty brow with the sleeve of his shirt. "I guess we'll never know. But since we took this guy alive, he can tell us all about what it's like to work for Lydell. Can't you, buddy?"

The man groaned and Dare began marching him toward the elevator, Seth on his heels. Evan pulled back slightly as if he too was going to follow but Josie shook her head, grabbing his arm to hold him there. He needed to know.

"Wait...Marisa..."

She had issues with the woman but she didn't wish her dead.

"She was alive when I came up here to look for you. Reed's with her and I think one of those sirens is the ambulance. I'm guessing she shot that guy so you could run. She always was damn good at her job."

That wasn't exactly how it happened. Torn in two, part of her wanted to leave Marisa's memory intact, especially if the woman didn't survive. But the other part, a deeper part, recognized the woman's jealousy and ambition. Marisa needed to answer for what she'd done.

"He shot her first," Josie finally said, burying her face in his shirt. Her stomach churned, making her sick to her stomach as she remembered that moment of betrayal. She'd thought she was dead for sure. "He shot her because he said she was a loose end and he didn't want to pay her the twenty-five thousand she'd been promised."

She didn't imagine Evan's swift intake of breath or the way his entire body stiffened. He pulled back, his eyes wide with disbelief as the wheels turned in his head. He was figuring out the truth.

"Twenty-five thousand?" he breathed, choking on the words. Josie could see tears forming in the corners of Evan's eyes. Being double-crossed by a good friend was a heavy-duty blow that she wasn't sure he'd recover from quickly. If ever. He'd trusted his ex-partner despite their lingering issues. "Marisa was on Lydell's payroll?"

Josie nodded, her own throat tight with emotion. "She came to the conference room and said she was taking me to you. I followed her and she led me here where those two goons were waiting for us. I'm so sorry, Evan. But in the end she might have had a change of heart because she was lying on the floor bleeding and managed to pull her gun. She shot him dead and that gave me an opening to run. So there's that."

Evan scraped a hand down his face, a muscle in his jaw working. He looked away for a long moment, clearly overcome with the events and she didn't want to intervene, but there were things going on downstairs. Police, two people shot, one beat-up guy.

Finally he turned and cupped her face in his hands, his expression fierce yet tender at the same time. His lips captured hers in a kiss that affirmed everything she already knew and a few things she didn't. He loved her. He adored her. But there was forever in this kiss. Maybe happily ever after and for better or worse wasn't out of the question. Not right away, but someday.

Hopefully, they'd had all the worse and it might be time for the better.

"I love you, baby, and I am so damn grateful that you're alive."

She smiled against his mouth, feeling his warm breath on her skin.

"I'm feeling pretty happy about that myself. You're a real badass former lawman, Evan Davis."

"Emphasis on the former," he smirked, beginning to lead them to the elevator. "Let's go talk to the police so we can go home. I need a bath, I need some food, and I need you."

Despite the horrors she'd witnessed today, she couldn't help but enjoy the flowering happiness that was unfurling in her belly. She had a new start. They both did.

"In that order?"

"No, but you already knew that, didn't you?"

She did and it felt good to come first.

CHAPTER THIRTY-FIVE

The next few weeks seemed to pass by in some sort of surreal reality for Josie. There were FBI agents, D.C. cops, and various other law enforcement individuals from the alphabet soup that was the nation's agencies. There was a point where she was on auto-pilot, repeating the same story over and over until she could have performed it with an interpretive dance number.

The only saving grace was that Evan and his friends were answering just as many questions, although Reed and Seth had returned back to Montana several days ago, leaving Dare behind. The burly lawman didn't like to be idle so when they weren't being questioned, he'd pitched in to help clean out the house. With the labor of all three of them, they'd managed to finish the kitchen, living room, and a spare bedroom for Dare. He teased that he liked the Florida heat so much he might drag Rayne down here and move in.

"Is it really over?" Josie asked as they settled into their regular booth at the diner. The young waitress Tammy knew their preferences by now and she didn't even ask for their drink order, instead sliding three icy glasses in front of them within ninety seconds of them wandering through the door. "No more questions? No more investigations? We can move on?"

Evan nodded toward the television mounted on the wall. Tammy had turned on a cable news network that was currently showing former Senator Lydell's perp walk over and over again. Skippy had sung like a bird when he'd been interrogated and thrown pretty much everyone he'd ever known except his mother under the bus. The FBI and DEA had already been building a money laundering case against Lydell and now they could add murder and attempted murder to the ever growing list of charges.

"For now," conceded Evan, sipping at his iced tea. "With any luck, he'll plead out and this will never go to trial. But if it does we'd all have to testify, I'd imagine."

Dare grunted as he perused the menu. "They'll drag this out in appeals for years. Rich people don't go to jail from what I've observed."

Evan's grip on his glass tightened and Josie placed her hand on his thigh, giving it a squeeze. He'd been incredibly supportive but there had been a part of him that had also been quite sad. It was going to be awhile before he'd be his old self again.

"Lydell is being held on three counts of conspiracy to commit murder plus facing RICO charges. I think he's going to do some time. Good people lost their lives because he wanted that recording."

Amy, Billy, and Marisa. Evan's ex-partner hadn't survived surgery and he was still having a hard time dealing with not only her untimely and violent death but also her betrayal. The henchman, Skippy, had been only too happy to detail his conversation with Marisa and how they'd reeled her in and convinced her to turn Josie over to them, promising money and a quick trip up the ranks.

Josie couldn't concentrate on her menu, her gaze constantly straying back to the television screen. They were now showing a portion of the infamous video but had blurred the nudity. "He wanted more than that recording. He wanted to keep doing all the things he was doing and make money plus gain power. Basically, he wanted it all and he thought he was special and deserved it. Didn't one of those agents say that Lydell thought that laws were only for the little people?"

Evan signaled to Tammy that they were ready to order. "I guess we'll find out. Personally, I just want to forget about all of this and move on with my life. I think once we get the house finished we should celebrate with a long vacation."

Tammy took their order - three fried chicken specials - and hurried back to the kitchen, leaving them alone. Josie wanted to know more about this vacation idea as she hadn't been on one since her mother and aunt took her to the Grand Canyon when she was twelve.

Then she remembered she didn't have any money and Evan wasn't gainfully employed either. The most they could probably afford was camping in the backyard and that was if Evan already owned a tent.

"Are we winning the lottery this weekend?" Josie elbowed Evan in the ribs and laughed. "If so, I better get my ticket."

Dare and Evan exchanged a glance and she immediately knew something was up. They did this every now and then, communicated without saying a word and it frustrated her to no end.

"No secrets," Josie reminded Evan. "That was the deal."

A slow smile bloomed on his handsome face and he lifted her hand, pressing a kiss to the palm. "No lottery ticket needed. But I guess I should have been more clear though. My parents are so thrilled with the job we've done on the house they've offered to allow us to live there completely free for as long as we wish or I can sell it and the land and keep the cash. I was thinking you wouldn't want to live way out in the country but I might be wrong."

She already knew the land itself was quite valuable and that there was a horse rancher who wanted to buy it.

"You shouldn't spend all your money on our vacation. You might need it in the future."

"I think it will be okay to spend a few thousand of it. We deserve to relax and have some fun." He held up his hand when she would have argued with him. "I'm going to insist on this, sweetheart. Start making a list of all the places you've ever wanted to go."

Josie turned to Dare and sighed. "He's not going to let go of this idea, is he?"

"Nope," Dare laughed, making a popping sound with the 'p'. "In fact, I'm not sure I've ever seen him this excited before. If I were you, I'd just go with it."

Evan waggled his eyebrows mischievously. "Do you trust me, baby?"

She had a feeling she'd be hearing that question a great deal in the coming years.

"With my life," she sighed, knowing in her heart it was true. "Just don't get us killed, okay? I'm enjoying this whole breathing and heart beating thing, especially after being shot at."

Evan leaned down to whisper in ear so only she could hear. "No guns. No blood. Only sun and sex. I promise."

"Add a couple of umbrella drinks and I'm in."

CHAPTER THIRTY-SIX

One year later…

The warm sand under Evan's feet felt amazing as he and Josie took their places among the guests on the beach. The sun was beginning to set and the sky had turned a fiery shade of orange and pink with a few shots of electric blue. It had been raining for two days but this morning had dawned clear and beautiful, perfect weather to recite vows.

Seagulls danced on the breeze and the tang of salt in the air reminded Evan why he loved this part of the country so much. He and Josie rarely had time to bum around the beach but they'd promised themselves that this weekend they'd relax and leave work behind. So far, they'd managed but it had been touch and go.

Josie's fingers tangled with his as he peered around the guests and down the aisle. Things should be starting at any moment. Dare was standing under the flowered trellis looking quite different than he normally did. Today he had a big grin on his face as he chatted with Griffin, his best man. It was Dare and Rayne's wedding day and it had been a long time coming. At least that's what Dare had said. Rayne had a slightly different story but it didn't change the fact that here they were, finally becoming man and wife.

"I think you're more nervous than the groom," Josie teased, looking up at him from under her lashes. She looked beautiful, dressed in an emerald green sundress that set off her auburn hair and highlighted the golden tan she now sported all year long. It was a casual beach wedding and he'd managed to get away with linen trousers and a sky blue button down shirt. No shoes. No tie. "Dare looks like he just won the Olympics or something. I've never seen him smile like that. It's actually sort of disturbing. I'm not used to it."

"He knows he's a lucky man," scoffed Evan, leaning down to drop a kiss on Josie's forehead. "He has had all of us watching Rayne this weekend just in case she made a run for it."

It was then that the music started, kettle drums and a guitar playing a song he'd heard before but couldn't place. All heads turned toward the bride who was walking toward them in a long white dress and bare feet, holding a colorful bouquet of flowers. Her jet black hair was loose around her shoulders and he would swear there was a tint of pink on the end of the strands. But that was Rayne. Colorful and full of life. Just like his Josie. He'd only been half alive before he met her. Now every day was filled with love, laughter, and yes, sometimes anger. You couldn't have the good times without the bad.

His gaze traveled around the assembled group, friends he hadn't seen in the past year. Seth and Presley, their two little ones having fun at Disney with the grandparents while mommy and daddy had a few adult days. Evan's throat constricted with emotion as he remembered the day he'd introduced them. He'd never imagined for a moment what he'd started but he couldn't think of a better couple.

Unless it was Tanner and Madison. Tanner had their baby girl in his arms, her head on his shoulder and fast asleep. Madison had been through hell and back to have that child, starting with fertility treatments and then in the hospital on bed rest while pregnant. When little Amanda had been born she'd had to spend weeks in the NICU, worrying her parents, family, and friends to death. But everything had only served to make the couple's bond even stronger. They were gazing at each other with a naked adoration that would make anyone envious.

The ceremony began and Dare and Rayne recited their vows to one another, bringing tears to every female's eyes. Perhaps some of the men as well. It was clear that Rayne loved her "grouchy bear" with all her heart and Dare worshipped the ground she walked on. They were going to have a good life together. Rayne had let it slip at dinner the night before that they wanted to have children right away but had started with a yellow lab puppy named Zeus. So far, the canine had chewed through Dare's favorite cowboy boots, Rayne's handbag, three throw pillows, and more newspapers than they could count.

The couple kissed and everyone clapped and cheered. Josie was dabbing at her eyes, a watery smile on her pretty face. "That was so beautiful. A beach wedding with the sunset in the background. So romantic."

Wrapping an arm around her waist, he pulled her close and breathed in her heady scent, a mixture of vanilla and all the wedding flowers. "You're not going to cry all night are you? I'm going to want the first dance."

Evan danced now. Somehow, Josie had loosened his inhibitions to the point they could both be seen boogying around the condo while doing the dishes or even working in the spare room they used as an office.

"I am not, I promise. I'm going to hold you to that dance though. I want to break loose and have some fun. It feels like we've had our nose to the grindstone for months."

"That's because we have."

The wedding had been held on the beach in front of a luxurious hotel so they didn't have to go far when the ceremony was over. Evan and Josie settled at a dinner table with Logan, Ava, Reed, and Kaylee. Griffin and his wife Jazz were at the main table along with Seth and Presley. Jared and his wife Misty had managed to make it to the wedding along with ex-DEA agent Jason Anderson and his wife Brinley. Those two couples were sharing a table with Rayne's sister Camy and her husband and Dare's sister Sophie, home from college.

Champagne flowed and conversation too as Evan laughed along with the men that had become his close friends. They had all been there for him in one way or another in the last year, and not one of them had tried to convince him to go back to law enforcement work. On the contrary, they'd encouraged his new career passion.

Ava took another sip and giggled, the bubbles apparently tickling her nose, much to her husband's delight. Logan hadn't taken his eyes off his wife all day and it was easy to see that having twins hadn't dampened the passion in that marriage a bit. They acted like a couple of besotted newlyweds.

"I saw your latest book climbing the charts," Ava gushed, leaning forward so she could be heard over the other guests' conversations. "I'm so proud of you, Evan. This is only the beginning."

Josie smiled up at him, cupping his jaw in her hand, her eyes soft with the love he'd come to depend on so deeply. He wouldn't trade her for anything in the world.

"It's only my second book and I wouldn't call it a bestseller or anything but I'm pleased with the sales." He raised his glass to Ava. "I couldn't have done this without you. You've been the best mentor anyone could ask for."

Kaylee rolled her eyes and snorted, acting with mock outrage. "And what am I? Yesterday's mashed potatoes? I helped too."

"You did and I can't thank you enough. I didn't have a clue as to what I was doing when I started out a year ago and you both walked me through every step. Because of you both I'm actually making money as a writer."

"A damn good one too," Josie retorted. "And I'll take the credit for recognizing his genius. The minute I read that story he gave me I knew he was talented. Now he has two crime thrillers out and a third in the works. I couldn't be more proud."

Once Josie had given him the confidence to really write he couldn't stem the tide of ideas. The words had flowed so quickly it was as if he was simply taking dictation from some crazy muse that wouldn't shut the hell up.

"I'm proud of you too." Evan whispered it into Josie's ear, the words for her alone. He knew she sometimes felt uneasy about how she'd started all over again. They'd moved to Orlando so she could enroll in the University of Central Florida and was working on a business degree. They'd agreed she had a knack for it, plus the business side of his writing was becoming a time suck from what he really enjoyed which was the writing. Josie, on the other hand, loved playing with his sales numbers, creating charts and graphs and putting together three year plans. She'd found her true calling as well.

Kaylee grinned, her eyes sparkling with mischief. "So you two look pretty happy. Might we hear wedding bells in the future? Or maybe the pitter patter of little feet?"

Logan and Reed groaned and shook their heads, Reed playfully placing his hand over his wife's mouth. "Pay no attention to the tipsy woman next to me. She's smart and sexy as hell but she wants the whole world to have a happily ever after. It's an occupational hazard."

Kaylee nipped at her husband's palm and elbowed him in the ribs. "I'm not pushing, I'm just asking. That's two different things."

Evan gazed down at Josie to find her cheeks a dark pink. He wasn't sure if he should answer or let her. It seemed like he should stay quiet at a moment like this. The fact was they'd quietly gone off to the courthouse about a month ago and done the deed, but had stayed silent because they didn't want to steal Dare and Rayne's thunder. There would be time to tell everyone.

Later.

"We've talked about it," Josie conceded finally, a shoulder lifting casually. "We're not in a big hurry. We've been so busy this year that it's not at the top of our list."

Kaylee seemed to accept the answer and instead turned her attention to Reed, whispering something in his ear that made the lawman's cheeks go red. Looked like they had plans after the reception. Everyone knew that Kaylee used Reed for "research" for her erotic romances. Although the couple was notoriously closed-mouth about their marriage, Kaylee was currently working on a series of stories regarding a couple where the man was a cop. That couple was trying to get pregnant so…It was a good bet that Kaylee and Reed were also trying.

"Dance with me?" Josie rested her chin on his shoulder and gave him the puppy-dog eyes he hadn't yet been able to resist. Not that he was trying all that hard. "I love this song. It reminds me of you."

Leading her onto the dance floor, Evan twirled her so her skirt flared out before pulling her close, her cheek on his chest. "Are you sure this song reminds you of me? Because last night you said that song the DJ played reminded you of me. And in the car on the way here yesterday morning, you said that song reminded you of me. And then the other day–"

"You've made your point," Josie cut him off with a giggle. "But it's true. All of these songs remind me of you in some way. I guess you simply make me a sappy fool for love. Are you happy with yourself?"

"Can't complain. I'm sappy too if it makes any difference." He let his hand slip down to her lower back, pressing her even closer so he could feel her heartbeat and sun-warmed skin. "Very smooth back there by the way. Nobody has any idea we snuck out in the middle of the night and married in secret. It's a little scary how well you lie."

"It wasn't a lie. We weren't in a hurry and now that we've done it, it's not at the top of our list. Let's face it, we were never going to have a big wedding or anything. That's just not us."

They'd both agreed that their vows were a private moment only for them. They loved their friends but the ceremony was theirs alone. The reception? That was a whole other kettle of fish. They both loved a party and planned to spend some time up in Montana to celebrate when they visited Evan's family.

The song ended and they made their way over to the main table. Evan hadn't spoken much with Griffin this weekend but Josie and Jazz had become fast friends, bonding over finals and professors. Jazz had returned to college part-time to work on an education degree to go along with the children's theatre she had opened. Both women had groaned and been quite dramatic when talking about reading, homework, and exams.

"How's your quiet little town?" Evan asked, remembering how Griffin liked it uneventful so he could fish, although he hadn't had much peace since Jazz came into his life. She constantly had a play going or a project she was working on. That girl had energy to spare and then some. "Catch anything lately?"

Griffin laughed and offered Evan a beer, which he gratefully accepted. Champagne was nice, but beer was better. "Not a damn thing. In my spare time, Jazz has me building sets for her latest production of *My Fair Lady*. Think adolescents with acne and bad British accents."

"Ouch," Evan laughed. "Sorry we're going to miss that opening night."

"It will be this summer so you could come. Isn't Josie out of school right now?"

"Yes, but we have a trip to D.C. planned. She wants to see some of her old friends plus we're doing some research for the new book."

"She gave up a lot to be with you. Her home, friends, a job. You're a lucky man and I should know. Jazz gave up everything to be with me."

Josie would have declared all day long that she hadn't given up anything but Evan knew better.

"Jazz doesn't look like she regrets it."

Neither would Josie if Evan had anything to say about it. He'd spend every day letting her know that she was *the one*.

Josie grabbed his hand and began to tug him toward the dance floor while Jazz did the same with a clearly reluctant Griffin. The man had two left feet but his wife didn't seem to mind.

"Come on, let's dance." Josie stood on her tiptoes and pressed a kiss to his cheek. "This song reminds me of you."

His answer would always be yes.

OTHER TITLES BY OLIVIA JAYMES

Danger Incorporated

Damsel In Danger

Hiding From Danger

Discarded Heart Novella (US Kindle Only)

Indecent Danger

Embracing Danger

Cowboy Justice Association

Cowboy Command

Justice Healed

Cowboy Truth

Cowboy Famous

Cowboy Cool

Imperfect Justice

The Deputies

Justice Inked - Amazon US

Military Moguls

Champagne and Bullets

Diamonds and Revolvers

Caviar and Covert Ops

ABOUT THE AUTHOR

Olivia Jaymes is a wife, mother, lover of sexy romance, and caffeine addict. She lives with her husband and son in central Florida and spends her days with handsome alpha males and spunky heroines.

She is currently working on a series of full-length novels called The Cowboy Justice Association. It's a contemporary romance series about lawmen in southern Montana who work to keep the peace but can't seem to find it in their own lives in addition to the erotic romance novella series - Military Moguls and the romantic suspense series – Danger Incorporated.

Visit Olivia Jaymes at
www.OliviaJaymes.com

Made in the USA
Columbia, SC
15 December 2024